****

THE NINE LIVES OF ALPHONSE

****

The Nine Lives of Alphonse

by

James L. Johnson

(A Code Name Sebastian Adventure)

J. B. LIPPINCOTT COMPANY
Philadelphia & New York

FIRST EDITION
Printed in the United States of America
Library of Congress Catalog Card Number: 68-19835

The epigraph from John F. Kennedy is taken from "William Manchester's Own Story" from the April 4, 1967, issue of *Look* magazine.

****

To

Those Christian Colleagues
in Whom the Flame of This
Cause Burns Bright

****

****

"The credit belongs to the man who is actually in the arena, whose face is marred by dust and sweat and blood . . . who knows the great enthusiasms, the great devotions; who spends himself in a worthy cause; who at the best knows in the end the triumph of high achievement, and . . . if he fails, at least fails while daring greatly, so that his place shall never be with those cold and timid souls who know neither victory nor defeat."

—John F. Kennedy

****

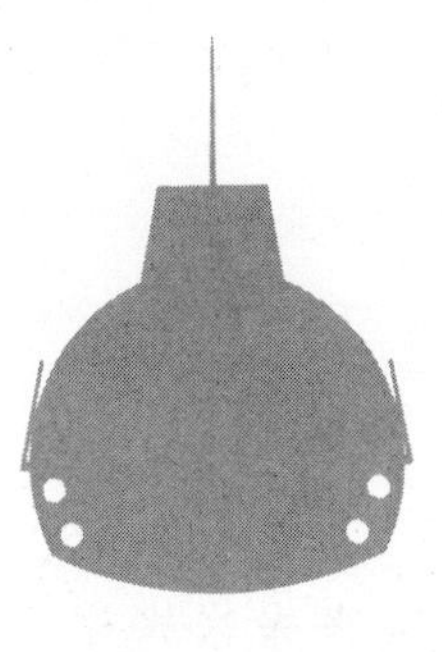

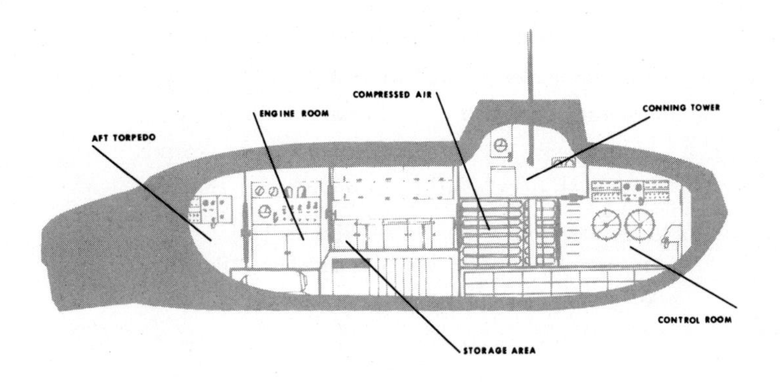
COMPRESSED AIR
ENGINE ROOM
CONNING TOWER
AFT TORPEDO
CONTROL ROOM
STORAGE AREA

alPHONSe

Prologue

****

Mr. H. B. Mathews
National Intelligence Agency
Miami, Florida

Subject: Operation Clean Sweep
Class: Top Priority—Destroy When Finished
Med: Teletype—Code R

This is to inform you that beginning on February 1 and running through March 1, inclusive, the USCARIB (U.S. Caribbean Fleet) and the SOUATFLT (South Atlantic Fleet) will concentrate their exercises on a search and destroy mission in the Florida Straits labeled "Operation Clean Sweep."

It is *imperative*—I repeat, *imperative*—that you do not authorize any clandestine operations to Cuba at that time. Fleet orders are to seek out any unidentified vessels, either surface or subsurface, attempting to run the Straits either into Cuba or out of it.

The fleet exercises are an approved operation of the O.A.S. to discourage Castro infiltration of the Florida and other southern coastal areas with guerrilla and other underground personnel and equipment.

I trust you to observe the quarantine on operations at that time, for there is no way to control our naval traffic or design after February 1. May I emphasize that the fleet has SHOOT–KILL go ahead—there will be no time to ask questions or consider benefit of the doubt.

Your cooperation in the above will save us any embarrassment or top-level kickbacks.

JOHN HOLLAND
Dir. Operations
State Department
Washington, D.C.

Chapter I

****

He knew there was a crisis the minute he spotted her standing off to the left of the milling crowd jamming the arrival gate. He remembered Jane MaConnel as being a composed, deliberate woman who had a firm control on life and a defying, resolute attitude about death. But that was eight years ago. Now there was a strange kind of flightiness about her in the way her head darted jerkily in all directions as if she were surrounded by a legion of shadowy shapes striking out at her. She was thinner, too, which gave her a gaunt, intense look, cutting away the natural lines of graceful beauty that had been hers once and which had made her a breath-taking person to look at. Now she appeared stark in her boniness, like a bare tree branch bouncing under the merciless whim of wintry gales.

When he came up to her, her eyes locked on him quickly, but only for a second. That was all she needed for recognition, for he knew his own gangliness was quite distinct and easy to pick out. She gave a fluttering, half smile that showed tiredness and uncertainty, and a quick hand flew to her dark hair as if she wanted to make sure none of her would come apart at the last minute. Whatever had transformed her from a confident, beautiful woman to a frayed neurotic had not checked her womanly instinct displayed in that single gesture with her hair, like a beaten soldier still gamely holding on to the tattered flag.

He saw pain in those clouded eyes that were once very blue, like sky after rain, but now had taken on a dull sheen like she'd been crying too much—or worrying.

"Thank you, Mr. Sebastian," she said, just touching his hand lightly with her cold fingers as he extended it in greeting. "Thank you for coming. . . ."

Her eyes shifted quickly again, as if she was trying to see someone on either side of her without directly looking. She turned, then, to lead him off before he could say anything, and she stayed two to three feet in front of him as if she didn't want to stop to allow him any conversation. "I have my car out front. . . . If you don't mind, we'll go right on home. . . ." She moved through the crowd, her body bouncing on her quick steps, the thin lines of her showing through the light trench coat. "You've been in Miami before, I take it?" But before he could answer, she went on, throwing her voice back over her left shoulder at him, but keeping her eyes straight ahead, "Well, January is the beginning of the tourist season, as you know, so it's a bit sticky with the crowds. . . . Did you have a good flight? Of course, most everybody does coming to Miami in January. . . . I suppose Chicago is cold as usual. . . . This will be a good change for you. . . . But I should say I'm so glad you came in response to my wire. . . . I hope you'll forgive me for imposing on you. . . ."

Then they were out into the main terminal area and heading for the escalator marked "Baggage Claim and Transportation." He still hadn't said anything, content to let her run with free rein. She didn't bother letting the escalator take her down; she insisted on taking the steps in the same rapid, nervous movements of her body. He noticed her head jerk in that nervous way to the right and left, either to make sure he was behind her or else to check on someone else she expected to move up on her at any moment.

They came to the lower ramp and to the damp Miami night. She led him to a cream-colored 1965 Plymouth and the man in the blue cap who apparently had been holding the car there for her. He got in, throwing his overnight bag in the back seat.

She drove out of the parking area and out to the road that led toward the city, but instead of turning with a couple of airport limousines in front of her she cut back to the right, running down a narrow ramp that apparently led back into the main freight passage of the terminal.

"You'll excuse me, Mr. Sebastian, if I deviate from the usual course," and she gave that quick, nervous smile, more into the rearview mirror than at him. "This will save me some time on the expressway."

But he knew it wouldn't. The road led a roundabout course all right, angling back around freight buildings and other structures with names of airlines on them, until they hit a small black-top road gleaming wet in the lights. He noticed that they were running parallel with the run-up end of the runway of the airfield where some of the big jets were parked waiting their turn to take off. Their engines thundered and whined and the smell of burned fuel was strong in the car.

She paid no heed to the aircraft. Their red flashing signal lights cast peculiar red hues over her taut face, contrasted with the blue and green of the runway lights that poked at them as they passed. She ran the Plymouth up to sixty and better down the uncertain road for five minutes; it appeared she wanted to get off this stretch before being stopped by anyone. Then she swung back to the right again on a wider strip of concrete that apparently led back to the expressway. All the time her eyes watched the mirror, but Sebastian knew there was nothing following them.

They came to a green light that was the beginning of the entrance to the expressway; she turned quickly, expertly keeping the car from going into a spin on the wet pavement. Finally she cut into the expressway traffic pattern, slowing down to forty-five to keep pace.

"I suppose all this has something to do with your wire?" he finally ventured, keeping his voice polite and pleasant, not wanting to increase the excitement that was already obviously pumping through her.

"It does, at least indirectly." She gave that quick, apologetic smile into the mirror again. "I must apologize for the tone of my telegram—I suppose it put you in an unfair position. I probably made things sound worse than I suppose they are. . . ."

"I would have come anyway," Sebastian said. "I often wondered in these past eight years how you were getting along —you and Joe."

"I wouldn't know about Joe." She gave a coughing kind of laugh that was half pain. "You probably didn't know that he cashed out of the Navy back in nineteen sixty. We moved here then . . . but it was no good for Joe to hang around in a house trailer the rest of his life. He's been active with the Cuban refugees and the freedom fighters all this time. . . . If I see him once a month I consider myself fortunate."

He let her go on talking, although he had his own questions he wanted to get in.

"I'm afraid he didn't appreciate my being suddenly very religious. When he came back from his tour of duty and found out I had become a serious Christian, something went out of him. He tried, I must say. But church and prayer meetings are not Joe's cup of tea. He took it for three months, then suggested we go to Florida. He was in the Bay of Pigs fiasco; barely got out with his life. He became bitter after that: bitter against the United States, against President Kennedy, against Castro, of course. From then on he became more and more involved with the Cubans, running guns, trying rescue operations. But it was all for money. He started gambling, drinking—and to tell you the truth I don't look for his coming home now; he's ugly and surly, mean. I've wanted to leave him long ago, but something inside tells me to stay. I guess my fourteen years with him has to count for something—and I'll stay until he doesn't come back or is thrown to me, a bloody pulp. . . ."

She slowed down to take the exit into downtown Miami. Sebastian wanted to ask her what she wanted of him. Her telegram had simply said: AM DESPERATE FOR HELP CAN YOU COME. He figured it was an appeal to get Joe out of his trouble, back on an even keel again, maybe even get him to consider Christianity so her world could have some sense of balance. But he didn't ask her. She was back to a reckless, desperate kind of driving. There were lights flooding them from behind now, and she had tensed up even more. Her hands gripping the wheel were knotted up into fists of bony desperation.

She cut off the main boulevard and into less congested streets. The lights continued to stay on them from behind. Her driving became more erratic as she fought to shake whoever was following, if anyone actually was. In the midst of it all, she managed to say, "I can't explain now . . . but I'm going to try to shake that car behind us. . . ."

She cut quickly around a corner and onto a wider boulevard again, poured coal to the Plymouth, and shot right, ignoring the four-way stop. Sebastian grabbed the door handle to keep from being pitched into her lap. The lights behind didn't come on them right away, but as they continued up the street he half turned and saw them closing.

"Anybody you know?" He put some banter in his voice, the kind he'd learned in the sweat of another experience not so long ago.

"No . . . but somebody who wants Joe pretty bad and figures I'm the easiest way to him."

They took another corner, and this time she almost hit another car broadside. She managed to spin out of it in time, beating the light by a second. The car behind ignored the light altogether and almost smashed another coming through on the green. Sebastian knew then that this was no drag race contest, that whoever was back there was very anxious indeed either to catch up or stay on her until she got to wherever she was going.

"We won't shake him this way," she said, and there was a fluttering sound to her voice, as if her breath was coming hard. He saw the big red PARK sign off to his right even as she hit the brake and swung hard. Before he realized it, they were gunning up the circular ramp of the unattended night parking pavilion, the concrete walls and yellow floor numbers flashing by him in a blur. He was jammed completely over now against the door as she pushed the car into the squealing turns up that ramp, barely missing the front or back ends of other cars parked in their stalls. One thought predominated as the wild, top-spinning ride went on—what would happen if another car was coming down?

He saw the yellow number 13 whirl by, and then she straightened the dizzying careen of the car and shot into an enclosure. Without a word, she reached out her open window and punched a red button. There was a loud whining sound in response, and Sebastian looked back to see the elevator doors come down behind them. The feeling of descent followed. He slowly straightened up as she put her head down on hands that still gripped the wheel. She was very still in that pose, as if she had deliberately crammed a tight lid down hard on her emotions.

The whine of the elevator stopped abruptly as the slight bump told them they were down. The doors lifted automatically, and he saw that they were facing the ramp to the street. No one was around. From somewhere there came the sound of a time-clock bell ringing in a long, raucous protest at the car running in without taking a time ticket. Above that he thought he heard the squealing, roaring of another car chasing up the ramp where they had been—or maybe coming down.

She didn't waste any time. Once they got out into the street again, she made a few more wild turns and then raced up a smaller residential street where there were fewer lights and less traffic. Finally, in a kind of desperate attempt to be relieved of the pressure, she cut into a driveway lined with Poinciana shrubs and slammed to a shuddering stop that landed them not more than three feet from a big white garage door.

The smell of burned rubber and hot engine grease was very strong in the car. She sat back with her hands clenched in her lap, her eyes staring fixedly at the garage doors. He waited with her for five minutes. No car followed them into the street.

"Well, you've done it," he said, giving her the tribute in his voice.

"I suppose I ought to act like a woman and cry," she said dryly, her voice empty of emotion. "Only there's no tears left to go with it. All that happens after one of these crazy rides in the streets is the swelling lump of bile that sticks in your throat—so all you do is keep swallowing and see if your lipstick is still straight. . . ."

Her voice spilled off, and he heard sounds like crumpling paper and realized it was her trench coat shaking with the shock tremors running through her. He opened the door quietly and said, "I take it you don't live here, so go on, move over, Jane, and let me drive. Just tell me where to go."

She moved over obediently. He got in and started the engine. "What a way to welcome a guest," she muttered, trying to push her tumbled dark hair off her face.

"Well, maybe the Chamber of Commerce ought to plan this for all their tourists," he quipped. "It beats the boring prelude to a tropical vacation anyway."

She tried a smile to match his attempt at jocularity. It was a tired, uncertain stab of forced optimism. "You can back out now and go back the way we came. The trailer park is two miles north on Twenty-seventh Avenue. . . ."

A half hour later they were in her trailer home, which was quite comfortable even in its compactness. She must have worked hard to give it a homey touch, and it was spotlessly clean. She made coffee and sat down at the table with him.

"Would you believe this is the fifth trailer park I've been in in the last few months?" she began, stirring her coffee slowly, cupping her other hand under her chin in a pose of reflection. She was calm now, though her movements were jerky as if the shock was still sending spasms of current through her.

"Can't pay the rent?" he said with a smile.

"I wish it were that simple," she returned. "Actually that car chasing us was desperate to follow me here to know where I'm at."

"Bill collectors?"

She smiled at her coffee, glad for his attempt to puncture the atmosphere of sordidness and tension that still clung to them. "It's probably Cubans, Castro's underground boys," she replied flatly. "Or maybe the N.I.A."

"And Joe fits into all this," he added, trying to help her.

"Well, it's no secret here," she said with a sigh, taking

hold of the cup with both hands. "The Cubans would like to start another incident with Castro, the N.I.A. tries to prevent it, and Castro's agents around here try to get information in between. Joe is a keyman, so I get caught in the middle. And it isn't getting any better. . . ."

Sebastian sipped his coffee again, taking his time, not wanting to push her, yet desirous too of knowing exactly what she had in mind for him. Looking at her now he remembered the night in her apartment in Chicago, eight years before, when he had helped her make living contact with Christ. She had been a blunt, outspoken, attractive girl of twenty-nine; she had argued intelligently against his position about spiritual destiny. In the end, though, she gave in, mainly because she was desperate. She was alone, a grass widow, her husband at sea, her mental and emotional needs crying out for satisfaction. He knew then that she was afraid she'd be unfaithful to Joe in satisfying those needs—and he had felt that she gave in to Christ only to keep from the sin she couldn't fight alone. In her faith, she had stood her ground against Joe, too, but now she had nothing to show for it; she was back to frustration, fear, and loneliness, maybe worse than she'd ever known.

"What can I do to help, Jane?" he asked bluntly, and she gave another sigh as if she was glad he had broached the subject directly, not making her come out with it by devious routes.

"I don't know what you can do," she confessed, avoiding his eyes. "Joe . . . well, he's in deep trouble now. He's somewhere down on Flagler Street—around Seventh and Flagler where the Free Cubans hang out—but I don't know where exactly. I got word that he ran up fourteen hundred dollars in gambling at some night club, and they're holding him until he pays. . . . I haven't the money nor do I know where to get it. I thought you might be able to go in there and talk to those people. . . . Your being a minister might help. . . ." Then, as if to justify it further, she added, "I read about your being in that Middle Eastern desert experience last summer; the papers said you figured big in that, so I just thought. . . ."

He nodded, assuring her that's he'd do what he could. "Is that all Joe is in for?"

She hesitated a moment, listening as a car went by outside. "No. Bingo—that's the Cuban kid who works for us and worships the ground Joe walks on—told me that he heard Joe was committed to a man named Hector Rodríguez to do some big rescue operation to get Rodríguez's family in Cuba. . . . If he did that, he must have been drunk. Nobody goes for the big ones in Cuba and lives; it's a one-way ticket to hell. . . ." She looked up quickly to see his reaction to that way of saying it.

"Who is Rodríguez?" Sebastian asked.

"The big man of the Free Cuban community here . . . lots of money . . . playing politics too, I guess . . . but nobody to fool with."

Sebastian felt the strange pulsations again that came with the slow feelers of entanglement. In the four months since leaving the church in Nashville, he had waited, wondering where he should channel himself, if perhaps he was wrong in setting himself aside for God's use in the suffering, infected areas of the world. In that time, his father had visited him twice in Chicago, appealing to him to reconsider, arguing with him, even praying with him and over him, asking God to send him back to the more "legitimate" ministry of the pulpit. Letters had come from his Nashville church, his former seminary professors, all lamenting his "pull out" from the ministry. Magazines that had carried glowing reports of his Negev experience now injected lamentations about his withdrawal from the ministry and his "retreat to oblivion." None of these had really bothered him, but there was the gnawing doubt at times that perhaps he was being a bit quixotic about his new role—that maybe the whole Negev experience had made him heady with idealism, that as much as he wanted to understand the burdens of suffering mankind where the church had no particular voice or stance, maybe those areas didn't want or need him. On top of that there always came the same sweating thoughts of not being up to the challenge when it did come; for once the Negev experience wore off, he was left with the nagging insistence within that he was still the same man with the same ineptitudes, the same clumsy approach to demands beyond him, the same serious lack of the dynamic needed to wade into trouble and successfully accomplish anything of worth. And then when the doubts were looming as a mountain in his future, the telegram had come from Jane—and with shaking hands and thumping heart he rose to it, not really sure what he was supposed to do or if God intended him to do much more than give counsel to an old friend.

But here it was now, more than counsel. How much more he couldn't tell yet. He swallowed the last of his coffee, feeling the old squeezing pressure within him, and said, "I can pay the fourteen hundred dollars for you, Jane." He waved his hand to silence her protest. "It's a loan if that'll make you feel better. Anyway, that part's easy. The rest of Joe's problem is something else again. Anyway, in the morning I can go down there and try to find where they've got Joe. . . ."

"I'll send Bingo with you," she responded eagerly, and a new glow of hope lit up her tired eyes. "He's a good kid, very trustworthy." She paused, then added, "I can't tell you how much your being here helps."

"I haven't done much yet, Jane," he cautioned her with a smile.

She got up then and went to the stove, to put the coffee back on the flame. She stood there a long moment as if thinking, then said, "I think you know how Joe feels about you without my telling you." Her voice sounded a bit apologetic. "When he came back from overseas and found me . . . going to church and all . . . well, you should know, he's mad enough to kill you . . . and the mood he's in lately, he could do it now. . . ."

Sebastian kept his eyes on his coffee cup, knowing she was telling him this to give him opportunity to change his mind.

"If Joe wants to kill me, this is his opportunity," he said lightly. "As I remember him in high school, he was always full of bluff—anyway, let's play that when we come to it, okay?"

She turned and smiled, but it was an accommodating one rather than one of confidence in what he said, and it was obvious that she was worried. "Your bedroom is ready," she said. "If you don't mind staying here tonight. . . . It's just good to have a man around. . . ." He nodded, and she added, "I'd appreciate it if you would pray for me before you turn in. And Joe? I might as well confess that I haven't been complimenting God much lately. I keep thinking my faith is what drove Joe into this Cuban mess—gunrunning, drinking, gambling—I need something, anything, some glimmer of light, to keep on track. . . . I hope I don't shock you?"

"Not at all," he replied. "I've been through my time of doubts too. I know how you feel."

She looked at him with some relief showing in her eyes. He talked to her about spiritual things for a few moments; then he prayed. At midnight he turned in. As he lay down on the small cot to stare at the moonlight coming through the small, round window over his head, he remembered Joe MaConnel again: the medium-built tank that he was, rolling with power and the ability to dismantle a man easily. He remembered those days in football scrimmage a short time after he'd whipped Joe in the school debate—because, though he wasn't much of a speaker himself, Joe was even worse—when Joe would deliberately seek him out on the field and deck him with the most painful tackles in the business. If there was such a thing as a human "killing machine," Joe MaConnel was that.

But now he rolled over and sought sleep, because dwelling on what Joe might do to him was not going to help him stay here very long. And as he drifted with the first webs of unconsciousness, he heard soft, choking sobs coming from the other end of the trailer, smothered now and then by the pillow. There was no question about it now; Joe or no Joe, he had arrived.

Chapter II

****

After breakfast the next morning, a battered, topless jeep came roaring and snarling into the carport directly under the window where Sebastian was finishing his coffee with Jane. As it came to a slamming, sliding halt with the painful sound of a thousand ball bearings spilling out on a wooden floor, the jeep kicked up a cloud of dust that swirled in through the screen. The young-looking driver, dressed in a loud green sport shirt and khaki bermuda shorts, with a face the color of creamed coffee, vaulted out of the seat and yelled, "Mrs. MaConnel, it's Bingo!"

"As if I didn't know," Jane called back, coughing on the dust and giving Sebastian a lifted eyebrow in apology. "Nobody makes an entry like that in a jeep except in battle maneuvers. Come on in."

A delighted, youthful chuckle preceded the young Cuban's entrance. Sebastian caught a glimpse immediately of white teeth contrasted with black hair and got the impression of effervescence running wild, like shook-up soda exploding from a pop bottle. There was so much buoyancy and restrained energy that he felt the Cuban was ready to start bouncing around the trailer like a rubber ball. There was not a static line in the face that gleamed with vigor and excitement, an eagerness to run, to compete, to move. Dark eyes flashed the boundless enthusiasm that goes with the young on a sunny day in the tropics; there was so much electric magnetism exuding from the newcomer that Sebastian felt a strong urge to do a jig just to keep pace with that flow of current.

"Mr. Sebastian, meet the one and only Bingo Gonzales," Jane said with a dry-sounding attribution that was intended as playful mockery.

"Good to met you, man," Bingo said, giving Sebastian a quick, firm hand.

"He's a reverend, Bingo," Jane warned.

Bingo looked confused for a moment, as though he were suddenly confronted with an altar full of candles and holy water. Then he made a quick sign of the cross. Sebastian sensed that it was a left-handed jab of respect, rather hurriedly performed to avoid having to switch off his glowing effervescent demeanor in favor of the more staid atmosphere of the church.

"Hey, I got news," Bingo said to Jane, turning his smile back on to full candle power.

"You found Joe?" She got up from her chair eagerly.

"Well, I think I know where he is." Bingo's body swayed with excitement. Sebastian noted the muscular ripple of his leg muscles, and the blacksmith arms, which said that Bingo was a man physically beyond his years who played lots of handball or worked regularly with weights. "I spent the night driving around town. . . . I hit every bar, night club, and"—he paused to look at Sebastian testily—"and other places where gusanos hang out, and I think I got enough information on Joe to zero me right in on the place."

"Good! Then you'll take Mr. Sebastian there immediately," Jane said. "He's a boyhood friend of Joe's."

Bingo hesitated. His smile remained on his face, but his eyes, intent on Sebastian, showed a little uncertainty.

"Ummm—well, it's no place for a padre," he said. "Least of all a gringo padre, you know what I mean? I could go there myself if I had the money—"

"Mr. Sebastian goes, Bingo," she corrected him. "You want some coffee?"

Bingo shook his head. A smile of resignation came across his face, and he began to snap his fingers in a fast Spanish rhythm, his body swaying, his feet shifting. "That's the kind of place it is, padre," he said. "Real hot and sweaty all the time—you know what I mean? Their biggest product is sin, and their code is to wipe out anything or anyone who brings goodness and light. You still want to go?"

Sebastian detected the Spanish accent that rode some of Bingo's words like unwanted passengers demanding more room on the train. There was also that debonair attitude about the church that said well enough that Bingo's Catholicism was not a very relevant force in his life.

"I'm ready when you are," Sebastian responded with a smile. "But why don't you call me 'man?' It'll make it easier on everybody."

Bingo paused in his finger snapping and looked quickly at Sebastian, not comprehending the request immediately. "A man of the church is a man of the church, padre," he remarked. "And me, I got respect for the church. Besides, it's the only way I got to remind me who you are—you got no collar, no robe. . . . Hey, are you a Protestante?"

"Call me 'man,' Bingo," Sebastian insisted pleasantly.

Again that brilliant smile broke out on Bingo's face, and

he said, while moving to the door in his shuffling half dance, "Okay, man, that's what I like—clear away the barriers to real friendship right at the start. We're off in twenty seconds minus zero."

Sebastian followed him to the door, then turned to face Jane. "Shouldn't that be—?"

"Oh, sure, it should be zero minus twenty seconds," Jane acknowledged with a shrug of her shoulders. "He picked that up a few months ago watching a rocket shot from Cape Kennedy on TV. But since his Spanish still gets in the way of his English, he gets it kind of fouled up."

Sebastian smiled at that and said, "I'll call you when I have news."

"God go with you," she said, and he could see the fresh fear in her eyes, perhaps over what Joe might do to him or whoever else might be standing in the way.

He climbed into the jeep and Bingo prodded the engine to life. There came that same loud sound of grinding bearings, and then they shot out of the carport, and the rest of the ride out of the trailer park was just one big blur as Bingo shifted and poured fuel to the jeep in motions that were impossible to follow.

"Junk," Bingo yelled to him over the sound of the motor. "They wanted to scrap it, so I buy it for ten bucks and look for parts. Now she running better than their new jobs—how about that?"

Sebastian didn't know who "they" represented, but he smiled his acknowledgment while looking for some kind of handhold in order to stay in the seat, especially when they rounded the corners. After they got into Miami traffic, the engine roar wasn't quite so constant, so Sebastian ventured, "By the way, what is a gusano?"

Bingo shot off through the light on yellow, geared down,

and said, "Gusano? That's Castro's name for all who leave Cuba—it means worm."

"Oh." And Sebastian settled back to concentrate on hanging on. After cashing a check for fourteen hundred dollars—which required a long-distance call to his bank in Chicago—and putting it into a sealed envelope, they went on. Sebastian had no idea as to direction at all. Miami was new to him. The sun was bright, the air brisk, and it smelled of salt water and expensive things. Palm trees waved their green bonnets in a kind of gay approval of the sparkling day. Fleecy clouds overhead danced like little lambs, giving their own promise of a perfect day ahead. For Sebastian there was a peculiar exhilaration in this vacation paradise, and he wished he could make a leisurely inspection of it today rather than be bumped around in this noisy, careening jeep that was as out of place in the expensive Miami traffic as Tugboat Annie at a debutante ball.

"Biscayne Bay," Bingo sang out as they slid to a stop at another light. Sebastian looked to his right, across an immaculate and cool-looking park, toward the blue water contrasted by the sleek white hulls of the fishing cruisers. While they sat at the light, the jeep bouncing with the idling engine, Bingo began singing the refrain from "Hello, Dolly," his finers snapping the rhythm.

Then they were off again in that same jolting take-off, roaring down Biscayne Boulevard. "Friendship Torch," Bingo called out, pointing to a monument on the right and the torch with smoking flame coming out of it. "Symbol of American-Cuban relationships, dedicated by President Kennedy."

The smile on his face was not entirely pleasant; Sebastian thought he detected a little bit of sarcasm.

"Freedom Tower," Bingo said again, pointing to a building on his left that had a large tower on it like Spanish architecture. "That's the Cuban Refugee Center—close to three hundred thousand Cubans gone through there since nineteen sixty."

"You too?"

"Sure. Only I swim out on a raft in nineteen sixty-three. Got picked up by the Coast Guard."

"Where'd you learn English?"

He hesitated a moment before answering. "At a Catholic mission school in Pinar Del Río Province."

"You still go to church?"

The smile flashed as he jumped the jeep off to the left and up a crowded thoroughfare. "Cubans always go to church—free Cubans, anyway. It is always good to say hello to God regular, comprene? You understand?"

Sebastian didn't know how to answer that, so he said, "What are all those thousands of free Cubans doing here now?"

"Try to make expenses and hope, man," Bingo said, gunning the jeep motor in emphasis.

"Hope for what?"

Bingo looked at him quickly, his smile a quizzical one as he tried to reconcile Sebastian's apparent total ignorance of the Cuban problem here.

"Man, another Bay of Pigs, what else?"

Sebastian let that go and waited for another traffic light. When one came up red, he said, "Isn't that proven hopeless by now?"

Bingo was whistling "Hello, Dolly" through his teeth, watching the light, ready to jump the jeep off again. "Padre"—he reverted now to that other title, apparently forgetting for the moment or perhaps reminding himself that only a minister of the church could be so ignorant—"if you ever get chased out of your home town by a gang of bandidos and told to never go home again, would you write it off as—what you call—hopeless? Say you get chased to Bimini out there sixty miles off Florida—how many times you try getting back to

Florida? You try, padre, or maybe you not much of a man, sí?"

Sebastian didn't meet Bingo's glance. The vehemence of the remark was obvious by the mixing in of Spanish, and Sebastian always felt some sense of shame when the obvious was pointed out to him.

He noticed that they were now on Flagler Street, one of the main arteries of downtown Miami. At Seventh Street, Bingo cut off and drove down several blocks, went off on a narrow side street, and pulled up in front of a building that had a dirty yellow canvas canopy over the door stretching across the sidewalk. A small red neon light, fighting to be seen behind a smeared window, spelled out *Libertad.* "The house of gusanos," Bingo said. "One of the many places a Free Cuban can drink and forget it all."

Bingo cut the engine of the jeep, and Sebastian was grateful at least for the comparative quiet. The sound of a fast Spanish rhythm came through a small loud-speaker over the canvas canopy, trying to be heard above the loud, scraping static.

"No place for gringos, this," Bingo warned. "You sure you don't want me to try it alone?"

"Maybe my going in there will help," Sebastian insisted, although he felt a certain queasiness about the prospects of being swallowed up in that cave. "Anyway, you run the interference, Bingo, and I'll carry the ball, okay?"

Bingo shrugged and got out of the jeep to walk toward the door. Sebastian followed. The doors were of glass; the one on the left had a long spider-web crack in it, the other was covered by grime. "Hold on to your money, man," Bingo warned before pushing inside. "We got experts here who are dying to go into the banking business."

The room was dark, and the only air came from one big propeller fan in the ceiling that moved in labored cycles, as if weary with trying to beat the battle with the stomach-constricting odor of stale beer and the foul breath of cheap disinfectant. It wasn't particularly hot, so there must be an air conditioner some place, but wherever it was, it was as weak as the ceiling fan. Sebastian stood blinking in the darkness, his eyes refusing to adjust to it after the brilliance of the sun outside. He was aware of Bingo moving forward toward the bar that sat vaguely silhouetted against a backdrop of macabre blue lights.

After a few more seconds, the shapes inside began to form for him. He saw circular, dark-stained tables in the center of the room, independent islands trying to find some identity with each other. Around a few of them sat some men, silent, staring, smoking long cigars, looking as stoic as philosophers in pain. Then his eyes shifted to his immediate right. Not four feet from him was a table around which sat three girls done up in brief red costumes. One of them was playing with a deck of cards but paused to look up at him with interest; another, busy filing her long red nails, gave him a slow smile that had solicitation written all over it; the third, most disturbing to him, sat back a bit, her long legs, encased in black net stockings, propped up on the fourth chair by the table. She was nearest, and her legs were close enough for him to reach down and touch. He couldn't help but look at her, from her legs to her tight bodice to the round face with the heavily made-up brown-black eyes and the exaggerated smear of lipstick on what probably was a good mouth. There was no indication of any emotion in her face; she simply looked up at him as if he were something the wind had blown in by mistake. But then, as if to communicate some message of distaste for him, perhaps because he was an American in strictly Cuban territory, she lifted one of those long legs off the chair, bent it at the knee, and began jiggling it in time with the loud Spanish music. It was undoubtedly intended to be some kind of obscene gesture, and he quickly cleared his throat, pulled at his tie, and decided that the safest move was forward toward that sickly blue ahead.

He walked away from the girls, leaving the powerful

scent of their perfume behind, through the tables where cigar smoke and animosity mingled together to warn him off. When he got to the bar, Bingo was already arguing with a big man who was standing behind it. The man didn't seem to be impressed, so Sebastian said loudly, above the music, "You understand English?"

Dark eyes shifted to him, measuring him as the others in the room had, the smoke from a long cigar curling up in a disdainful kind of dance before his eyes.

"Gringos not allowed in dis place," the bartender said with a scraping sound to his voice.

"I'm a friend of Joe MaConnel. . . . I've come to get him. I have the fourteen hundred dollars he owes you—"

The music stopped at the precise moment Sebastian was shouting about the money. Bingo shot a warning glance at him. The room behind him had gone very quiet.

The big man folded his arms and removed his cigar to get a better look at Sebastian. As he leaned forward, a long scar on his left cheek showed like a white thread against the dark color of his skin. Part of his left eye was pulled down, too; he was anything but an angel of light.

"The money," he said, holding out a big brown hand.

"When we get MaConnel," Bingo cut in.

"Money," came the insistent reply.

Sebastian handed him the envelope, and Bingo said, "Dios mío," in an exasperated tone of voice.

The big man counted the bills and then handed over an official receipt. "That is what MaConnel owes me in gambling debt," he said. "Now he is paid up."

"All right, now show us where he is," Bingo ordered.

The big man turned to glare at Bingo as if he were a pesky house fly that had either to be tolerated or swatted down right there. He shook his oversized head in the angry gesture of a bull getting ready to charge. "He is not mine to give. He belong to Señor Rodríguez."

"What?" Bingo yelped. "We just paid you fourteen hundred dollars to get MaConnel out of here!"

"No!" the big man cut back. "You pay me for what that gringo owed me. I did not say he could go! You see Señor Rodríguez, then you get MaConnel!"

"Who's Rodríguez?" Sebastian asked Bingo. Although Jane had said something of him the night before, he wanted more details in the light of this situation. But Bingo was already walking out toward the street without even looking back. Sebastian followed, ignoring the three women by the door as he went, but feeling the same sense of headiness as he passed through their perfume.

After they had climbed back into the jeep, Sebastian asked again, "Well, what about this Rodríguez?"

"He's like the mayor of the town," Bingo explained. "You got your Jimmy Hoffa—we got Rodríguez." Bingo's smile was there again but not quite so genuine. "If *he's* keeping Joe in that place, then it's something pretty big."

"I don't want to leave until we've tried everything possible to get Joe out of there," Sebastian insisted.

Bingo sat quietly for a long minute staring fixedly down the street, his hands gripping the wheel. Then he turned to Sebastian, his eyes dancing with new inspiration. "You not afraid to sweat a little, padre? You pray for me to the Blessed Virgin if I do what will get Joe out of there?"

"As long as nobody gets hurt, fine," Sebastian said, "although I'll send my prayers by the more direct route."

Bingo grinned. "Okay, padre, we're in business. Come on, let's check the side door."

Sebastian followed Bingo into the alley. They tried the side door and found it unlocked, but when Bingo opened it a crack Sebastian saw a man sitting in a chair at the top of what must be stairs to the basement, leaning against the wall reading a newspaper. There was no way in there.

"Okay," Bingo said, closing the door quietly. "I'll go

inside and make smoke. When you see it or hear trouble, wait to count of ten. Then open the door, go down those stairs, and look for Joe. Okay, padre?"

Sebastian wasn't sure what Bingo meant by making "smoke," but he nodded anyway and Bingo went back toward the street. Sebastian waited, standing by the door, feeling the heat of the Miami sun for the first time. Sweat began to trickle down the back of his neck, and he resisted the temptation to go see what Bingo was actually up to.

Then it came: a soft puffing sound from inside like someone had touched a match to a can of gasoline. Even as he started ticking off the seconds, Sebastian heard the commotion inside of people moving quickly in some kind of panic. For a moment he was tempted to run back to see what it was all about; perhaps his place now was to rescue people from whatever was going on. But he knew that this was his only opportunity to get Joe. He pulled open the door. The man was not in his chair; the newspaper was on the floor in a heap. Smoke, columns of it in a blue-black cloud, was already pouring into this dingy back corridor. He went down the stairs ahead of that smoke, getting the new smells of rotting garbage, stale liquor, and the mustiness of a basement that wasn't used for much of anything except refuse.

In the darkness at the bottom of the stairs, he groped around looking for a light switch, calling out to Joe as he did so. There was no answer. Finally, as his foot struck something solid, he heard a gasping sound. He reached down and felt the bulk at his feet. He felt the clothes, the skin—that was enough. He hadn't time for identification now. He picked up the body, staggering under its weight but managing somehow to get it slung over his shoulders. He found the stairs again and half stumbled back to the top, gagging and coughing on the smoke and trying to see where he was going through running eyes.

When he staggered out the side door and into the alley,

he found the jeep already there and waiting, Bingo gunning the motor that beat a tremendous howl against the brick buildings in the alley.

"We're on a short fuse, man!" Bingo called out, and Sebastian carefully but hurriedly dropped the body into the back seat, trying not to let the head strike the jeep's side. He heard the sound of sirens even as he did so and realized that the fire department was already coming down on them—and the police? He glanced at the face in the back, but he couldn't tell if it was Joe MaConnel or not; it was a face swollen and bluish, with heavy gouging cuts over both eyes. There was blood too, matted in the thinning dark hair, creasing down the left temple, drying there to form a trail that led to a shirt already turned reddish-brown with it.

"That's him!" Bingo said, as if sensing Sebastian's question.

"Off to the nearest hospital, Bingo!" Sebastian snapped, as he hopped into the front seat.

"Man, this chariot already she burn rocket fuel!" Bingo responded, the excitement garbling his English again. Then he shot the jeep back in reverse with full power, careening out into the street that had become choked with a curious, excited crowd. Smoke was pouring out the two glass doors in front, and, as Bingo stopped the reverse slide of the jeep to throw it into low, Sebastian found himself looking into the face of the girl with the long, shapely, black-netted legs who had wiggled her contempt of him earlier. In the sun there were striking lines of beauty behind her garishly painted face, and the whole of her was a communication of disturbing dimension—only now her lips curled up with a remark she shot at him in Spanish, and he knew it was not a very complimentary one by its tone.

Then Bingo shot power to the jeep, and they were off down the street. Sebastian lifted his hand to the girl in a kind of lame salute, not knowing how else to reply, continuing to stare at her until she was lost in the crowd behind them, her red costume standing out like the color of the anger that probably roared inside her.

"She called you a pig," Bingo yelled at him, his smile flashing the exuberance of his victory and at the same time jumping the barriers he had apparently always felt between himself and the sacrosanct man of the church. "A special American pig, at that!"

"I don't blame her," Sebastian yelled back. "How much in damages will all that smoke cost?"

"Odorless smoke bomb!" Bingo replied. "All that gusano has to do is open his windows for a day, and it'll be gone—it will do him good to get fresh air into that place!"

They got Joe to the emergency room of Mercy Hospital, where doctors worked on him for over an hour, closing up the head wound with ten stitches and taping his ribs, one of which they were sure was cracked. They spent some time making sure he didn't have a concussion and then moved him to a room where he could get some whole blood into him.

"He'll be okay," the intern said finally, "but it'll be a few weeks before he's mobile."

Sebastian saw to it that Joe had a private room and signed for it himself. Joe was still unconscious two hours later, so Sebastian put a call through to Jane. She was so relieved that her words over the phone were garbled, and he knew she was trying to fight off the tears of relief. He went ahead and explained what had happened at the Libertad to give her time to recover, for she was a proud girl who hated to show tears or emotion of any kind. When he finished, she had regained her calm, and he told her to come on over and he'd meet her in the lobby.

It wasn't until nine o'clock that night that Joe came out of it. Sebastian was having coffee in the coffee shop when the nurse came in and told him. He took the elevator to the ninth floor, not knowing what to expect when he saw Joe or when Joe saw him. To his surprise, when he walked into the room, Joe was sitting on the edge of his bed, clad only in the white smock that hospitals provide, which gave him the look of a man wearing an oversized bib. The lumpy bandage on the left side of his head gave him a disbalanced look, as if he were hanging over on a thirty-degree list. His lips were still puffy and both eyes discolored; he looked disheveled, older and dissipated. Sebastian hadn't seen Joe MaConnel since a high school alumni day in Chicago in 1959. At that time Joe had been sparkling in his chief petty officer's uniform with the submarine patch on his shoulder. He had been the picture of authority, the kind of military man that speaks out of recruiting posters saying: "Uncle Sam wants you!" There had been that same dash about him, almost a kind of swashbuckling air, from his youthful crew-cut head, to his ready, perpetual smile, to the flashing sparkle in his iron-gray eyes. Joe had been golden gloves champion and most valuable football player at Central High, the man who always made people look twice at him because of the aura of athletic smoothness and power that radiated from him and gave him the character of a walking Gibraltar. In Joe there was a sense of Fourth of July fireworks, flashing, multicolored fountains of bravado that went with the soldier of fortune he portrayed.

Now Sebastian could only barely see some of the old Joe MaConnel in the man who sat on the edge of the bed. The slight smile, that dangerous smile—a hallmark of his that nobody else could duplicate—the kind Joe always wore when his inner self was churning or getting ready for a contest, as if he was secretly relishing the thought of what he was getting ready to do . . . that was all Sebastian could identify at the moment as belonging to the man he once knew. "Happy Mac" they called him in high school, because he was probably the only tackle in football who could smile across at his opponent before the ball was snapped; but it wasn't really a happy grin, it was a flash of the sadistic streak in him, the mocking kind of smile that said life was full of rotten breaks and practical jokers and all you had going for you was your willingness to hit first and smile while you're doing it.

Sebastian, though, was prepared to run through all the warning signs of that smile, and he walked over to the bed and leaned over in front of Joe to put out his hand in greeting. Though he saw Joe's quick movement, he couldn't get out of the way in time; the fist caught him on the chin and snapped him upright and backwards off balance. He tried to catch himself, but there was nothing to grab, so he went down on the seat of his pants in a long, sliding glide, picking up acceleration from the smooth, polished tiles underneath. He heard a cry of dismay from Jane and a "Dios mío!" from Bingo, and then he hit the wall in the far corner by the door, winding up in a tangle of his own legs and arms. He lay there, blinking uncertainly, trying to get his double vision shaken loose and also forcing himself not to reach up to touch his stinging jaw. At the same time, he saw the white-stockinged legs of the nurse next to him in the doorway and looked up at her, putting on what must have been at best a sloppy grin to explain that all this was but normal procedure for visitors calling on Joe MaConnel. The nurse made a move to put down her tray and help him, but Joe's voice called out a warning to her.

"Leave him alone, honey! He's a big man now; he can get up by himself—can't you, preach?"

"Mr. MaConnel, this is no place for gymnastics," the nurse shot back in a scratchy voice that went with a crusty kind of spirit of her own.

"And what kind of greeting is that, anyway?" Jane chimed in, her voice gone shrill on the taut strings of her nerves. "Especially for the man who helped save your life?"

"He didn't save anybody's life!" Joe retaliated. "All he did was put a few more necks in the noose, that's all! Anyway, what I gave him is only down payment for what's coming. You hearing me good, preach?"

Sebastian got up slowly, shaking his head to clear the fog, and slowly walked back toward the chair in front of Joe, waving off Bingo and Jane, who reached out to help him. "That's just a sample of what you got coming for what you did to my wife a few years back when Daddy was off playing submarine—remember?" Joe continued, his voice grating over his own weakened condition and the hot stream of genuine anger that rode with it. "For getting her all fouled up in religion, see, and for making her what she is now. Take a good look at her, preach; do you see the same lovely lady you met back in Chicago in nineteen fifty-nine? No, she looks like a refugee from a nut house, that's what. And that little love tap on your button, preach, is only earnest money for what I'm going to do to you when I pay back those fourteen hundred bills you put up to spring me from the Libertad. Ouch!"

The nurse, a big, blonde woman, grinned impishly and with some vindictiveness as she pulled out the needle from Joe's right arm. Joe's smile broadened to reveal one chipped incisor in an otherwise perfect set, a gesture of tribute to someone who had managed to get in a blow of her own without his looking, and his smoky gray eyes took on a kind of stormy green against the yellowish purple of his shiners.

"Lady, if you ever try attacking me again without notice I swear you'll get a gymnastic experience that you'll remember long enough to tell your grandchildren!"

The nurse only grunted her disdain and, on her way out, said to Sebastian, "Are you all right?"

"All right?" Joe contradicted with a yelp and a scornful laugh. "He's never been all right since the day he was born! He's got all his gears twisted around inside so that every time he moves he registers tilt like a cockeyed pinball machine!"

"Joe!" Jane tried again to cut off the rising flow of liquid heat that seemed to pour out of him.

"There'll be a few tilting moments for you, my friend, before you get out of here," the nurse called back from the door, waving the bent hypo in her hand.

When she disappeared into the corridor, Joe turned quickly to Bingo. "Get my pants!"

"What?" Jane put her hands up to her face in a gesture of horror.

"You can't go anywhere in the shape you're in," Sebastian said.

"Ahora mismo!" Joe snapped at Bingo again, pointing to his pants on the back of the chair that Sebastian was sitting on. Bingo, with a confused glance at Jane and Sebastian, made a move to obey.

"You can't," Sebastian insisted, leaning back against the chair and holding the pants there with his body.

"Okay," Joe said, his eyes flashing his vehemence and contempt for Sebastian, "you sit here and wait for the pick-up committee. Because what you did today, preach, was to steal Señor Rodríguez's prize pawn from under his nose. You don't know Rodríguez, but I can tell he can get very ugly when he's crossed up. . . ."

"How does he know you're here?" Sebastian tried, taking time to rub his stinging chin.

"Where else would a couple of stupid would-be commandos take a beat-up prisoner but to a hospital?" Joe barked back. "So now you got your choice—any minute now people are going to walk through that door looking for me. Either Rodríguez's caballeros coming to get me to throw me back into that sweatbox you stole me from—and you'll probably go with me this time, all of you—or else it'll be the N.I.A. coming to put me out of circulation for a good long time, and you'll have some explaining to do; or, worse yet, it could be Castro's goons, and, if them, we'll all be buried in cement and dumped in the Atlantic before the sun sets. Do you want me to spell it out a little more?"

That did it for Bingo. He snatched the trousers from the chair with a vicious jerk before Sebastian could do anything about it. Joe pulled them on and tossed the white smock into a corner. After he got his bloodstained sport shirt on, Sebastian said, "You'll never walk out of here—they won't let you."

"Joe, get some sense for once," Jane added. "You can't even walk."

"You just watch me, doll," Joe retaliated, standing to buckle his trousers, then sitting down on the bed again as an intern passed the door and looked in for just a second before moving on. "And all you have to do is help me a little—including the preacher boy here, who can let his little light shine now that he's bustin' to crusade. . . . Bingo, you go down the hall to the service elevator and wait there. . . . Hold the car on this floor. . . . Preach, you go outside the door and make sure the coast is clear, and don't let any bright sawbones come bustin' in here; tell him I'm praying or making my last confession and don't want to be disturbed. . . ." Joe flashed that grin at Sebastian again, the smile that communicated nothing but his mocking disdain for the symbolic elements of religion. "And Jane, honey, you can wheel me out in that wheel chair over there. . . . It'll save us time going down the hall and maybe cause less suspicion."

Jane just stood there hanging on to the end of the bed with her hands, her head bowed in resignation, as if she'd come to the last stroke that she could take in all this wild business. Sebastian didn't want to argue any further with Joe, so he went obediently to the door to scan the hall. The jaw still hurt where Joe had connected, and he wondered what would have happened if Joe had been in good health. As it was, the blow was only glancing, delivered off a weak energy plant. There was something else, though, that smarted and dazed him even more—he had never been hit by anyone in his life like that, certainly never for trying to do something good as was expected of him as a man of God. The shock of that would not wear off very soon. And the thought of having to look for more of the same, perhaps, as long as he stayed here didn't help much either. But he put it aside for now, looking down the corridor again for any sign of traffic.

With visiting hours about over, the corridor was empty except for a few stragglers on their way out. A nurse entered a room three doors down; an intern was at the front desk talking to the receptionist. In a moment, he might come down the hall again, and then it would be too late for Joe. Then, even as he made his move to signal that all was clear, he saw something else—three men in light tropical suits came up to the desk and began talking to the receptionist and the intern. That didn't look good at all.

"Now," Sebastian said over his shoulder, and Jane pushed Joe out into the hall in the wheel chair.

"Come on, doll, come on," Joe prodded her, his eyes checking the hall and focusing quickly on the three men by the main desk. "This is no stroll on the sun deck."

"I'll take him," Sebastian said and moved Jane aside.

"Take your hands off, preacher boy," Joe snapped. "I don't want a holy man setting course for me. . . . Jane, get back there!"

Jane shot an exasperated glance at Sebastian and took over the chair again. They got down to the service elevator where Bingo was waiting, holding the doors.

"One minute there!" The voice sounded from up the corridor behind them.

Sebastian turned to see the intern coming rapidly, the three tough-looking tropical-suit boys with him.

"Inside!" Joe snapped, and shoved on the wheels of the chair as Sebastian pushed along with Jane. Bingo was the last inside, hitting the down switch even as the intern let out another warning yell to them to stop.

The doors closed with the intern just a few feet away. They started down.

"She's slower than the main traffic elevator," Joe commented, more to himself than to any of them, his grayish-green eyes staring up at the lighted numbers that bounced off ever so slowly as they descended. "If we beat them down, it won't be by much. . . ."

His face was gleaming in a greasy paste of sweat, giving it a ghoulish appearance, the two blackened eyes looking like a weird clown's mask over the top of his face, the lumpy protrusions around his mouth twisting his lips out of shape, all topped off by the white crown of bandage that gave him the lopsided, bizarre look of a New Year's Eve celebrator.

"Let her go to the basement," Joe said to Bingo as the lighted numbers hit "main" and continued on. "They'll think we'd get off at the main floor; our best chance is out the ambulance exit. Doll, is the Plymouth out back?"

"In the rear lot . . . not far. . . ."

"Okay, get ready now; we may have a wild ride out of here."

The lower corridor was empty. Sounds of pots and pans banging together, of a heavy motor running a cooling plant—these followed them as Sebastian tried to put a hand on the wheel chair to help Jane push without Joe noticing it. Bingo hesitated a moment to check the main traffic elevator as it came down, then ran to catch up as they reached the ambulance ramp.

"She comes down fast, the elevator," he said.

"All right, let's pick up the pace," Joe said, and he got up out of the chair and led them in a half trot down the ambulance ramp and out into the rear parking lot. There were a few seconds of disaster-building tension when Jane couldn't immediately remember where she'd parked, and Joe snarled something at her that only increased her sense of confusion and panic.

"That it?" Sebastian said, after crossing one lane of cars and pointing to the end of another lane.

"Yeah," Joe growled, and they ran for it. Joe climbed into the front seat, Sebastian in the back. "Bingo," Joe said, "you take the jeep. If we have to split up, you can be the decoy."

"Bueno," Bingo chirped and was off on a run across the lot to his own vehicle. Jane got behind the wheel of the Plymouth, fumbling for the keys, fighting for control as Joe stabbed her with his eyes. She finally got the car started, backed out, and shot off for the exit with a loud squeal of tires.

"Keep your eyes out the back, preacher boy," Joe said to Sebastian without turning around. "If you see headlights staying with us, you let us know. . . ."

There weren't any headlights. They made it all the way back to the trailer park without incident. But even then Joe had pushed Jane to a wild driving bout, wanting to be sure he was well out of sight of anyone who might be just far enough back to see them.

When they got to the trailer park, Joe told Jane to park the Plymouth in the village lot rather than by the trailer. Then they walked down the black-top road, and Joe deliberately cut across two other trailer lots, approaching his own from the rear. He waited five minutes, studying the trailer before going in. When they got to the carport, Bingo came sliding in with the jeep.

"They follow me down Biscayne," he said, "but I lose them when I cross the canal!"

"Okay, park down the road," Joe told him. Bingo swung the jeep around and parked fifty yards down the black-top; then he came back to stand with them in the dark under the carport canopy.

"All right, preach, this is the end of the line for you," Joe said. "Bingo can take you to the airport and you can get a plane in a few hours back to wherever you belong. . . . I don't want you cluttering up the scenery here any more."

"I just got here," Sebastian argued, "and I don't intend to leave until I finished what I came to do."

"If you think finishing the job is converting me to what my wife has hanging around her neck, you can forget it," Joe retaliated, and there was a new sound of bristling anger Sebastian could feel there in the dark. "Besides, I'm giving you a break—you hang around here and you're one dead pigeon sooner or later."

"Car coming into the park, pretty fast," Bingo hissed in the darkness.

Joe swore and said, "All right, let's get inside."

They stumbled into the trailer, slamming the door behind them, and Joe threw the lock. They waited, only their eyes alive and discernible in the dim glow from the approaching headlights that cut a latticework of exposure through the drawn Venetian blinds. They waited. The car seemed to slow, and the lights hung on the blinds a long time.

"Dios mío!" Bingo said softly in the dark, and then the motor revved up again, and the car moved on, plunging the trailer back into its welcome darkness.

"What about it, preacher?" Joe asked, continuing his conversation where it had left off before. "Now's the time to make your run out of here."

Sebastian waited, instinctively sensing that he was facing a mountain here that defied him to climb. What was going on was again far beyond his own abilities to comprehend or affect; he sensed that to stay was going to chafe Joe even more and maybe force him into action he wouldn't normally consider. And Jane? Perhaps that's what made him hesitate; he could just see her hunched-up form vaguely in the dark, and he knew that all she had left now was him; for him to go meant she would face this nightmare alone again, and he knew she wouldn't be able to; the lean, spent, burned-out woman would crack under the strain. There was too much at stake here for her—her health; most of all, perhaps, her faith. It was this last consideration that moved him to say,

"Joe, I think we ought to talk about it over a cup of coffee."

Joe didn't answer. There was a long minute of silence, and then Sebastian heard a low, trembling sigh from Jane, either in relief or out of the mounting pressure that was squeezing the breath out of her. Sebastian expected to feel the hard knuckles on his chin again, to be flayed by the unleashed fury of a Joe MaConnel who was now probably tested to the point of murder because of bitterness over what had happened to his wife and what was happening to him at the hands of Rodríguez.

"I said I'd kill you when I saw you again," Joe said, his voice gone quiet but very heavy with hostility. "Now you want me to drink a cup of coffee with you. What kind of an ass do you make me out to be?"

"I got fourteen hundred dollars invested in you, Joe, and a clip on the chin on top of it," Sebastian said evenly. "That buys me a cup of coffee and some conversation at least. . . ."

Again the silence. Then there was the rattle of a pan, and Sebastian caught Jane moving around the sink, preparing to make the coffee. Joe moved and flicked on a small night light by the table. The orange-yellowish glow seemed to dispel some of the sharp edge of vehemence and anger in the room. Bingo was smiling as usual, as if finding this moment one to relish, as if he witnessed for the first time a kind of halfway surrender on the part of Joe.

"He is one gringo padre, Joe!" he said.

"Shut up," Joe said. A smile had suddenly come to his mouth, a strange, dangerous grin that didn't do anything to cover the sinister thoughts that lurked underneath.

He kicked a chair for Sebastian and then moved slowly around to sit opposite him on the other side of the small table.

"Your meter's running, preach," he said, digging out a crumpled pack of cigarettes from his shirt pocket, smoothing out a crooked one carefully, and putting it between his puffy lips. He lit it with a paper match and blew a column of smoke deliberately across the table at Sebastian's nose. "And fourteen hundred dollars runs up fast—so you better start your talking. . . ."

Sebastian thought of trying to approach him on spiritual matters, but it was obvious that Joe was not ready, and he didn't want to have that cut out so quickly and finally right now. Instead, he said, "What's this man Rodríguez got you into?"

That's when the cement was poured. And it was at that moment that Sebastian put both feet into it. Any other question at that particular time would have ultimately led him back to Chicago by morning. And he knew it the minute Joe laughed, that knowing laugh, as if he was saying that the answer to that question was bound to demand more than fourteen hundred dollars and a love tap on the chin.

It was at that moment that Sebastian knew it was going to cost him plenty—maybe his life.

Chapter III

****

As reluctant as Joe was to say anything or even take the time to share his problem with Sebastian, whom he despised—and made no pretense about it—he seemed to be eager to talk, as if he had waited a long time to get it out. Now and then he blew smoke ceilingward in long, jabbing explosions like a locomotive puffing up a steep grade, to indicate either his frustration or disgust at himself for saying as much as he did. At other times his voice took on the note of an appeal, as if he was trying to justify his past actions, to lend strength to his rationale. Now and then the smile would come, as if he was secretly enjoying the misfortunes piling up on him, or at least the challenge of them. But never was there anything apologetic about his tone, nothing to indicate his mistakes, no indication of desire to be out of it and somewhere else. That was Joe—

with the ship going down under him he'd never admit he'd done wrong or that he wanted it some other way.

". . . so this Señor Rodríguez agreed to pick up my gambling debts and extend credit," he went on, smashing one spent cigarette butt into the overloaded saucer he was using for an ashtray and lighting a fresh one. "I knew that sooner or later he'd be into me for a chunk I couldn't pay—but that's what he had in mind. Once he got me in that position, he threatened to foreclose on me unless I took on the big caper of his, make the run to Cuba to get his family off the island. So when I ran up fourteen hundred bills at the Libertad he decided to let his goons put it to me: pay up the whole bill of chips or take the option of the rescue job. I refused—so they put me through the grinder and let me bleed in that basement until I changed my mind."

Nobody said anything, so Sebastian finally prodded with, "Nobody else will go for Rodríguez's family? I thought the Free Cubans here were anxious to run these operations just to beat Castro."

"Hogwash!" Joe exploded. "The Cubans here got a good life now. The old war chants about beating Castro are gone. Nobody's interested in sticking his neck out for anybody—for any price."

"That is not true," Bingo cut in. He kept his voice politely respectful but his eyes snapped in renunciation of Joe's remark.

Joe only looked at him with a smile of indulgence and went on dragging on his cigarette as if he hadn't heard.

"Rodríguez will pay, then?" Sebastian asked.

"Oh, sure, up to a hundred thousand bucks—but there's no money in the world big enough to get anybody around here to try it."

"Why?"

Joe looked at him with eyes narrowing, probably wondering if he should go on, hating to divulge information that could be explosive stuff to the wrong party. "Look, preacher boy, every rescue of people off the island has a hundred-to-one chance of succeeding—it just isn't done with Castro gun-boats sitting around waiting."

"There's the airlift out of Cuba, two flights a week," Jane countered, her back to them as she did the dishes in the small sink.

"They will wait forever!" Bingo almost shouted in contradiction.

"Why?" Jane insisted again. "Others get on the list and come out."

"These—Rodríguez family, they are not the same."

"Shut up, Bingo!" Joe warned, and Bingo looked quickly at Joe, sensing he might be pushing too far.

Jane looked at Joe quickly, then at Bingo, and Sebastian saw a new look of concern pass over her face, pulling her already tense features into sharp points of resistance. "That means they're military," she said, half to herself, half to Joe. "That's why they can't get out on the flights; they are already hooked into the militia, or else Castro's youth movement. Anybody who tries for them is dead before he starts!"

"Okay, okay, so let it go," Joe shot back. "You want the preacher boy here to get it all and spill it to Castro's goons or the N.I.A.? Then where are we? If Rodríguez finds out that I said anything—"

"What difference does it make? You don't intend to go on that rescue anyway. Now that you're here, we can make a run for it."

Joe blasted a salvo of smoke rings toward the ceiling. "I ain't runnin'," he said quietly, staring at the rings as they dissolved over his head.

"So you're going," Sebastian offered, trying to nip off Jane's building tirade.

The go-for-broke grin on Joe's face said that's the way the mold was shaped.

"What for?" Jane demanded.

"For the hundred thousand what else?"

"What good is money when you're dead?" she railed back at him.

Their voices bounced off the walls of the trailer in a metallic ring, falling on everyone with the finality of a funeral bell. Their conflict had rushed in on them in just a few words, shaping up on the jagged ends of their opposing values. Sebastian saw the gulf between them; even though they were trying to reach out across that chasm toward each other, they couldn't touch, like two runners passing in the dark.

"It is more than money," Bingo said quietly.

His words caught Joe by surprise, for there was in Bingo's voice a note of determination, a deliberateness that contrasted with his usual light and debonair personality. Joe opened his mouth to try to silence him, but then he apparently thought better of it and jammed the half-lit cigarette back into his mouth.

"It is for more than money," Bingo added, sure now that Joe wasn't going to oppose him, and there was a set line to his jaw, a peculiar hard shine to his eyes. "For us Cubans here, it is what you call a—a—"

"A symbol," Joe finished for him with a kind of exaggerated patience, as if he had argued this with Bingo before.

"Sí, a symbol," Bingo continued, and the word seemed like a kind of switch that threw on the dynamo of his magnetic side. "Everyone here in Miami—the Cubans—with children left in Cuba, they give up hope. They say it is too late now, that Castro has put their children in the militia—already they are taught communism, to hate the old ways, even their parents. If the Señor Rodríguez's children can be rescued, then there is hope, new life; we can go on fighting."

"Sure, sure," Joe cut back with a sardonic tone to his voice, snipping the optimism in Bingo's voice. "Hope for what? There are only a few thousand kiddies in Cuba—all in Castro's machine—whose daddies are here in Miami. You think we can get 'em all?"

"I don't know," Bingo said doggedly, "but if we do it once, who knows?"

"Can't they try for it like the rest who came out by boat?" Sebastian asked again. "They do it all the time, I understand."

"Sure, about eight hundred came out that way this past year," Joe admitted, stuffing out the cigarette butt. "But Rodríguez's kids are military so they're watched too close—they can't walk ten feet without secret police on their tail."

"How do you intend to get them out, then?" Sebastian asked pointedly.

Joe laughed, trying to shove the question aside on banter when he probably didn't know himself. "Well, as sure as God made the devil, preach, I don't intend to pray them out of there. . . . A new gimmick, for sure, will have to be used . . . but that's no concern of yours, anyway."

"What gimmick?" Jane chimed in, half turning from the sink. Joe didn't answer. He dug for another cigarette in the crumpled pack, lit it, and built up a screen of blue as if he wanted to hide behind it. "You don't have any idea, do you?" Jane went at him. "All you can do is try to run a boat straight in there, something nobody can pull off around a military establishment and get within five miles of the place! In the name of decency, Joe, let's run now!"

"Run where?" Joe shot back, his face going puffy with anger. "You think Rodríguez is going to let me walk out of this town with all the money I owe him? The country ain't big enough, doll! We got no choice, get it?"

Sebastian saw the fires stoking again, so he said, "You might consider her feelings in this, Joe."

"Sure, don't I know it!" Joe slammed back, his jaw muscles bulging as he bit hard on his anger. "I had feelings for my wife too before you came along, preach! But when you got through with her, she had none left for me. She belongs to God now"—there was a mocking tilt to Joe's voice at that—"but did anybody care two hoots in Hades about my feelings about it? No, sir, preacher, you filled her with the heavenly light and then vamoosed to your fortress in Nashville, leaving me with a religious psycho on my hands! No, neither of you touch my heart with all this feelings jazz."

"Car coming!" Bingo suddenly cut in, and they all looked up quickly to see the lights flash against the Venetian blinds, holding on there a long time. Then the sound of the wheels sliding in the gravel outside and the crunching stop told them it had turned in. "Dios mío!" Bingo said in awe, peering through the blind slats. "It is Rodríguez!"

"Oh, God," Jane moaned, grabbing the sink with both hands.

"All right, don't panic," Joe snapped, but his tongue had reached out to moisten his lips, showing for a moment a startling chink in his usual façade of toughness and indifference. "If he was out to murder, he wouldn't choose here to do it, so play it easy in low key. . . ."

Sebastian heard the footsteps coming across the gravel carport. He moved his chair away from the door and around to the head of the table, so that his back was almost flush against the small icebox behind him. He noticed Joe fumble with nervous fingers in the half-empty cigarette pack, draw one out, smooth it, stick it into his mouth. He hunted for a match, couldn't find any, and sat there with the cold cigarette in his mouth as the door opened with the look of a man who had been caught indecently exposed.

The power and authority of the man filling the trailer door seemed to crowd them all, making the room stuffy as if he was sucking all the air for himself. His face in the saffron light was darkly tanned in color, just a shade above caramel;

his eyes were a startling gray-black, which didn't seem to go with his face, except maybe the inch of gray-white mustache that was like a strip of adhesive over his upper lip, cutting down the long angle of his wide mouth. The eyes held steady, indicating a mastery of inner forces and a dominance of everything they touched. His hair was completely white and long and thin on top, so that the scalp showed through with its uneven bumps looking like careless thumb marks on fresh wax. It was a sign of premature age. The rest of his hair was cut close around the sides; its crew-cut appearance clashed with what was on top and gave the contradiction of youth and age in one. He lifted his hand and put a glowing long cigar in that wide mouth, and all the angles seemed to stand out on him—the gray eyebrows working to and fro with the smoke, the pointed nose with the spreading nostrils letting the smoke leak out as if he was some legendary species of dragon—but with it there was that unmistakable bearing of Spanish aristocracy, of the old class of barons who owned ranchos in Mexico or Spain, sat in ringside seats at bull fights, and took the homage of the toreadors. He was dressed impeccably in white dinner jacket and black trousers, and a diamond stickpin flashed its signal of wealth. A man couldn't help but feel small in his presence.

But even in all that splendor of power, Sebastian saw something else in those peculiar gray-black eyes that now surveyed the room with disinterest—a shadow of pain, of suffering, of inner torment. Not predominant at all, but there just the same, detected only by men like himself, perhaps, who had looked into eyes like that before many times.

"Good evening, Señor Rodríguez," Joe began amiably.

Rodríguez puffed on his cigar once, them removed it and said to Jane, "Forgive me, Mrs. MaConnel." His voice was modulated to a pleasant-sounding bass. "I did not wish to disturb your house at this late hour. . . . I find, however, that my business cannot wait for a more expedient time."

"It's—it's all right," Jane managed in a voice just barely above a whisper.

Rodríguez gave a curt nod of his head to express appreciation for her understanding and then barked a quick Spanish command to a swarthy Cuban standing half in the door behind him. The man disappeared outside and closed the door.

Again Rodríguez puffed on his cigar with careful gentility, surveying them all, his eyes moving from Bingo, to Jane, to Joe and then stopping on Sebastian.

"A friend from up north, señor," Joe said quickly. "Mr. Raymond Sebastian, Señor Hector Rodríguez. . . ."

"The padre," Rodríguez said flatly, his tone contemptuous of Joe for trying to hide the real identity.

Joe tried a laugh that sounded uncertain and tinny in the small trailer. "You knew that?"

"I knew who raided the Libertad this afternoon five minutes after it happened," Rodríguez replied, taking his eyes off Sebastian to stare at Joe. "You should know that I never allow a detail to escape me, old man of the sea. I must say that this is not a very respectable group of bandidos to perform such a rescue. I would not think that a man of the church would identify himself with such an operation." His eyes came back to fix on Sebastian again. "You have made peons of my men, padre. But then I underestimated Chico, here," and his eyes lifted slowly to take in Bingo, just off to Sebastian's left elbow, measuring him with the look of a father who wanted to give his son a whipping. "And how did I know where you lived? Unfortunately one of you gave this address to the hospital."

Jane sucked in her breath, and Rodríguez lifted his white, bushy eyebrows toward her.

"It is quite all right, Mrs. MaConnel," he added. "In an hour of stress, all of us are prone to become careless. Fortunately, I have the hospital record, so you need not fear anyone else will trace you here."

There was an awkward silence, during which he puffed on his cigar again, removed it, and stared at the glowing ash for a long time, his smooth face wrinkling up in concentration.

"Now, let us get to the point of my visit. . . . You have one week, amigo, to put a plan of action on my desk for the operation we are mutually agreed upon."

"I'll need more time, señor,"Joe said, leaning back and folding his arms, in an attempt to appear relaxed, a pose from which he hoped to bargain.

"You have had all the time we agreed on. . . . You will be in my office at the fraternity one week from tonight at seven o'clock with a plan of action, a foolproof plan. If not, you can be assured that I will collect on my outstanding debts with a finesse that you are already aware of. Do I make myself clear, amigo?"

Joe sighed and tried that daring grin, but it seemed tired against the drawn, starchy look of his face. "You have always had a gift for communicating your wishes—and your threats, Señor Rodríguez."

"Good. Now, you are ready to carry out the operation of tomorrow night?"

"If the N.I.A. turns its back, all is in readiness," Joe said. "The boat is ready, too."

"The N.I.A. will not be a problem." Rodríguez looked at Sebastian again, and there seemed to be some doubt in his eyes about the wisdom of such conversation with an alien man of the cloth present. "You are in reasonably good health?"

Joe kept the tired smile on his face. "Señor, I have never been in good health since I came to Florida—but I have always managed to stay mobile."

Rodríguez said nothing. He put his cigar back in his mouth slowly and carefully, as if it were a stick of dynamite, his eyes moving from a flicking glance at Joe back to a study of Sebastian. "How is the confession business, padre?"

Sebastian looked at Joe for the word of explanation that would clarify his own religion, but Joe simply sat with the cigarette hanging between his puffy lips, one eye squinted against the smoke, giving a peculiar, unfriendly, uncooperative leer to his mouth. "I'm not in that particular field, Señor Rodríguez," he offered finally.

Rodríguez thought on that a moment and then, with a shrug, added, "Well, then, I trust the offering plate is fruitful?"

Joe laughed at that, but Rodríguez's expression did not change. There was intentness in his eyes like that of a rattlesnake waiting for a rabbit to jump out of a hole. "The Lord is not one to welsh on His promises, señor," Sebastian replied, trying not to sound flippant or give a false note of bravado.

Again Rodríguez removed the cigar from his mouth, blew a column of smoke toward Sebastian, and said, "I take it you are soon to return north again?"

"In due course . . . yes."

Rodríguez flicked a half inch of gray ash off the end of his cigar into his right palm, and Joe hastily shoved his overloaded porcelain saucer toward him. Rodríguez ignored it. "May I advise you, then, that what business we carry on here has little to do with the church. . . . In fact, you could say the ugliness of it at times melts the hardest and toughest of men." He paused and then, as if coming on a sudden revelation added, "Joe, perhaps it would be well to give the padre an exposure to the elements tomorrow night."

"Into the Straits?" Joe asked, coughing on his cigarette smoke.

"Of course. In fact, I insist. The padre strikes me as one who feels his sacraments have a place in all this. It would be good for him to be aboard—better than a rabbit foot, perhaps?"

Joe looked at Sebastian with some wonder, as if he too had suddenly seen the possibilities of this idea. And then he smiled, and it was there again, the design, the relished thought coming to fruition, the obviously anticipated adventure.

Joe got up slowly out of respect for the idea conceived by Rodríguez and said, "Señor Rodríguez, there are times when I really think you and I are destined for a pact against the world—and the church."

"Sit down," Rodríguez said shortly, turning to the door quickly as if anxious to be gone. "You look more ready for a pact with death than life, let alone against the world. And I dare say a priest could knock you down with a well-timed belch. Good night, Mrs. MaConnel—and to you, Chico. Boys should not play men's games unless they expect to suffer the penalties of men. The firecracker will go off in your fingers some day." And then to Sebastian, he added, "I will light a candle for you, padre—adiós!"

There was silence in the room until the sound of the car motor died away in the night. Then Jane moved forward and, laying her hands flat down on the table, leaned toward Joe until her face was only a foot from his. "You let him do it! You sit there and let him commit an innocent man to your crazy trip down Murder Alley! Sometimes I think—I think you are nothing but scum!"

"What?" Joe said with mock incredulity, holding out his hands in appeal, while his puffy mouth worked to control the smile. "Is that any way for a Christian to talk? Anyway, what did I do?"

"You know well enough that Rodríguez deliberately wanted Mr. Sebastian on that boat, hoping he'd get killed or else get enough Castro lead thrown at him to send him flying home. That's Rodríguez's way of getting even for what Mr. Sebastian did to rescue you today—and I know too that it's your way of getting even with him too, and I'm telling you it's a pretty rotten way to even the score."

"All right, all right," Joe retaliated, bristling in defense. "So the preacher boy, here, comes down on a mission to win a soul? Well, let's let him work for it. Anyway, it'll give him something to talk about to his Sunday School class; it's a lot more dramatic than marlin fishing! Now he can say he was on a rescue run for Free Cubans—think how that'll pack them into the church! We're doing him a favor."

"Let it rest," Sebastian cut in quietly. He touched Jane on the arm, felt the taut muscles there, the chords of tension carrying all the rushing emotion that had already burned her down dangerously low in these years of similar encounters with Joe. "Maybe it is a good thing that I get the chance—anyway, I was just about to ask why it is so difficult to get a boat into Cuban waters for rescue. This is a welcome way for me to find out."

One side of him rebelled at what he was saying even then, although the other thought it was right to say it for Jane's sake.

"See?" Joe chirped, and Jane slowly straightened up and walked back toward the bedroom, dismissing any more discussion.

Bingo began to snap his fingers in slow rhythm, and Joe sat back smoking the last of his cigarette, grinning in that same knowing way at Sebastian. As for himself, Sebastian could only feel the tickling of cigar smoke that still hung in the air like bad news and soon became a slight palpitating cough in his chest.

After a while, Joe got up and said he was going with Bingo to a motel. Sebastian insisted that he stay with Jane.

Joe paused to peer at him from the door, his eyes alive even yet with those strange fitful fires. "Amigo," he said, "if I stay in this place Jane will start climbing the walls, right? Nope. Like I said, she's got feelings only for God now, so let a man of God be her comfort. Good night, preach, and say a few Hail Mary's for me—okay?"

Sebastian had no choice but finally to crawl into the bed in the small compartment with the round window by his head. He slept some, but every time he awoke he smelled that same cigar smoke, strong and pungent, clinging like the smell of death or the portent of it. And the sweat. It was there too, soaking through his pajamas, smelling sweet like the sap from maple trees, the kind that squeezed out of glands pumping too hard with inner tension. He was not yet used to it—this brush with the hardness of man, these challenges laid down for him beyond his depth. There was no safe ground here either. No point of commiseration, even. If a man had to die, he should at last have one friend who understood what he stood for and what he was trying to do.

But then Christ didn't have that either. So he rolled over, wiped at the sweat that tickled his hairline around his neck, and willed himself back into the escape of sleep.

When he woke again, the sun was slamming into his face through that round hole of a window, and there was the welcome smell of bacon and eggs and coffee replacing the smoke.

Chapter IV

****

When he came out of the small cubicle, he sensed that she was not around. There were dirty dishes left in the sink, and the frying pan showed use. There were two eggs and a half-dozen strips of bacon on a sideboard for him to fry.

He found the note by his plate. He sat down and read it:

Dear Mr. Sebastian:

Since I have to work for a living, I must leave you to get your own breakfast. Forgive me. You were sleeping so soundly I did not want to wake you. I called the airport and got you on the 11:00 A.M. *flight today. I hope you'll take it. You can't prove anything by going out with Joe on that boat. All you can do is get yourself killed.*

So please take that plane today—you'd make me very happy if you did. Thanks for coming—you've helped me.

Jane

He fried the bacon and eggs, thinking about it. He knew he couldn't leave now. The note did more to dictate the course of action than if she hadn't said anything. He detected the same note of frantic desperation even in the crisp handwriting, the way the sentences did not fit the areas between the blue lined paper. That was but symbolic of Jane's life right now—her emotions spilling out of their normal channels and running wildly across everything she touched.

He ate his breakfast and had hardly gotten things cleaned up when Bingo was there with the jeep. He went out and got in, carrying his light beige jacket with him. Bingo said nothing on their ride to wherever the boat was. Once, while they paused at a light, Sebastian asked, "You not afraid of getting killed today, Bingo?" He asked it as a kind of hint as to what to expect himself.

"You get killed choking on a piece of meat," Bingo said simply. "You die for nothing that way—but out there you die for something, sí?"

"Sí," Sebastian replied, but it was lost in the thunder of the jeep jumping off again.

They crossed over a bridge and Bingo designated the channel as the Miami River. They swung right off the bridge past gray and maroon-colored buildings that sat forlornly, crowding the river like disgruntled old men waiting for the fish to bite, and finally turned into a small area next to a large gray building that sagged peculiarly as though a large hand were pressing on it, slowly forcing it to lean.

They went inside. The sharp smells of oil, fish, and salt water hit them immediately; the inside was dark but the slamming glare of the sun from the water through the open entrance to the Miami River to his left provided a garish glow so that weird fingers of light danced on the walls.

They didn't waste much time. The boat was much like any cabin cruiser he'd ever seen, except that he sensed it was more powerful. "Old PT boat!" Bingo sang out to him, as if he was particularly proud of it. Joe appeared finally from the forward cabin; he had on a greasy yachting cap and an oily undershirt. His khaki trousers didn't look much better. He paused momentarily to look at Sebastian in the way a general would look at a private who had volunteered for a dangerous mission—with skepticism, even contempt, but also with a kind of half smile of resignation. His face still looked white and drawn from his ordeal at the hands of Rodríguez's men, but his movements were quick enough and there was that same cracking, snapping-whip-like tone to his voice.

"All right, Bingo, let's crank her up," he said. "Have a deck chair, preacher boy, and make it look like a day for marlin!"

Sebastian did as he was told, while Bingo dropped down into one of the open deck hatches. The boat coughed to life and growled there in the boathouse, gargling and muttering like some angry sea monster. Then slowly it moved out of its tight quay, creaking against the already squashed tire fenders. The sun struck them in contrast to the cool damp of the boathouse, and the boat took on new power as it moved around to head down the river.

Sebastian tinkered with the fishing pole Joe had stuck in his hands, trying to look the tourist type but all the time sensing the power under his feet and realizing that he was heading into the jaws of an experience that could see him chewed up by the time the sun went down or the moon came up. "Lord, into Your hands I commend my spirit," he said softly, but he smiled at himself, for right now this boat ride had nothing portentous about it—it was all sun, blue water, and gentle breezes.

He stayed in the deck chair most of the way—they cut out through Biscayne Bay, then on the busier government cut to the Atlantic. When they hit the long ocean swells, Joe threw on more power, and the boat settled in a gliding clip across the waves.

There was no conversation with either Joe or Bingo all day. Only once did Bingo come up out of the engine room hatch and bring him coffee and a fish sandwich. Joe stayed at the helm, sipping a can of beer and ignoring him completely.

Around nine o'clock that night they pulled into a darkened pier area north of Key West and refueled. By ten they were on their way out into the Straits, and, unable to sit around any longer without some idea of what was coming, Sebastian went up to where Joe stood at the helm and asked, "How far in are we going?"

Joe sipped from his can of beer, keeping his eyes straight ahead. "The Baria Mariel light, thirteen miles out," he said. "That's where they are supposed to be."

"How'd they get that far out?" Sebastian asked again.

Joe looked at him quickly as if that was a stupid question. "Built a raft of chicken-coop lumber, probably—swim with the raft by day, ride it by night. That way they don't give a good target. It ain't exactly the nicest way to commute, preacher!"

Sebastian, watching the water shoot over the bow in cascades of fluorescence, didn't say anything to that immediately. "How many are there?"

"Six adults, seven kids, that's all I know," Joe replied sullenly, as if he didn't want to talk about it any more.

Sebastian wisely refrained from any more probing and stood back, watching, waiting, wondering.

They had been traveling at a fast clip for more than an hour when Joe suddenly cut the engines, and the boat sank down into the water, bow down, moving easily with the swells, the engine gargling quietly. From somewhere in the heavy night there came the sound of a bell, and Sebastian realized they must be coming up to a marker buoy. After a few minutes he saw the yellow light flashing, pulsing in tune with the nervous tinkling of the bell.

"Okay, stand by the cargo net, preacher," Joe said, and Sebastian walked back to the stern of the boat where the bulky cargo net was anchored to two deck cleats. He stood there holding on to it, waiting for word as to what to do with it, staring into the uncertain night, trying to keep his balance as the boat slid with the long swells. The sound of the marker buoy bell grew louder now, and the light was almost on top of him, winking its big yellow eye in spasmodic stabs as it rolled with the buoy in the heavy sea. Then the boat engines stopped altogether, and the only sounds were the bell and the sucking of water around the plywood hull. The human voices he waited to hear didn't come, that shout of recognition from thirteen people on a chicken-coop raft.

He heard the engine-room hatch open and he turned as Bingo moved up halfway to look out toward the buoy, waiting for the same sound, probably wondering too.

"There's a boat out there," Bingo called to Joe.

"I know it," Joe said, his voice sounding quiet and steady but squeezed too by some of the awesomeness of the tension now building up rapidly. Then, after a pause, he said, "I'm going to throw a light around the buoy."

"If it's a Castro boat, she'll pick it up in a hurry," Bingo called out in warning.

"If it's a gunboat, she's probably got us on radar anyway," Joe replied.

"She can't pick us up very easy; we don't give much to show," Bingo argued, wanting to sit here and wait rather than expose too early.

"We can't wait around all night," Joe returned shortly.

"Maybe they're a little late." Bingo tried again, referring

to the people who should have been here by now. "Give them some time."

Joe did wait. It seemed a long time. Sebastian waited too, holding the cargo net in his hands, rocking with the boat, feeling the nausea building in his stomach. The flashing buoy light was throwing weird designs over the boat now, and Sebastian strained to see some sign of life in the water below.

Then something bumped the side of the boat right below him, and he gave a start and peered down the five feet of free board toward the black, oily sea.

"Something bumped us!" he called out.

"Get the cargo net over!" Joe yelled back. "Bingo, stand by the engines!"

"You can't let the padre do that work!" Bingo shouted back.

"Shut up and get to those engines!" Joe roared.

Sebastian threw the net over the side, wondering why Bingo should be so concerned about his doing this kind of thing. He tried reaching down to feel whatever might be there. But he couldn't reach that far down even lying prone, so he grabbed the long boat hook next to him and began feeling around with that. He finally hooked something firm and pulled on it, straining against the weight of it as he pulled it on the deck. Then with it half over the side and on the deck, he reached out with his free left hand and felt the wetness, the slick, slimy wetness. The horror that shot through him almost forced him to let go. It was hair, human hair, soaked in salt water.

"I got somebody!" he yelled, and there was a tremble in his voice. At the same time that he reached both hands down to pull up on the body, the night was suddenly illuminated by a long, probing shaft of light. He felt himself exposed by it so that he froze for a moment, staring at it like a cat caught in a dark basement by the steady beam of a flashlight. He glanced up to see Joe huddled against the wheel in the protection of the cabin housing. Now he knew why Joe put him back here —there simply was no place to hide.

But there wasn't time to wonder about it. He was taken now with what his hands fought to lay hold of and land in the boat. And then he got the feel of the wet cloth in his hands, soggy almost like wet clay, and he pulled, bending his back to it. He got the body finally over the side, and it dropped with a final, sickening thud to the deck. The light showed him the horror of it—it was the body of a young boy, in his late teens, maybe even younger, the upper part of the face covered with matted blood, the arms frozen in a half-bent position reaching upward in a poignant, heart-wrenching pose of appeal.

"How many more?" Joe yelled as the boat's engines came to life.

Sebastian swallowed hard, fell against the deck again, and looked over the side into the murky, greenish water. Again he reached out with the pole and caught another firm weight . . . and all the time the light grew stronger, and from somewhere in the hollow cave of his mind he sensed a peculiar sound, loud, puncturing, and he felt the water around the boat kicking up into his face, stinging his eyes. . . . But he kept at the work. One by one he fought the dead weight of water-soaked bodies up over the side of the boat, letting them drop with a final clumping sound like so many dead fish landing there . . . and his hands were sticky with the blood and the salty grease and the dead cold feeling that stuck with it. . . . He couldn't count them now—maybe six already—and the light was everywhere, turning the night to day, flooding the grisly scene with unkind fingers of exposure . . . and the puncturing sounds were louder and there was a snapping sound against the boat that communicated the danger to him . . . but he went on with it, yelling over the sounds roaring to a peak of finality, yelling at the light, the sounds, yelling his protest at the sea that kept coughing up its indigestible flotsam of butchered bodies . . .

and he went on working, clawing at those soggy mounds of death, pulling them into the boat . . . and after a while Bingo was there, laying his hands alongside and shouting, "Dios mío! Dios mío!" in a voice that was half sob . . . and then the engines of the boat suddenly bellowed into action, and he felt the powerful surge forward, so that he was knocked backwards, sprawling on the duckboards, sliding on the blood and greasy salt . . . and he saw geysers explode around the boat and the light kept trying to hold on to them as the boat smashed its way out of the graveyard, rising to its one glorious moment of destiny, flying over the long swells of the ocean, fleeing pursuit and the carnage it had witnessed around the clanging bell of the marker buoy. . . .

When the light finally died behind them, Sebastian crawled back to stand upright, looking around the deck now strewn with misshapen lumps of death. "Oh, God . . . Oh, God . . ." he heard himself mutter above the sound of the wind and the sea and the diesels. He searched among them for life, passing over the stiff bodies of the children, one still clutching a rag doll, or was it a dead puppy in her arms? Seeing the blank stares as final as the battened shutters on a mansion, he turned away, afraid he would be sick—and then Bingo clutched him by the arm and led him forward and to the small compartment below.

Sebastian hung on to a stanchion against the motion of the boat. Bingo opened a flask, poured a small portion, handed it to him. Sebastian shook his head, his stomach still refusing to stop its nauseous swirling. Bingo downed the drink, screwed back the cover, and put the flask into his back pocket. Sebastian looked at him then and saw the faint streaks of wetness on his cheeks that rubbed out his normal demeanor of laughing buoyancy; he looked fragile in his youth now, as if grief had stripped him of any maturity he had once displayed.

"What happened to them?" Sebastian asked, shouting the question above the roaring of the boat.

Bingo sniffed and swiped at his nose with one finger. "Castro's boats got to them . . . sometime. . . . They don't have much chance. . . ."

Sebastian could only stare back at him, wanting a better explanation than that, for he could not admit that anyone could be that bestial, to shoot helpless children in the water and leave them to the sharks. But there wasn't time to pursue it, nor was there much sense to it anyway. For now he heard a peculiar cracking sound above the roar of the diesels, and the boat pitched wildly to the right. Bingo jumped for the ladder first and was well ahead of Sebastian going up to the deck.

When he came up, Sebastian first saw the orange flash, behind, off to the left. Then a thumping sound followed and a geyser of water shot up not more than twenty yards astern.

"Who's that?" he yelled at Joe.

"Coast Guard!" Joe shouted, not turning his head.

Sebastian looked back again and could vaguely make out the running lights and silhouette of the larger ship. "What do they want?"

"They want us to heave to—what else?"

"Well, why don't you? You've got no fight with them!"

"Who says I don't?" Joe fired back, hurling his answer on a half snarl of defiance. "You know what they'll do with this boat if I heave to? Yeah—scuttle her! And that means no more rescue runs down Murder Alley! It's the only boat of its kind that can do the job, get it? Now, you think it's so simple just to heave to, preacher boy?"

Again the cutter shot, and once more the PT boat yawed wildly as the geyser came closer.

"They'll blow you out of the water!" Sebastian yelled the warning.

Joe laughed, and it was a wild laugh, expressing the kind of nose-thumbing that characterized him when the odds were ten to one against him. "Whatsamatter, preacher, you wanna live forever?"

Again the geysers came in close, and this time water sprayed over the cockpit. But Joe only hit the throttles harder, trying for more revolutions. And after another five minutes of wild running, it became obvious that the cutter was losing out to the smaller, more maneuverable, and faster PT. The distance continued to lengthen until the geysers no longer appeared. But it wasn't until they had left all sign of the pursuing cutter behind that Joe cut the engines and Bingo disappeared into the engine room to check. The smell of burning grease came up from below, the smell of engines pushed too hard.

After a while Bingo came back up. "You got a shell in the port fuel tank," he said, "and you almost burned out a bearing. . . . Can we go easy now?"

Joe didn't reply immediately. Then he said, "Can we make Miami?"

"If you go easy," Bingo said.

They said no more. Sebastian and Bingo found canvas tarp below and covered the bodies on deck after lining them up in a neat row astern. Then they sat down on the deck behind Joe. Sebastian finally leaned his back against the bulkhead and folded his arms, looking for warmth as the cold cut through his lightweight jacket. He watched the wake astern as the screws churned away, and he began to shiver uncontrollably, so that he bit down hard on his back teeth. He knew it was shock—the kind that started way inside. Once Joe turned to look at him, as if he knew and was waiting to see him shake apart, and Sebastian bit harder and squeezed his arms tighter against his stomach, keeping his eyes off Joe's, forcing himself to stare at the anonymous undemanding darkness behind.

Joe had tried to kill him by exposing him to that murderous Castro gunboat fire. It left him shook up now that he realized it, even more than the slaughter he had witnessed at the marker. He was out of it, but not by much. It sobered him and left him feeling weak.

"'In Rama was there a voice heard, lamentation, and weeping, and great mourning; Rachel weeping for her children, and would not be comforted, because they are not.'"

And Bingo turned, hearing the words but not understanding—and then he too went back to his solemn vigil, his head down.

Chapter V

****

It seemed as if the dawn crept in reluctantly, coming with a few exploratory fingers of light to switch off the night stars one at a time, leaving patches of night shadow here and there like mourning ribbon. The new day was caught in those half shadows, waiting in the wings like a confused actor who has missed his cue.

When the sun finally raked the horizon with one bony red arm, the boat was in the Miami River, quietly gurgling its way up toward its misshapen haven of rest. Sebastian had slept off and on in fitful jerks during the long run home; each time he awoke, with the sweat mingling with the salt of the sea and the smell of human blood and hot engine grease, he saw those mounds of death under the coarse canvas and he would start shivering again. He was aware that the nightmarish journey was about over, but what now of the relatives who waited in Miami to claim this carnage? He had little stomach for facing up to them, nor did he have the ready words to comfort them.

He was sensing again how sensitive he really was yet—even after the Negev. The rawness of this death was new to him. He could not reconcile in his mind the insanity that perpetrated this kind of slaughter. It was that same old grinding of the gears again, violence vs. spirituality, the disheveled, wrinkled, chaotic world vs. the prim, starchy, well-pressed theology of love. He was coming to realize now more than ever that living in this world was nothing more or less than grabbing a high-voltage wire with his feet planted in a bucket of water. If he intended to keep going on, he'd have to start learning to take these jolts with a greater sense of outward aplomb—to say nothing of his inner lacerated spirit—lest he be reduced to what Joe and Rodríguez expected.

So now he got up from his half-lying position against the side of the cabin wall, stood stiffly on his feet, and peered ahead, watching that yawning hole of the boathouse reach out to swallow them. He saw the people there, knotting up around the side entrance, about the same time Joe did Joe yelled for Bingo to come up. When the Cuban appeared, Joe shouted, "Who told those people we were coming in? If they know, it's a sure thing the N.I.A. knows!"

Bingo only shrugged. It looked like Joe might change his mind and go on back out again, but he was almost in now, so he throttled back the engines and cut into the boathouse. When the engines were cut, the silence pressed in, the kind that hangs around grave markers, as if the rushing torrent of time had suddenly been trapped and dammed up for these awful seconds, straining to be on its way but backing up with terrible force. Sebastian saw the faces up the stairwell, peering down at the canvas-covered lumps in the stern of the boat, and someone screamed and began to cry softly.

And then someone pushed through the tangle of people, and a voice shouted, "Joe! N.I.A.!"

Joe began to swear, his voice rising to a chant, bouncing off the walls in that confined space, lending a peculiar atmosphere to the heavy feel of death. "Come on, Bingo!" he yelled. "You too, preacher boy!"

Sebastian didn't understand. He saw the people coming down the stairs now, carefully, reluctantly, not wanting to have to identify their next of kin but knowing they had to. Sebastian felt his place was here with them, to give what comfort he could, but Joe wasn't allowing him that. He grabbed Sebastian and shoved him bodily over the side of the boat, so that he fell to the planking on the opposite side from the people.

"You can't take the time to make any scores for God here, preach!" Joe pounded at him from behind, and then Bingo had a small trap door open in the wall and was scampering on through. Joe shoved Sebastian through and followed Bingo as they moved from one boathouse to another, through small trap doors and narrow passageways, built undoubtedly for just this kind of emergency.

When they finally came out, they were a good half mile from the boathouse. They walked up the stone steps to the road; a black car moved up quickly, and they got in.

"Where now?" Sebastian asked in some bewilderment, chafing in the knowledge that he was running from something he knew nothing about.

"To Señor Rodríguez, who else?" Joe snapped from the front seat next to the driver.

"What for?" He wanted to get out of this, to get away for a while, to find some place to think, to try to find some spiritual balance to the godless night he'd just experienced. The thought of Rodríguez and the choking cigar smoke and perhaps more invective heaped on him for his religion was not one to relish.

"Nobody asks what for," Joe replied sourly. "When Rodríguez gives the order, we jump. And you're in it now, preach—if you'd stayed back there the N.I.A. would have you, and there'd be a lot of explaining to do."

All Sebastian could do then was sit back and try to accept this for what it was. He was totally exhausted. He felt the bad taste of the night in his mouth, but something else was happening inside him: the same kind of fire that had torn at his innards in the Negev with a man named Brelsford who insisted on being a spectator to the ignominious defeat of God. He felt it rush through him again, but then it died, as if there were no fuel to keep it alive. For he was helpless here; there was nothing he could lay hold of to effect any change. He was being mastered by elements he was not at all familiar with. In the desert he had but to decide to walk it, to lead, for who else was competent enough or more equipped anyway? But here—here there were people who knew the sea and the heartache of it and the failure. And it was this sense of futility he had to let rest heavily inside him as he prepared to face Rodríguez.

He thought of those bodies on the boat and the poor people coming to claim them—to have to take those tarps off and see that mangled flesh they once loved and kissed and fondled as their own! He should be there, not here! Driving to meet a gloating, domineering, calculating, probably unmoved Spanish baron! Running like this, as if he'd committed some dirty crime by going out there in the Straits—as if such an act of mercy had to be judged as evil! God, if one had to feel guilty in trying to save life, where would this all end finally?

The Asociación Fraternal Latin America was located at Flagler and Tenth Streets. It was a small and unimposing brick building, four stories high. The upper three stories included various recreational activity rooms for young Cubans. The ground floor had offices and a few other rooms for storage. One room on this floor was strictly the haven of Señor Hector Rodríguez. It was a large room, carpeted wall to wall, with a giant pool table in the center. A fireplace, various trophies on the paneled walls, antique guns, photographs of athletes, and one large painting of a very attractive woman, carrying that mysterious Spanish beauty, made the room into a comfortable sportsman's retreat.

When Joe, Bingo, and Sebastian arrived and were ushered in, Rodríguez was playing pool. He did not look up when they entered; he went on expertly knocking the balls into the pockets with obvious skill and mastery.

After a long moment, during which the three of them could only stand and wait, Rodríguez said, "Help yourself to coffee, gentlemen." Joe went over immediately to the half-filled Silex on the sideboard and poured himself a full cup. Sebastian did the same and handed one to Bingo, who remained subdued and meditative. Rodríguez did not ask them to sit down.

"How many did you get?" Rodríguez asked of Joe then, as he leaned over the table to study a difficult shot, removing his long cigar to lay it on the corner of the table carefully. Sebastian wondered if he ever smoked a cigar beyond an eighth of an inch; it was always the same length.

"We got seven."

"All alive?"

Joe sighed. "All dead."

Rodríguez made his shot. It was perfect.

"What about the others?" Rodríguez took a chalk and rubbed it on the tip of his cue carefully.

"We didn't have time to look. . . . The Castro gunboats were on us."

Rodríguez went on chalking his cue, studying his work as carefully as he did the angle of the shots he made on the table. "That is thirteen thousand dollars we will never collect, amigo."

"I know that. . . ."

Sebastian looked quickly at Joe. "What's money got to do with it?" he ventured, feeling a bit surly himself now.

"Mind your own business," Joe retorted.

Sebastian turned to face Rodríguez. "Señor, as long as you invited me to go on that boat and now here to your safe harbor, I beg at least to have answers in exchange for risking my neck."

Only a hint of a smile touched that wide mouth, though the black-gray eyes remained unchanged in their steady, disquieting penetration. "Rescue is a business, padre," he said, then. "For some of us it goes beyond sentiment, though I know that that must scrape meanly on your tender skin, no? I get one thousand dollars for every Cuban I bring back alive—the families here are willing to pay that. After all, what is money when it means a united family again?"

Sebastian could only sit there and remember those people claiming their dead. As he was thinking, the phone rang. The swarthy Cuban answered, listened, hung up. "The N.I.A. has found the boat," he said. "They have taken it down the river."

Joe looked up quickly from his steaming coffee cup. Rodríguez went back to his game. "You ran into trouble with the Coast Guard last night," he said factually.

"Yeah," Joe said. "And I outran them."

"I have told you repeatedly you are not to tangle with them." Rodríguez's voice now had taken on an icy brittle tone.

"You want me to heave to with a boatload of bodies, and with the one and only boat that can do the job?" Joe appealed, sounding indignant that he should be blamed.

"So what do you have now?" Rodríguez snapped and rapped the ten ball into the corner pocket. "The only boat we have is impounded. You were stupid to think that the Coast Guard cutter you outran would not radio in to check on you when you got into Miami or Key West. They had you tracked all the way into the stall, amigo."

"Besides, there were two Americans on our boat," Joe

argued. "I couldn't let them pull me over with that kind of setup."

"The Coast Guard has never made smoke over who runs the rescue."

"No, but the N.I.A. does!"

"I told you I will handle the N.I.A.!"

Rodríguez's voice had a warning pitch to it now that implied caution. Joe paused, gulped at his coffee once to help keep his words down. They all waited while Rodríguez went on to line up on the eleven ball, as if it was imperative he succeed on the pool table before conversation could go anywhere from there.

The bank shot was perfect. Rodríguez leaned back from the table, picked up his cigar again, and replaced it slowly in the corner of his mouth.

"One thing I detest in you, old man of the sea," he said quietly. "And that is your foolish desire for war when war is an embarrassment to strategy. You are—what you say in America—a gringo who shoots from the hip, no? I do not like war lovers, amigo. I admire courage and willingness to fight when the time calls for it, but I cannot afford commandos who shoot first and talk later."

Joe shrugged, though by the look of the reddish burn on his neck he was anxious to say more in defense of his action. But Rodríguez's voice had put the blanket on that.

"All right," Rodríguez went on, staring at the two balls left on the green table top, the twelve ball and the cue ball. "It is time now that you give me your plan for Freedom Seven."

"You said I had a week," Joe complained.

"Events have altered that. I have word now from the underground that it will be the night of February twelfth—that is exactly twenty-eight days from now."

There was a moment of silence during which Joe appeared not to have any adequate words. Then, shaking himself from the paralysis of the moment, he said, "I had planned to use the boat. . . . We'll have to try to get another one."

"The use of surface craft has proven quite impossible," Rodríguez contradicted. "There is no way to get into Cárdenas Bay in a PT boat without Castro getting to you first."

"Cárdenas Bay!" Joe exploded. The coffee slopped over on his hand in the reaction, but apparently he did not feel it. He just stared at Rodríguez. "That is right under the nose of a naval and military outpost at Pena de Hicacos!"

"I am aware of the problem, amigo, but I expect answers from you."

Joe snorted. "Well, señor, I don't have an answer for that one." He licked his lips again in that way of his that hinted he was feeling pressure. "We–we can't go on the sea, we can't fly over it–"

"Under," Sebastian said, half in response to the only other alternative Joe had, but sensing too for the first time the beginning of a wild idea. Up to now he hadn't had much to contribute. This, he realized, had been the building flame in him: to have to be in this as far as he was but not able to articulate, to become, somehow, a welcome or accepted part of a very sordid corner of life and death. He had learned to hate being classed as "limited"; the Negev had taught him that. He didn't want to admit it now either, but he wanted something by which to make Joe retreat a few steps, to make him backpedal a little. It was not a good motive, but he had allowed it anyway just for what value it might bring.

"What do you mean?" Joe demanded, turning to him, his eyes flying those fiery pennants and his body leaning into the words as if they were spears he could throw at Sebastian.

"I mean go under the sea, what else?"

"By sub?"

"There is no other way in my limited knowledge to go under," Sebastian tried the quip.

Joe's laugh was intended as ridicule. "So all we got to do

is go down to the Fleet Submarine School at Key West and ask for a sub." He turned back to Rodríguez in a move of dismissal.

"No, I don't mean that way," Sebastian pursued, and he felt a flush of excitement as Rodríguez paused in his preparations to knock off the number twelve ball and turn toward him with some curiosity.

"So what else?" Joe pummeled, his half smile anticipating the stupidity of Sebastian's reply, wanting Rodríguez to share it too.

"I mean there's Alphonse."

"Al—" Joe's face froze in an expression both of disbelief and of the beginning of a good laugh. Only it was the kind of look a man has when he realizes that he's been cheated in a card game or trapped into a conversational ambush.

"Why not?" Sebastian went on, eager to press this home, realizing that it wasn't as ridiculous as it sounded.

Joe laughed, putting all his derision into it. "Señor Rodríguez, we have a practical joker among us. . . . I must apologize for him, for he takes precious time telling his bad jokes at a moment of crisis. . . . Give me forty-eight hours, señor, and I will have another surface boat that will do the job."

But Rodríguez had laid his cue stick down on the table, and he lifted one hand to silence Joe. His eyes, though, remained on Sebastian, studying, as if he were trying to bore through Sebastian's skull and look into his brain. Then he removed his cigar and began rolling it between his fingers slowly, all the time watching Sebastian carefully.

"Gentleman, I am not in a mood to be amused," he said, quietly but with the quality of deadly finality that goes with a judge's verdict. "Now, what is this—this Alphonse?"

"Señor," Joe said, putting his coffee cup down on an end table and displaying his hands palms upward in a pose of appeal, "in nineteen forty-two my father, who was an inventor of various naval gadgets, presented plans for a five-man midget submarine to work in the shallow water of enemy harbors. He was given the go-ahead to build it—and he did. But a year later the Navy canceled the contract. That little sub never got out of the barn; she's still there, twenty-five years later, never been near water except for the rain that's leaked in through the years. My old man was left with an untested monstrosity that cost him a fortune—in fact, a week later he died of a heart attack. We kept Alphonse in the barn as a kind of memorial to him; kind of a family heirloom, a museum piece. But, señor"—and Joe made a great flourish out of desperation to cancel this crazy idea now—"she's never been in water. She would probably sink."

"What about it, padre?" Rodríguez said to Sebastian, ignoring Joe's appeal.

"In nineteen fifty-nine," Sebastian responded, avoiding the withering look of Joe, "Mr. MaConnel here took fifty-seven of us, alumni of Central High School, to visit that submarine in his family memorial. He said at that time—and he was a chief in the submarine branch of the Navy then—that Alphonse was a kind of work of genius and that whenever he got the time he would prove that the idea could be a tremendous asset to present-day naval submarine strategy."

"I was drunk, drat it all!" Joe bellowed. "You—you think I'd say anything so ridiculous if I was sober? Besides, all we got is twenty-eight days; it would take a good three years to try to make that pile of junk operational, provided such a thing were even possible! Señor, I am not in the mood to be amused either or waste your time—"

"It is a good plan," Rodríguez said, snipping off Joe's words with a decisive tone to his voice, his eyes still on Sebastian. Then, satisfied with his contemplation, he added, looking at Joe now, "You will begin to get it operational immediately. The padre has come up with your answer—all you have to do is follow through."

"It will take experienced submariners, equipment—"

"Money is no object, I told you that a long time ago."

"But you can't buy experienced submarine people—"

"Enough!" Rodríguez snapped, and his voice was like the slap of a whip on bare flesh. Then he went back to his pool table, picked up the cue, and put the twelve ball into the corner pocket without seeming to aim. Then, laying the cue down, he added, "You will report progress to me every three days. . . . You will make that—that Alphonse run, amigo, or you become shark bait, comprene?"

Then he left, and there were only the three of them. Sebastian put his cup down on the mantel of the fireplace. Joe just stood there looking at him, not yet comprehending the enormity of what had occurred but fully cognizant of the fact that Sebastian had committed him to a plan of bizarre, if not disastrous, proportions. Only Bingo appeared to demonstrate a clear, positive response. He kept looking from Joe to Sebastian, a new light rising in his face darkened by mourning; it was the sun coming through the clouds.

"Alphonse!" he said, and it came from him like a song, a prayer of hope, and his fingers began to snap in rhythm again.

"Shut up, Bingo!" Joe said, without looking at him. "Go on home to bed."

"Let him alone," Sebastian returned mildly, feeling a new sense of bravado now that he had put Joe on the defensive.

They stood facing each other for a long moment, each waiting for the other to thrust, like two weary assailants getting their wind for the last furious round. Then Joe smiled, and it became a laugh that started as a shaking, rippling motion around his narrow waist, until finally he threw his head back and let it come, and his greasy yachting cap almost fell off so that he had to clutch at it. Bingo stood uncertainly aside, wondering at the laugh, then allowing the smile to come to match it, sensing that perhaps the laugh after all was one of good humor and a portent of victory.

But the laugh died as suddenly as if a bug had flown into Joe's open mouth and slammed into his windpipe. Only the smile remained, hanging there mockingly, lifeless as usual, the unwilling grimace of a man who could only express his anger and hate in this way. Contradictory as it seemed, it was the highest and most dangerous point of Joe's vehemence, and yet it was, at the same time, a kind of asbestos coat he was throwing over that vehemence, as if he was afraid of what he might do if he let it have full lead.

"You picked a beautiful way to die, preach," he said, the words coming through his teeth, being chopped off one at a time by the flashing blade of his barely controlled anger. Then, pausing as if hunting for the words, he pointed his right index finger at Sebastian, waving it in a kind of stabbing eloquence of its own. "You think you can play with Rodríguez—you think you can experiment with that polliwog of a submarine and if it doesn't work come back here and tell him that there has to be some other way? Well, I'll tell you something, preacher boy. You just sold Señor Rodríguez a bill of goods, and he won't accept anything but an operation with that tin can."

"I'm well aware—"

"And there's something else," Joe went on, cutting off Sebastian's attempt to reply, his finger still waving. "You think now that you've got me committed to that tin coffin you can walk away, to go and do your watching and praying while I do the sweating and bleeding? Well, preach, you're going with me in that steel strait jacket—I want you there when we go down, I wanna look into your eyes when the Atlantic comes down on us, I wanna see what kind of man you really are when the salt water comes up over your chin and your next breath is going to be a throat full of death." He paused again, and his breathing was heavier now, and his smile had faded to that twisted leer of contempt. "Yeah, you'll be there all right, preach; I'm even going to let you call the shots . . .

I'm going to let you make the decisions . . . I'm going to let you sweat, preach, with every move of that poor excuse for a Moby Dick . . . and if you're lucky enough to get out of that belly of a whale after the first try, then I wanna see what you do when the first depth charge comes down at you from Castro's expert antisubmarine gunboats. . . . I wanna see how you get a dozen people into a sub built barely for five . . . I wanna look at you when the air runs out down there and there's no place to go . . . or when the pressure starts making wrinkles in that rusted, paper-thin hull that'll fall in on you just by bumping an air bubble. . . . Yeah, preacher boy, it's going to give me great delight to have you along. . . ."

And he laughed in that way again to seal all that he'd said, to sound the note of the ridiculous, the impossible, and the final. And he stood there with his thumbs hooked into his belt in a salty pose of defiance, like he'd made a point too difficult to refute successfully.

"Did you have a better way in mind?" Sebastian asked, keeping his voice as cool as he could in this atmosphere of mounting heat.

Joe swore in carefully chosen words, driving them with slow deliberation into what he knew was a tender side of Sebastian, trying to draw blood.

"I'd rather take my chances in the open and die with some kind of honor," he concluded. "Any way is better than what you suggested; it's like drowning cats in a gunny sack and a tub of water."

Sebastian had nothing to say to that immediately. Then, in order to get to the end of what was but a design for an extended exchange of mounting diatribe, he said, "You know there isn't any other way. No matter which way you look at it, you'd die if you didn't come up with a plan—or at least you'd probably wish you had, if I take Rodríguez for what he is. And there's always a chance you might pull this off."

"The chances I'd be taking under Rodríguez are far less

than what I get committing myself to that Alphonse monstrosity," Joe retaliated. "Or at least it would be cleaner, by far. . . ."

There came that sense of stalemate in the conversation again, so Sebastian tried with, "But suppose you pull it off, what then?"

"You mean *we,* don't you, preach?"

"Okay, we. . . . What then?"

"What do you mean, what then?"

"Well, that means a hundred thousand dollars for you and a canceling of the gambling debt. . . . I thought there was no risk too high for that. That's what you told Jane."

"I'm really touched by your consideration of my interests." Joe paced back and forth on the opposite side of the pool table, trying to work off his anger. "I'm sure you got that in mind for this trip. . . ."

"No, there's what I might get out of it too."

Joe stopped his pacing and glared back at him. "And what might that be, preach? Just what do you want out of it?"

"Well, like seven people who'll be waiting out there on February twelfth—seven people I help get out from under communism."

Joe laughed again, the kind that has a scraping sound to it like bitterness rubbed raw on a bad joke.

"Straight from corn alley!" Joe chided. "The old 'rally round the flag, boys,' hey, preach? But I know what you want out of this trip—you want a pocket-sized miracle from God to crow about. You want as tough a job as you can find, so if you pull it off you can tell everybody that God did it—and maybe you think I'll wind up saluting God, too. Well, I'll tell you one thing, man of the cloth, if you are thinking of taking the same God out on Alphonse as you did last night on that PT boat, forget it!"

Sebastian let that ring to a silence in the room, and then

he said, "Okay, I've got my reasons for going; you've got yours. In any case, we don't have much choice. And if we pull it off, you stand to come out smelling of money. And I get the miracle I expect. . . ."

"And if we lose?"

"Then neither of us wins. . . ."

Joe paused on that a moment, then pulled out a fresh pack of cigarettes from his shirt pocket. It was a sign that something new was forming in his mind. He went through the ritual of lighting up, and then, with the smoke pouring ceiling-ward, he said, "The stakes in the pot are too small to even deal the cards, preach. I'm going to up the ante." He removed his cigarette, letting the smoke leak out of his nose, past his eyes; the smile was gone now, but there were hard chips of light in his stormy gray eyes. "You know now that our skins ride with getting Alphonse operational, right?"

"Right," Sebastian said, not knowing where this was going.

"You believe God told you to mention Alphonse to Rodríguez, right?"

"Since the name didn't even enter my mind until ten seconds prior to mentioning it, yes, at this point I'd say God did put it in my mind."

"Okay, then if God told you to mention Alphonse, then you must be pretty sure that God'll get us out and back with the pay load on the twelfth?"

It had gone really quiet in the room, except for the sounds of the building Miami traffic outside. "What you want me to do is put God in the middle, the pot we gamble over?"

"Why not? It's your hand against mine; if you believe God is in this, then you go all the way. If you pull this off, then I'm willing to admit there is a God in the universe and that He might even have something to say to me. If you change your mind at any time or we get clobbered out there, my hand wins."

"I can't presume on God like that. It's forcing Him to move contrary to His will."

"Then why were you so sure Alphonse was the answer?" Joe retaliated.

Sebastian had to think on that. "Actually, it was the only way to get the pressure off at the moment. . . ."

"Then in that case you're not sure God was in it—yet you committed us to a big gamble. You haven't got any more faith in your God than I do!"

"Suppose I did make a promise," Sebastian tried, sensing the trap closing on him now. "That would force me to take unusual risks to back it up later on."

"What *unusual* risks?" Joe demanded. "Once we get moving toward Cárdenas Bay, we can't back out—we've got to come back with a full load or face Rodríguez, and that won't be easy. All I'm asking you to do is put God up as either consistent with what you say or inconsistent, master of events or victim of those events—is that too hard for you, preacher boy?"

"I can't presume on God like that."

"You had no trouble presuming on God when you pumped my wife full of faith back in nineteen fifty-nine!" Joe shot back. "That's what you told her then—or has your memory failed?—God is all-powerful, God can overcome the mountains, have faith in God and see the miracles. . . . Well, I keep telling my poor wife that that's a lot of bunk!" Now Joe came around the table to face Sebastian directly, the cigarette hanging between his puffy lips and giving him that leer. "Now, preach, you're changing your mind, and I've got the right to tell Jane exactly that: that you committed me to a totally suicidal operation but wouldn't come through in the belief God could work the miracle—you want me to tell her that? You'd do me a big favor, preach, if you'd back out right now, a great big favor. . . ."

Sebastian took his time. He didn't know if this had come

about by Joe's careful design or if he had stumbled on it by accident. One thing was sure—there was a rightful quality to Joe's challenge. Even the way Bingo looked proved that, for the young Cuban had folded his arms in a pose that indicated that he too sensed that the challenge was fair. It was so right that to deny it, to refuse to meet it, was in essence a true declaration of his own lack of faith. It would mean starting out on a very sticky operation with a total disbalance against himself, and it would indeed do more to destroy what Jane had of God in her life than any other single act. If he hadn't mentioned Alphonse, he might have had an out. But how much could he dare assume of God anyway? Did he have the right to face the issue? In short, was his faith really so strong that he could bluntly state that this operation would be successful—or was it pure presumption? What if God wasn't in it? But then if God wasn't in it, what right did he have to commit Joe and the others to such an operation? What was it that Barbara Churchill had hit him with? "The test of your faith is not that you're willing to die but that you have confidence to perform and live!"

"How do I know that you won't deliberately try to scuttle the operation to prove my faith and God all wrong?" he asked then.

"What do I gain?" Joe replied. "If I scuttle it to prove you wrong, I hand myself over to Rodríguez to get buried in cement! I'm laying my life on you, preach, that's the way it is!"

But that wasn't really it. Joe knew the facts, that the chances were a hundred to one of pulling this off—he knew Alphonse better than Sebastian. If he was sure of defeat, he wanted to be sure the idea of God was defeated too—if not to prove anything to himself, at least to Jane. Sebastian realized then that Joe really was desperate to get Jane out of the spiritual realm altogether, even if it meant he would die in the process; he could go gladly if he knew he had destroyed the idea of God forever in her life.

"You must hate what Jane has and love her awfully at the same time," Sebastian said to him.

Joe didn't say anything. He waited, dragging slowly on his cigarette. Bingo waited. Sebastian looked at them both, and he saw what all of humanity was hung up on when it came to faith in God. A sign. A tangible indication of reality. They were wrong to let their faith stand on that visible manifestation. But from what position did he argue back? He had allowed himself to be caught in a clever impasse. Not to follow through simply meant he would have to withdraw altogether from the operation—for he would have lost anyway, because Joe would have what he needed to strip Jane completely of her faith. If he intended to go on with it, he had no choice but to follow through.

"You dealt yourself into this game, preach," Joe said quietly. "For fourteen hundred bucks you came in. Now you either play your cards or I say you're bluffing—and I'm going to call you on it, that all this faith-in-God jazz is about as sure as snake oil for gout. All I'm asking is if you're willing to put your money where your mouth is."

Sebastian hesitated a moment. The awful pressure of the decision was almost too much to take in the time he had. "Okay," he said then, with a sigh. "I'll go on the line—I believe God will do it. I stake my life on it."

Joe looked at him steadily to make sure he had heard right. There might have been a flicker of disappointment in his eyes. He had undoubtedly hoped that Sebastian would not commit himself. But then that daring smile came slowly across his face, that expression that said he'd already won.

"One thing we need to get settled right now," Sebastian added. "You can kill me any time or wherever you want to—but from now on we quit this check and countercheck about God. From now on we concentrate on the operation—you keep your profanity to yourself and we concentrate on getting Alphonse ready to go. Clear?"

Joe grinned like a boy who had gained more than he had

given up in a trade. "Preach, you got yourself a deal," he said with a mock salute. Then he moved to the door.

"Where are you going now?" Sebastian asked.

Joe paused at the door and looked back. "I'm going to Chicago—where else?—and get Alphonse out of mothballs, what else? Then I'm going to find a way to get her down here and a place to hide her from the N.I.A. and Castro's goons, which will take a bit of doing. And then outfit her and find a crew—all in twenty-eight days, remember?"

Sebastian said, "I expect you'll stay in touch?"

"Preach, I'm gonna be jabbing you even in your sleeping hours," Joe replied, and then added, "By the way, I don't want you staying with my wife any more. I got a feeling you ain't doing her a bit of good. I got you a room at the Flamingo Hotel on Miami Beach. Ocean view and all. Come on, Bingo."

Bingo followed, pausing only a second or so to give Sebastian a quick glance, a look that showed his uncertainty about whether to leave the conversation where it had ended. Then, with a smile, he said, "Things are looking up for gusanos," and he went out whistling "Hello, Dolly."

Sebastian was left alone, feeling the constriction of the empty room. He was both exhausted and irritated. He had been boxed in. He had begun all this with a driving urge to command a deteriorating situation. He had thrown Alphonse in as a kind of left jab to get Rodríguez and Joe to think of some more practical undersea rescue operation. He hadn't expected Rodríguez to jump for the idea so fast or so finally. Now he had been victimized by it. He thought of Alphonse, that strange naval design that he had seen a couple of times, once during high school, when Joe invited the General Science class to look her over; again in 1959, when the alumni group studied her. She was a clumsy, awkward, grotesque-looking vessel as she hung on timber supports in the old barn back of Joe's house. He remembered those years after Joe's father died of the blow to his reputation when the Navy turned his design down.

But a lot of time had gone by since. Time in which Alphonse had aged without being tested. Twenty-eight days was indeed a short time at that. He picked up the white cue ball from the corner pocket and rolled it slowly down the table top until it plunked into the far corner pocket. The law of diminishing returns. Did the same law exist in his relationship with God? The sight of those bodies falling into the boat was still a fresh, stabbing nightmare to him.

Well, O man of God, is this not a familiar place? Aye, but never was it so dark!

Chapter VI

****

He picked up his belongings at Jane's and left a note for her telling her he was at the Flamingo. Then he checked into the hotel. It faced the ocean, all right. It had a bed, plywood chest of drawers, one chair, a TV, and an air conditioner that hummed loudly. That was it. It was all the Flamingo had left, probably.

After he showered, he went to bed and fell asleep immediately. The phone woke him. It was nearly four in the afternoon as he made it out from his watch. The voice was male. "You are requested to attend a garden party at the residence of Señor Hector Rodríguez tonight at nine o'clock," the voice said. The address was given as 415 Cardinale Road, Coral Gables.

There was no question as to his availability. It was an

order. He tried to shake the cotton-batting waste of sleep that still clogged his mind, wanting to ask for more details, to ask who was speaking. And then the line went dead. He stared at the dead receiver a long time and then hung it up. He rolled over and sat on the edge of the bed, taking time to ponder. He had a sneaking feeling that events were beginning to move too fast and he ought to stop and check everything out. How did he know that that voice had anything to do with Rodríguez, anyway? So why go? What if it was someone out to lure him off the familiar trails and finish him?

But he shook that off as being far too melodramatic and decided he'd better go. He reached for the phone and called Jane. He was surprised to get her at home at that hour, but she told him she worked only until three. She also cautioned him that the line might be tapped and that he should be careful what he said. He frowned at that, not comprehending the reason for this at all.

"Besides," she added, "Bingo filled me in on what happened last night—and the conversation with Joe on Alphonse. Incidentally, Joe told me to tell you that he went to Chicago to get Alphonse and would be back in a few days, depending on the complications." There was a pause, and Sebastian didn't know how to proceed with the consciousness of another party possibly listening in. "You'll never make it," Jane went on, and he thought he sensed a hard coolness in her voice.

"It may not be as tough as you think." He tried reassuring her.

"I wouldn't even go near that thing on a bet, let alone get into it," she responded tartly. "I think you might be pushing this one a little too far."

"There wasn't any other way." He tried again, wanting desperately now to at least have some indication of confidence from her.

"Anything is better than that. . . . Besides, you don't have enough time."

"We'll have to try it—anyway, don't worry, Jane."

There was a pause and she said, "Who me?" and then, in an attempt at jocularity that was sprinkled too heavily with pain, "You're speaking to Calamity Jane, remember? I just bleed, never worry."

"Don't count God out of it."

"I may sound bitter, but I don't think He wants any part of this either," she said bluntly. "After what happened last night, I'm almost positive. It's all over this evening's edition—did you see it?"

"No."

"Well, I don't think I better keep the line open. . . . They're probably tracing if they're on. I'll be in touch with you some other way." The click at the other end of the line was final, too final. He wanted to ask who "they" were—Rodríguez, Castro, or the N.I.A.?

He had his dinner in his room after ordering the desk to rent him evening clothes. Then at nine o'clock he went out and caught a cab for the Coral Gables address. Ten minutes later, the cab pulled up at a gate in a high white stucco wall. The sign on the gate said: NO ENTRY, so he had to get out and walk up the long circular drive to the house, set on a small rise glittering in the pinks and yellows of balloon lights. As he walked he noticed the fountains and green grass and marble statues that were mostly military figures either marching or on horseback. It was like entering the private grounds of some war museum.

When he got to the front steps of the main veranda, he was stopped by two men dressed in maroon uniforms who looked half general and half bellboy. He gave them his name. One of the men took a phone out of the box behind him, checked through, and then nodded to the other, apparently indicating Sebastian was bona fide.

Then he followed the one maroon guard into the house itself. He wondered about this, since the sound of calypso music was coming from somewhere out in the back gardens where the party was obviously taking place. But he stayed behind the ramrod back of his escort, through the big mansion with its marble statues of more military heroes. When they got to a big mahogany door sprinkled with gold ornaments, the escort knocked softly. There was a muffled voice from within, and Sebastian was ushered in to face Rodríguez.

"Come in, padre," he said, and he was standing by a huge desk, decked out in a maroon and black military uniform with medals and gold embroidery that probably dated back to another century of Spanish dragoons. "I have been expecting you. . . . thank you for accepting the invitation."

As usual the voice was well modulated, unaffected in its tone, sounding like he'd said those lines a thousand times before. Being alone with Rodríguez was no less awesome than meeting him in the company of his bodyguards; it was like seeing a judge in his chambers rather than in court; the same sense of authority and power remained, even though an attempt was made to dilute the atmosphere to some semblance of relaxation. The room reflected a heavily masculine and warlike taste, paintings that showed war scenes of various eras and the usual photos of athletes, mostly Cuban. On the mantelpiece were two glass cases showing crossed pistols welded together.

Sebastian moved forward and stood by the empty fireplace, waiting for Rodríguez to get steam up, which meant the ritual of a cigar. And no sooner had the maroon escort gone than Rodríguez found one, bit the end off, and put it between his teeth in careful, deliberate movements, as if he were saying the rosary. He picked up a gold lighter, flicked it, and held the flame off long enough to say, "Cigar smoke offend you, padre?"

"Help yourself."

Rodríguez grunted his thanks, and his eyes stayed on Sebastian steadily as he puffed on the cigar, holding the lighter flame to the end of it longer than he had to, as if the flame was giving him a better look.

"You have caused me some moments of amazement lately," he said, snapping the lighter off and putting it back on his desk.

"I would imagine the fact that I came through last night without getting killed is one of them," Sebastian responded with a smile, trying to get in a stroke or two here to see if the apparently imperturbable demeanor of the man could be scratched.

But Rodríguez never flicked an eyelash. He was as cool and as impassive as the hard, white face of the Napoleon statue directly behind him. "Yes, that is one. . . . The other is the matter of this submarine. Let me say that these are not things that match a padre, do you think?"

"Perhaps the image that we of the church have had in the past has not been a fitting one, señor," Sebastian replied. "Perhaps all I'm doing is seeking to correct that image a bit."

Rodríguez did not answer immediately. He stood there clouding the air with smoke screens, as if the smoke eventually would reveal some kind of pattern that would tell him all he wanted to know about Sebastian. The faint sound of the calypso leaked into the room, sounding a little tinny like an amplifier on half power.

Rodríguez picked up a gold-framed photograph on his desk and handed it to Sebastian. An attractive, dark-haired woman stood in a proud, regal stance; on either side of her were younger children in a casual grouping, faces that smiled back at the photographer—dark faces, reflecting Spanish blood, and one or two lighter ones—good looking, all of them. The woman was the same one whose portrait Sebastian had seen on the wall of Rodríguez's room at the downtown fraternity earlier that day.

"My family," Rodríguez said, and his voice had dropped

just a half note from its usually ironlike control. "Are they not handsome?"

"Very," Sebastian admitted.

Rodríguez came around the desk and began pointing out each of them one at a time. "Carlos, he is seventeen now, the oldest, already in Castro's militia serving at Príncipe Castle overlooking Havana . . . then comes Pepe, he's fifteen and he will be moving up from Castro's youth movement to the militia next year . . . then Juan, at fourteen, who is in school and living at home with his mother but already is an organizer of work crews in Castro's sugar farms . . . then comes Pedro, he is twelve, training in one of Castro's antiaircraft units . . . then there are the nine-year-old twins, my two sweet girls, born just before I left Cuba; their future is the same as the others, olive uniforms and a rifle serving Castro . . . and then my dear wife, Pila, who alone has kept freedom alive in the hearts of them all at great cost to herself. . . . You see now why money is no object to me in getting them out of Cuba?"

"I can see that," Sebastian said, and Rodríguez went back behind his desk and put the photograph on the desk top at the same angle. He puffed on his cigar a long moment, staring at the photograph, and then he looked up and studied Sebastian again in that long, hard way of his. He was getting ready to say something more when a knock sounded on the door, and he said, "Come."

He thought it was the girl from the Libertad the moment she walked in and stood hesitantly for a moment in the half light. And the beauty he had sensed before behind the garish make-up was now breath-takingly evident. She was dressed in a long greenish evening gown of some kind of silk material, off the shoulders; the dark cream of her skin was beautifully emphasized in that contrast as well as by the balancing effect of the crown of upswept black hair that showed the smooth, natural richness of oil. She walked with slow, easy grace, controlled as an athlete but delicate as a debutante. And as she approached, it was like having an apparition come through a smoky, dreamlike haze into reality until she stood before him—and he could only look, transfixed by the large dark-brown eyes that changed color to black, then to brown, then to a kind of greenish tint, depending on how the light hit them or how she smiled, almost as if she had as many different personalities within her. The mouth was lightly done with a pale-white lipstick, accentuating the creamy skin; an expressive mouth it was, disturbing in its curve, soliciting in its half pout, sometimes receding into a soft line of childlike innocence. She was a composite of balancing forces: beauty, mystery, vivaciousness, precociousness, and an almost irritating knowledgeableness, as if she knew she commanded a man's continual attention—which she undoubtedly did—and knew exactly what he was thinking about her before he realized it himself. When she looked at him, he felt a flush of heat in his cheeks, as if she did look through him and saw what he felt, and her smile was a flashing salute to him that he was after all a male animal, clergyman or no clergyman. But Sebastian had another woman too deeply entwined within his emotional machinery to allow himself more than a healthy admiration. Barbara Churchill still commanded all of the ramparts of his life, and he was willing to leave it like that.

"My dear, meet the man who has produced the fish for Freedom Seven," Rodríguez said, as he reached for her extended hand, took it, and kissed it delicately while she let her eyes slowly come around to Sebastian. "Meet the padre—or I should call him the reverend?—anyway, padre—Mr. Sebastian?—this is my niece, María San Roman."

She gave him her hand. He said, "It's my pleasure," and he felt the small delicateness of the hand, the warmth of it, the surrender of it in his own, like a little bird. She would have left it there, but he dropped it quickly as if it too would tell more of the peculiar turbulence she created in him.

"I have already read of what happened to you last

night," she said, in an even voice that sounded lazy, as if she had just gotten up from a sleep. "It is hardly an experience for a man of the church, is it?"

"Hardly," he said, and managed a smile. He began to feel stupid standing there, wondering if he should acknowledge having met her at the Libertad, yet not really sure it was the same girl.

"I shall leave you to María," Rodríguez said then and moved around the desk to the door. "You will excuse me, but I do have guests to entertain. You are in good hands, padre." His uniform crackled as he moved out, as if it were made of wrapping paper.

She went to the desk and removed a cigarette from a box sitting next to the cigar case. She stood with it in her hand, held halfway up to her mouth waiting for him. He moved quickly, hitting the leg of the desk with his toe. He found the lighter, lit it, and held it to the end of her cigarette. Her dark eyes remained fixed on his face as she puffed delicately, and he realized that the eyes were not friendly or warm at all—they looked like black ice on a frozen bay.

"Then I'm correct in thinking that you are the same girl," he said to her, standing back while she blew smoke ceilingward.

"The one and only, of course," she returned simply.

"Your uncle knows all about that?"

"Of course not."

He looked at her quickly, not sure what she meant. "Is he that naïve or doesn't he care?"

"I get him information. He is not a man to question where it comes from just as long as it is accurate," she said factually.

"You enjoy that kind of job?"

"What kind of job?" she replied with disinterest, as if she had that put to her many times before by her own conscience.

"Well, I would assume, from what I've seen, that the nature of the Libertad—"

"We entertain men, yes, if that's what you are getting at, reverend. It's a price we are willing to pay for what we get back."

He felt a sense of disappointment in this revelation, almost a kind of jealousy that both puzzled and startled him, for the thought of that beautiful body making the rounds was jarring to him.

"Suppose your uncle knew?"

She held the cigarette away from her mouth, pausing a moment to study him. "It'd kill him, I expect."

"How did you know I wouldn't tip him off that I had met you already at the Libertad?"

"I didn't. I was holding my breath, if you want to know. But I know too that it probably will come out sooner or later."

She dragged at her cigarette.

"You expect I'll tell him?"

"Church people often feel a godly duty to expose sin regardless of the hurt it costs."

He savored that, feeling the sharp end of the truth.

"You seem to know about the church."

"We were all Catholics in Cuba—a long time ago. We have since learned to put aside lesser things."

"Well, if it will make you feel any better, I'm not interested in exposing your sins."

She half nodded, as if this was something of a duty for him; there was no indication of gratitude on her part. "I suppose that will make us what you Americans call kissing cousins?"

"Any way you want it," he said, and it was very hard to keep his eyes off hers, to watch the lights move and change in them as her mood and personality changed.

She moved from the desk, as if to finish that line of

conversation, and headed for the balcony. He followed, and it was as if she knew he would follow, as if she had control of him.

He waited, staring at the long line of her bare back that plunged down into the green folds of her gown below her waist. He cleared his throat and looked beyond her to the vast, rolling greenery of the estate.

"It might interest you to know," she said, "that I study at the University of Miami three nights a week. The other three I work the Libertad, and two days more on top of that. I allow myself to be touched, squeezed, embraced, and made drunk for the information I get in return. That may sound like a poor excuse for promiscuity, but my uncle uses the information I get in planning his rescue operations in the Straits."

He waited awhile, then said, "Is that the only way you can get information?"

She paused a moment, then flipped the half-smoked cigarette out into the dark night, its glowing red ash kissing the night a fiery good-by as it headed for a dismal end in the water fountain below. Then she turned slowly, the smoke trickling out of one corner of her mouth in lazy loops as if it were coming from a smudge fire inside her that was close to popping into a crackling flame.

"You are speaking, of course, from that high and lofty plateau of American morality," she said in a mockingly categorical tone, "which you as a clergyman can't help but link up with your own idea of spiritual morality—like the two go together? Well, some of us have learned to survive only by learning to use anything and everything available to us, even our own bodies. And I learned most of it in your puritanical America, citadel of western civilization and morality. Every dime I ever raised for the Free Cuban cause from your American entrepreneurs has cost me something in moral virtue—nothing really comes free, reverend, and if God has anything to do with it, then I thank Him for the lovely body he's given me that makes it easier to barter with—anyway, think of the lives I've saved by doing so. Have you ever debated the right or wrong of morality in those kinds of balances?"

Her English was perfect, without a flaw, even more precise in the slow burn she was experiencing now. He had to marvel at it, the cool, direct way she had of nailing down the words for effect.

But she sensed now that she was revealing a side of her she didn't want to, so she shrugged and removed a folded check from the bodice of her gown.

"My uncle doesn't trust you," she said bluntly, without allowing him time to change gears. "And neither do I. Here is a check for ten thousand dollars. He wants you to have it for what help you gave with that submarine. You can do with it what you wish. You are welcome to stay here in Miami, of course—in fact, we'd like you here where we can know where you are until after February twelfth."

Sebastian looked at the green check extended to him, actually thrust out at him between her carefully manicured fingernails and a long, creamy arm that carried an angle akin to an insulting jab. "I don't want the money," he said simply.

"Then give it to your church."

"I don't think I can be bought out this way."

"Then what is it you want?" she demanded, letting her arm drop.

"To be where I'm supposed to be, that's about all. I started this submarine thing; I'm going on with it until I'm more of a hindrance than a help."

"You are a hindrance now," she said flatly.

"Why?"

"This is no place for a man of theological views such as you hold—this high stock on human values in terms of God."

"You don't know my views."

"We checked you out—your church, your Negev experiences," she countered.

"Okay . . . so why is it that men of all walks of life can lift their hands on behalf of others, but as soon as a clergyman does it's as out of place as a musical saw in a symphony orchestra?" He didn't like the way his voice sounded defensive.

"Human values don't count in a war."

"I thought it was your uncle's concern for the human values of his family that started all this?"

"In one sense, yes. But you may have to kill to get them out. Are you prepared to do that?"

"I'll cross that bridge when I come to it."

"You won't cross it when you come to it," she contradicted, and she was staying ahead of him as if she knew every line he was coming up with. "You'll stand on the edge of it, trying to decide, and in that moment you'll be smashed yourself. It's that moment of hesitation that we can't afford—that's why we want you out."

"Is that all?"

"No. . . . I said I don't trust you. My uncle doesn't. There are too many questions hanging over you—why you came here, why you left your church, why you got involved with MaConnel at this point. . . ."

"Then ask me!"

"I don't have the time—we'd rather you were out of the picture from now on."

"Well, I'm not taking your way out," he managed to say, pleasantly enough, but feeling a scratch of irritation at the way she pummeled him with those abrupt answers. "It's Joe's show from now on, and I'm afraid he wants me on this thing pretty badly."

"Yes, your boy Bingo told my uncle about the contest you and Joe have going on between you."

"He told—Señor Rodríguez?" Sebastian cut in quickly,

baffled by that revelation. "I didn't think anybody got to Rodríguez except the Maharajah himself."

"Bingo was in on the talk early this morning," she countered. "My uncle considers him in on it—anyway, there's no Free Cuban in this town that can't get to my uncle when he wants to. . . . Bingo is concerned about this spiritual tug of war between you and Joe. So are we. And we won't allow it—not on this operation."

He looked at her a moment, searching for a flaw, some indication of deceit. She was as cool as her uncle. "I don't think Bingo gave you that information voluntarily. You got it out of him, maybe sweated it out of him, like you're trying to do with me right now only not quite so genteelly."

She smiled as if she expected the remark. "You don't understand us gusanos, reverend. Bingo came out of Cuba the same way I did, fighting currents, sharks, and Castro gunboats. When you have to leave your homeland like that, you don't forget easily—and every time you get a chance to even up the score a little you want it to go right. . . ."

"There has to be more than that," he insisted flatly.

"That's it," she retaliated, her eyes turning a hard, glaring black.

"He wouldn't go that far in the concern you say he has—there's got to be something rubbing deeper!"

For a moment it looked as though she would walk out on him; apparently she was not used to being pressed like this. Then she relaxed against the railing, looking at him closely with her head bent to one side as if debating whether to go on.

"Very well," she said with a sigh. "Bingo we know pretty well. He was once an altar boy in the Church of Guadalupe in Havana. His father and mother were very religious. When Castro came in, he began rounding up all the men who might have been sympathetic to Batista. One day they chased Bingo's father to the statue of the Virgin of Guadalupe outside the church in downtown Havana—there's a fountain there, and the statue is in the middle of it. Bingo's father jumped into the fountain and moved across to the Virgin, and while he was praying to her in waist-high water they shot him. Bingo was there to see it, to watch the water turn to blood—the boy hasn't forgotten that and never will. The lesson taught him one thing: that the Blessed Virgin is more of a mockery than a help, that the church only complicates matters in the big things that count."

"But he's been more than friendly to me," Sebastian said, with a note of defensiveness he did not intend, but which came out of his bewilderment at this side of Bingo. "He's even shown real respect for the church."

"Of course," she said evenly, her voice controlled now to a velvet kind of purr as if she was deliberately trying to give it to him in easy doses. "Bingo can tolerate the church or anyone connected with it just as long as it doesn't infringe on complicated matters like this operation. But like all Free Cubans he covers up for his true feelings. There is a kind of ambivalence we have for spiritual things; we can respect the church as tradition but we abhor it when it comes to using it for practical ways. Bingo is like that—he can tip his hat to the altar, but he will throw a bomb at it if it gets in his way. So don't think for one minute that you have potential converts here, sympathizers for your clerical elements."

Once again the long arm came up in that poking jab. He looked at the check, then at her, the eyes still flashing sparks against the black ice, communicating her own sense of disdain for him.

"Put the money away," he said. "As far as I'm concerned, whether I go or not is up to Joe MaConnel. We better leave it at that."

She dipped her head in final acknowledgment and put the check back in the folds of her dress. "It is time then to return to the party." She turned to move back into the library. She stopped, as if remembering one further point. "You will be watched from here on in," she said.

"Oh, I'm really sure of that," he replied with a smile.

"We are checking on your credentials," she went on, her eyes turning to him again, raking him with a kind of mean, probing, measuring look, almost of contempt, as if she had concluded he was already something far less than he claimed, though what he claimed to be was anything but complimentary to her. "If anything shows up that doesn't match, we will get you out of the operation finally in our own decisive way. Meanwhile, we will talk to Joe about dropping you."

"Fair enough," he replied, and gave her a smile of acknowledgment which she did not return. He followed her through the library, out through the many rooms of the mansion, and finally to the sound of calypso and festivities that went with a party already well along and building to reckless momentum.

She turned on her most radiant side at the party. Though she stayed close to him as her uncle had asked, she danced with others, but never out of range of where he stood discreetly sipping a glass of punch. Now and then he caught her eyes over the shoulder of her partner, and he would each time lift his glass in salute to her. She would never acknowledge, of course, because her constant watchfulness was purely one of responsibility.

It was near midnight when Sebastian decided to leave. He paid his respects to Señor Rodríguez, who was in the middle of entertaining a number of people and showing some effects of what he had been drinking. Once sure that María was with Sebastian, Rodríguez was quick to turn back to his company without a further word.

She accompanied him to the front patio. When they got to the steps leading down to the parked cars, a tall, lanky man in dinner clothes too small for him stepped out of the shadows of bougainvillea vines. Sebastian noticed watery gray eyes that kept blinking rapidly, as if taking a thousand quick camera shots, storing them up in the brain for later examination. She did not look particularly happy about his confronting them.

"Mr. Mathews," she said in a well-played approach, disarming and innocent. "How good to see you!"

Mathews blinked at her, smiled thinly, and looked beyond her to Sebastian with some interest.

"Oh, may I introduce Mr.—the Reverend, I'm sorry—the Reverend Raymond Sebastian? Mr. Sebastian, this is Mr. Harold Mathews. . . . I should say that Mr. Mathews is with the N.I.A., National Intelligence Agency, so I would advise you to be very careful about what you say; it could be held against you."

Her light, bantering way was a cover for what she was trying to tell him, that he should play it very cool right now. Mathews took Sebastian's hand in his own briefly, his eyes blinking furiously all the time.

"Mr. Sebastian is an old friend of my uncle's," she added.

"Oh?" Mathews said politely. "I didn't think your uncle had any desires left for the church."

"He—he doesn't. Mr. Sebastian is what you might say a kind of hangover from other times. . . . Oh, there's your car, Mr. Sebastian."

She gave his arm a squeeze to urge him down the steps. Below them a big, black Cadillac pulled up and the driver got out to open the back door.

"We must get together some time for a walk on the beach," Mathews said from behind them as they moved down the steps.

"Love to," Sebastian called back over his shoulder. María gave him a light shove in the back so that his head barely cleared the top of the door as he half tripped into the back seat. She slammed the door on him, waved to the driver, and as he pulled away from the curb he saw her again for a moment as he'd seen her outside the Libertad, defiant, fierce in her anger, and ever so much more beautiful.

But then she was gone behind him, and he turned to face the front, wondering what a N.I.A. man was doing at Rodríguez's garden party anyway. His mind shifted to Bingo, the finger-snapping, enthusiastic, buoyant Bingo, who was all the time covering up his true feelings about the church and churchmen. What bleeding emotions lay under that youthful, zestful Cuban's exterior? What kind of environment could have produced such dimensions in a boy, to make him appear so readily friendly to the church but underneath so bitter? Why did he bother to cover what he truly felt? But then, maybe María San Roman wasn't telling the truth either.

He was still thinking of Bingo when he got to the hotel, got out of the car, got his key from the desk, took the elevator up, and slid the key into the lock of his door. He turned once, but it remained locked. Funny. He twisted it back the other way, and this time it worked. He pushed his way into the dark room. He knew immediately something wasn't right. He smelled something almost immediately: sweet, almost perfumed, like flowers. He lifted one hand as if he wanted to push the darkness aside, his other going along the wall to the light switch.

The blow caught him in the solar plexis—it bent him over, forcing him to cough and suck for air in a gasping groan. He tried to straighten, but a second blow, on the back of the neck, dropped him to his knees. He kept his shaky arms under him to hold himself on all fours while the darkness took on purplish-red lights. Then he felt an arm go around his neck and a hand gripped his arm, twisting it up behind his back. "The wind blows quieter in the home country, padre," a voice hissed near his ear. He felt the heat of it on his skin, smelled the sharp stench of alcohol. "We warn you now to find those calm breezes or face the storm. . . . Comprene, padre?"

And again a blow caught him on the neck, and this time

he went down flat, and a shoe hit him hard on his lower back so that he cried out. Then he was heading straight down into that black hole, and there were no lights now, nothing to grab, and he let it come, hoping when he hit it would be soft, as soft as the blanket that came down over him in a kind of finality.

Chapter VII

****

When he opened his eyes he caught the sun coming through the Venetian blinds, stabbing a shuttered shaft of light at him, like it was chopping up the day in easy doses. He let time come to him, filtering through a frothy liquid of pain, bringing awareness. He opened his mouth once as the pain hit hard in his back, and the sound, a gagging kind of sigh, seemed strange to him, as if it had come from someone else. He lay there a long time wondering if his back was broken, for there was a numbness that kept pricking him around his neck and shoulders. Finally, with all the dribbled-out will he had left, he managed to grip the end of the bed and pull himself up inch by inch until he fell across the bed, rolling over on his back and letting go with a yell as the pressure hit hard.

He lay there panting a long time, staring at the spotted

cream ceiling, wondering what to do. The phone wasn't too far from him now. Call the house doctor? Jane? No. He would arouse suspicion on the one hand, perhaps panic on the other. It would do no good in either case. Better to weather this himself and force no unnecessary questions.

Instead he lay there, letting his mind feel around on its own in this puzzling thing. The big question was who? N.I.A.? But nobody really had enough of a line on him yet to know what he was up to here. Castro's boys? Could be. But they would do more than beat him up; they'd want to know some answers as to what he was trying to do and how. Rodríguez? Most likely. And more specifically María: the cool mint of her, that disarming low-temperature chunk of green ice that covered a calculating, almost ruthless, manipulating mind capable of anything to get her wish. María probably was no novice at this thing either. And she wanted him out of this operation—pretty bad.

But after a while he stopped the senseless tail chasing. He had no proof either way, and he had no intention of facing anybody with it. Right now he had to stop feeling sorry for himself; that could wreck him more than the beating.

The pain, meanwhile, stayed with him, harsh, howling. But he began to force himself to move in inches, until by afternoon he got to the shower and let the hot spray hit his back. He yelled when it first hit, but then the needle-sharp edges began to cut into the tender flesh and relax him. Some of the pain began to subside.

It was late afternoon when the phone rang. He was sitting on the bed by then, his back propped up against the pillows. It was Bingo. "I come up, okay, padre?" he said.

Sebastian thought maybe he shouldn't tell Bingo what had happened. On the other hand, maybe the kid knew all about it.

"The door's unlocked," he said, and he hung up and

pushed himself back a little more to make sure he didn't have one of those spasms now.

Bingo came in with his usual slashing blaze of good cheer. "A good Sunday to you, padre!" he chirped. Sebastian hadn't realized it was Sunday.

"It has started a bit off color," he said casually, watching Bingo to see if the Cuban would show any hint of knowing.

"Sunday is your day, padre," Bingo shot back. "Big business day for the church!" Sebastian caught the light barb mixed in there. Bingo tossed a copy of a newspaper on his lap and then busied himself with a paper bag containing coffee and rolls. Sebastian noticed that it was the previous evening's edition; it had the story about the rescue operation and the seven bodies found on the PT.

"They say they are looking for two Americans," Sebastian said, reading down the story. "How do they know there are two?"

Bingo put coffee on the chair by the bed for Sebastian. "The N.I.A. knows," he said simply. "Probably Peter Rabbit. . . ."

Sebastian looked up at him quickly, but there was no smile in return.

"And who is Peter Rabbit?"

Bingo took a bite of his roll, chewing on it slowly. "Sometimes he sells information to Rodríguez, next day to Castro, maybe the third day to N.I.A. When you don't think he's there, he's there. He was at the boathouse maybe when we come in . . . maybe saw us come out and get into the car. Anyway, you can do nothing without N.I.A. finding out. . . ."

Sebastian didn't pursue that any further. He put the paper aside and sipped of his coffee. "By the way, do you know María San Roman?"

Bingo's jaws slowed as if that had caught him off guard. "Sí, I know María." His voice was guarded even though not changing its light note of banter. "Met her once at the Refugee Center. . . . She is one beautiful señorita, no?"

"Yes," Sebastian admitted, and toyed with the idea of asking Bingo if he knew she worked at the Libertad. But then he figured that wouldn't reveal much in any case. "What's the news from Joe?"

"Mrs. MaConnel, she tell me that Joe called at four this morning. Says Joe is having much trouble with this Alphonse. Like working with—what she say he say?—a Egyptian dummy ten million years old. Everything fall apart in his hands. . . ."

"You mean mummy."

"Ha?"

"Never mind. When did he say he'd be here?"

"Don't know. But he try for Tuesday. You know, I don't think you look so good, padre. You sick?"

Sebastian looked back at him, but all he saw was genuine concern. "No, I'm not sick. . . . Just get me one of those rolls, will you?" Then, to keep the conversation running, while he chewed, he said, "Do you have any girl friends?"

Bingo took a bite of his roll, examined the part that was left very closely, and said with a shrug, "Sure, I got one."

"She live here?"

"No, not here."

"What's her name?"

Bingo paused, staring again at the half-eaten roll. "I call her Dolly."

Now Sebastian knew the reason for the song, at least. "She live very far?"

"No, but she not easy to get to."

"Someone in Cuba then," Sebastian offered.

Bingo nodded. He looked suddenly at Sebastian as if he were a father confessor and said, "Havana, padre, it is Havana. . . . She one beautiful girl. I know her all my life; now I miss her. . . . You think that is funny?"

Sebastian smiled. "No, I think I know what you mean." He would have tried to swing Bingo around to thinking about the kind of girls it was more wholesome to become emotionally attached to, but he knew it was something deep with the boy.

"Well, I got to go, padre; many errands for Joe," Bingo said then, suddenly getting to his feet as if the conversation was getting too close to him. He stood there a moment, the remains of a roll bulging in his cheek, his eyes running over Sebastian's sprawled-out body on the bed. "You sure I can't get you something?"

"Better run your errands, gusano," Sebastian said. "Keep in touch."

"Me, I gonna jab you night and day," Bingo said, in a parody of what Joe had said earlier, and then he laughed, and Sebastian wasn't sure he liked the sound of it. "Adiós, padre!"

He was left to ponder the strange ambivalence of the Cuban. It seemed as if Bingo knew he had suffered something, but how much he couldn't tell. Well, so what? He was going to put that aside now anyway. He read from the Scriptures the rest of the evening. With the pain in his back still digging deep into his nerves, and with thoughts of Alphonse coming up to new and real proportions, he closed his reading in Proverbs: "The lot is cast into the lap; but the whole disposing of it thereof is the Lord's."

He let it rest right there and turned off the light. There was no more final way to look at it. Perhaps the Lord would dispose of this. But if his experience was any norm, it would be as much through him as anyone. So, man of God, climb your mountain now—it's always easier coming down than going up.

He slept well enough and called Jane the next morning. "Are you all right?" he asked.

"I meant to call you and ask the same thing," she replied. "I wanted to have dinner with you so we could talk; I'll go crazy if I can't talk to somebody. How about tonight?"

He didn't think he was in shape yet to meet her without arousing her suspicions, so he said, "Give me a day or two. . . . you hear from Joe?"

"One call—Bingo tell you?" Sebastian said he had. "He really didn't call me," she added with a kind of apologetic laugh, clipped with bitterness. "He tried to get Rodríguez. When he couldn't, I was all there was left. Nice way to live with a man, isn't it?"

"That'll change some time," he said, trying to get her out of that disturbing kind of mood.

"Sure," she said in a dry tone. "Anyway, I feel just terrible that I got you into the Alphonse thing."

"I got into that one myself. . . . Now, how about a dinner date for Wednesday night? How about over here on the beach?"

"Well, I can't guarantee you won't be on another midnight ride like the first one; I'm being watched regularly lately."

"Let's try it anyway, Jane," he replied, and he was glad for her short laugh. "Here at the hotel at six—okay?"

She agreed and hung up, and he was left with that same awareness that she was a desperately lonely, frightened woman. He felt guilty about not going to see her right then, but he knew that at best all he could do was walk in a half crouch some of the time—and he knew that it wouldn't help to explain that to her.

By the next day he was able to get around better. That afternoon he caught a cab to the Cuban Refugee Center. He had to have a look himself. He was given the tour by a short Cuban lady who spoke broken English. He watched them being processed, clutching brown paper sacks, all the possessions they could carry out of Cuba. They were a different kind of flotsam that went with wars. Not yet killed in spirit, though sometimes the flame burned low in them as they thought of the hopelessness of Castro communism, while at other times it leaped as fresh argument poured fuel to the dampened wicks of their hopes. Some wept when they told of their families still there. When he left the center, he didn't feel as tired or as lame—he felt the urge to do something to rebuild those fires, but the sense of frustration hung on him too.

At nine-thirty that evening the phone rang. It was Bingo. "Joe is in, padre," he said. "The señor Rodríguez wishes you both to meet with him at the Asociación Fraternal on Flagler Street immediately. Comprene?"

"I'll be there," he said, and forced himself to do some bends to get his back limbered up so he wouldn't show any signs of trouble when he got there. Then he went out and hailed a cab.

When he got to Rodríguez's downstairs den, the rest of them were already there. They all appeared to be strangers to him now. Circumstances in the past hours had altered all of them to him, him to them. He saw María first, standing by the mantel just to the right of the pool table, across which were spread blueprints and charts. She was dressed in a white, open-necked blouse with a green handkerchief in the breast pocket, that touch of mint kept alive in her, a kind of sweetener to soften what was her real self. Her tight skirt was a brown tweed. Her arms were folded and she held a burning cigarette in one hand, which was halfway to her soft, delicate mouth. She had paused in that pose of half uncertainty as he walked in, and he detected a quick, measuring flick of a glance over him, questioning his right to be there.

Bingo was standing behind Joe and Rodríguez, behind the shadows of the light that hung over the pool table. He was content to stay back now, apparently as if all this was a job for people much older than himself. His face, what Sebastian could see of it, was set in somber lines, studious, reflective.

This was no time to be singing "Hello, Dolly" or clicking the Spanish rhythms. The room was charged, the kind of atmosphere in a developing storm just before the lightning hits.

Both Joe and Rodríguez stood together at the pool table. Rodríguez as usual chewed his fresh cigar and stared at the blueprints, almost unmindful of Sebastian's entry. Joe simply looked up once. There were crude lines of exhaustion on his face now, cutting jagged smudge patches under and around his mouth and building sagging pockets of blue-black under his eyes. His eyes were red and half closed, and the greasy yachting cap rested at a crazy angle away from the yellowish lump of bandage, offering sick contrasts that intensified the air of belligerence in Joe that rode over everything else.

"So what did I have to do?" Joe went on, apparently continuing with the conversation they were having before Sebastian came in. "Well, I'll tell you—I managed to get this sagging monstrosity to the railroad yard only after I cut off the conning tower bridge. Fortunately the periscope well unscrews from the bridge mount and bolts down to hook into a coupling in the control room or it would have been impossible. Your man there almost had a heart attack when he read your note ordering him to get a flat car for delivery—but he did. Just so happens that those flat cars go exactly sixty feet, no more, so there was a lot of haggling about whether to ship her like that with the margins of safety so close. When we got her down here, we sat around for two hours before that special low-bed trailer showed up, the special kind they ship those Cape Kennedy rockets on—I dunno how you managed to get one like that, but it was a touchy business getting into your property up north, then backing around into the hangar and all—."

"Let us get our minds to what is ahead, amigo," Rodríguez cut in then, showing some irritation with this recitation of details.

Joe sniffed once to indicate his disdain at being cut in on

like that, and then he jerked his head to the blueprints spread out on the green pool table. "It's a mess, that's what," he returned tartly, not bothering to put on his usual respectful manner with Rodríguez. "The hull peels off in your hand like it was made of putty. She's got no equipment in her at all, except for a compass, a helm, and the ballast control valves. We'll need to check over her circuits and probably replace most of her wiring. And we have to cut a hole in her afterdeck and lower in a new diesel—to say nothing of welding that conning tower bridge back into place. In short, this poor excuse for a boat needs a Navy repair yard. And even then she probably will take to water like a locomotive—which all goes to say, señor, that I think the whole operation with Alphonse is as screw-loose as"—he looked up quickly at Sebastian, intending to make the comparison, and then finished with—"as trying to fly with an umbrella!"

"The flying with umbrellas is good, they say," Rodríguez countered, peering closely at the blueprints again. "So—it is our only way. And I will say it again for the last time, amigo"—and now he looked up at Joe, and there was no smile, instead a kind of boring gaze that reached in with a long hand and poked Joe in the left ventricle where life and death was in balance—"we will work with Alphonse. You will do what you have to, but on the morning of the eleventh of February, old man of the sea, you will be sailing for Cuba."

Joe fished for a cigarette in his shirt pocket, took one out, stuck it in his mouth, lit it, and puffed angrily, as if all this were a language only he and Rodríguez understood. "Señor, I've still got to have a crew—"

"I have checked all of your leads," Rodríguez said. "I offered every man I could trust ten thousand dollars to sail with you. They all turned it down."

There was a moment of silence, during which Joe tried to assess the enormity of that fact. "So now what?"

Rodríguez squinted at the charts as if they were a problem in billiards and said, "We will have to—what you say in America?—"

He couldn't find the word, and he snapped his fingers toward María, who said, "Improvise."

"Sí, improvise," he continued. "So, for one, María goes as part of your crew."

Joe pulled the cigarette from his mouth and stared dumbfounded at Rodríguez, then at María, who gave him a quick, flashing grin as if she had scored one on him. It was a forced salute, though; she seemed to dislike this arrangement as much as Joe.

"We don't have any room for a woman," Joe began, his voice rising to a point of weary indignation.

"She goes as insurance for me," Rodríguez said shortly and removed his cold cigar a moment to pick a fleck of tobacco off his tongue with a long forefinger.

"Insurance for what?"

"In case you get to think maybe you would like to run Alphonse somewhere else besides Cuba, sí? María will be there to guard against that moment of weakness. . . . In the meantime, she can learn from you to be a very practical part of the crew."

"Like what?" Joe demanded, pushing aside all caution now. "We got no room for cooks, or laundry specialists, or morale officers—"

"Do not play games with me, amigo," Rodríguez hissed. The blue-black veins bulging out on his forehead were as dangerous-looking as the puffed-up head of a cobra. "You will teach María what must be done to keep that boat running, sí?"

Joe shook his head slowly, his face gone even more pale so that the smudges of exhaustion showed up like the purple stains of a grape. "Señor, you don't understand what it takes to run a submersible boat—"

"María, she learns fast."

Joe got the metallic edge of the voice now. He put his cigarette back into his mouth with a hand that shook perceptibly. "Okay, okay, so we got a woman crew member as of now." The note of resignation and defeat was heavy in his voice. "It's your niece you are committing to the deep, señor."

"On the contrary, amigo, I am committing her to your capable hands as a submarine officer, no?"

Joe sighed. "Well, I can't go with just a woman. I need an engineer, a man on the bow planes–"

"Chico, he will go also," Rodríguez said with finality.

Joe turned to look at Bingo, who had jumped forward out of the shadows as he suddenly realized what Rodríguez had said. The surprise and shock was evident on Bingo's face too; it was a new look, one that Sebastian hadn't seen on him before, as if there never was anything left in the world to shock him.

"Bingo?" Joe appealed. He took off his greasy cap and dropped it on the charts as he would throw in a bad hand of cards. It was a gesture of total futility. Then, as if it struck him as ludicrously funny, he began to laugh, and the laugh rose to borderline hysterics as his apparently tired nerves couldn't check it.

Rodríguez let him finish and then said coldly, "He runs your engines on the other boat. He can run the motor for Alphonse too."

"Sure," Joe said, rubbing at eyes that had gone watery with the laugh. "But what does he know about running a delicate problem of diesel and battery motors ninety feet under the ocean? It takes quite a man to keep a sub alive down there, a man who knows his equipment and can spot trouble before it happens. . . ."

"I can do it, Joe!" Bingo cut in eagerly.

"Hogwash!" Joe contradicted, his voice whipping out like a lash. "That's a seven-hundred-horsepower monster you got to handle down there in a space that won't let you do more than take a half breath at a time."

"He goes, amigo," Rodríguez said flatly. "There is no other engineer in town who will do it. There is no time to look elsewhere. Chico goes."

Joe said nothing. He was staring at the green table top, his eyes reflecting something of the horror of trying to run a complex boat underwater with a crew of novices. "I cannot go without even one man who knows subs," he said then, and this time there was that firm biting note of the categorical in his voice, a sign he was not going to budge any more.

Rodríguez sighed. "Well, then, I think perhaps I have the answer." Just then a buzzer sounded, and Rodríguez said loudly, "Come in!"

One of Rodríguez's bodyguards stepped in first, and then came a medium-built Negro, who stood there in the open doorway for a long minute surveying the room, as if testing it. He was dressed in a simple blue denim shirt and dungarees that had seen too many washings, his feet covered with a pair of dirty white sneakers. He held a guitar in front of him as if he'd just gotten up from playing in a band. His eyes showed both gentleness and withdrawal, as though he'd looked on a world of constant suffering too long. A long jagged scar ran down from his left eye to the corner of his mouth and pulled the muscles of his mouth upward so that he had the look of a clown, a half-leering grin as if all people were subjects of laughter to him. He couldn't be much more than twenty-five, but the marks of dissipation on his face gave him a much older appearance.

"El Dorado Santos," Rodríguez said, and the note in his voice was that of a ringmaster introducing an act that he knew wasn't the best. "Soldier of fortune, beachcomber, but important to you, Joe, he is a former Cuban, was brought to this country when he was thirteen, became a citizen, served two years in the U.S. Navy in submarines, was in the Bay of

Pigs, escaped, and is now. . . ." Rodríguez's voice trailed off, as if he didn't know how to identify Santos's present way of life delicately.

"Law student," El Dorado said, and stepped into the room, seemingly satisfied that it was safe. Sebastian saw that the guitar hung on him by a maroon cord over the shoulder, and as Rodríguez introduced each of them to him, he shoved the piece around on his hip, bowing to each of them in a kind of mock display of politeness. When Sebastian was introduced as the "padre," he paused halfway over in his bow to look up quickly, and a quick trace of a smile tugged at that scar as if he'd suddenly thought of a good joke that he couldn't fully repress.

"What's the law student crack all about?" Joe said disdainfully, not liking this new idea of Rodríguez's any more than the others.

"I got him out of the Miami City jail," Rodríguez said bluntly, and he flicked a lighter and held the flame to his cigar, trying to puff up a distracting pillar of smoke to lessen the impact of what he was saying. "It seems that Ellie here is in for assault with a deadly weapon. I paid twenty-five thousand dollars to get him for two months until his trial comes up in March."

"The law knows where he's goin' for the next thirty days?" Joe demanded.

"Amigo, I pay lawyers a lot of money to cover tracks," Rodríguez retorted with some irritation, as if it was an insult for anyone to ask him that.

"Assault on who?" María cut in abruptly.

El Dorado looked quickly at Sebastian again, and for a moment there appeared just a flick of hesitancy almost akin to apology. "Some preacher," he said, then, and his grin was a flash of ivory in the room, an invitation to the others to share the irony of the moment. Then to Sebastian he added, "No offense, padre, since I do not lump all men of the cloth with the lesser breed."

"Why a preacher?" Joe prodded. He was suddenly very interested.

El Dorado shrugged. "He just wouldn't perform the wedding like I asked. . . ."

"She white?" Joe coaxed.

El Dorado rocked on his heels a moment as though the question had started some inner mechanism running, and his look at Joe was one of acknowledgment that he'd found a man who could cut expertly to the bone. "You might say that's one issue that would get a white preacher excited, man. . . . Right, padre?"

Sebastian didn't have the answer to that right away, and Joe cut in again. "So?"

El Dorado studied him a long minute, that crooked, almost twisted grin coming on slowly as he saw how anxious Joe was to have it all. "So I cut him up a bit, man . . . you know? A little here, a little there, enough to educate him, okay?"

Joe waited a minute while the room stayed quiet, and then he said, "Yeah, you're the same guy, all right. . . . Ain't we met before?"

"Yeah, man," El Dorado replied, his body loose but his feet spread apart, ready. "You cheated me in a poker game here in Miami, not long ago, and I called you with a knife, remember?"

Joe's eyes narrowed, and Rodríguez looked at his cigar, as if he didn't want to watch what might be coming now. "Yeah, you got quite a reputation with that knife of yours," Joe said, his voice controlled on the sharp edge of his own killer instinct.

"This is no place to settle ancient scores, old man of the sea," Rodríguez cut in, making a game try to head off what was coming.

Joe said nothing for a minute, watching El Dorado rock in front of him, and then he quipped, "Well, we got a padre here who needs some cuttin' up, El Dorado, any time you get that old feelin'. . . ." El Dorado grinned again, turning it full on to Sebastian, who suddenly found the painting of a fishing schooner on the far wall worthy of his attention. "What do you know about subs?" Joe went on, and the atmosphere of tension drained off with the question.

"Man, I ran the control room of the *Exeter,* the biggest of the subs we got before the *Nautilus*—I kept the bubble in the boat, you know what I mean? Steering, bow planes, the whole trim was my baby. . . . That answer your question, chief?"

"It'll do," Joe said, and, though he wouldn't show it, Sebastian knew he was pleased, both with El Dorado's submarine know-how and perhaps especially his controversy with clergymen.

"There's one man here who hasn't been assigned anything." María's voice came in again clearly, and she folded her arms and turned to look at Sebastian. "I take it we all agree that he stays ashore."

Joe's moment of placidity faded, and he looked quickly at María, then at Rodríguez.

"She is right," Rodríguez said with a shrug. "The padre stays."

"That part you don't buy me out of, señor," Joe said flatly.

"What can he do?" María challenged.

"I'll find plenty for him to do, don't worry," Joe snapped.

"He doesn't fit," María argued, jabbing a long finger toward Sebastian as if he were a leftover piece of bread dough that wouldn't shape into anything worthwhile.

"We got a deal, the preacher and me," Joe said simply.

"You can't put God in the middle," Rodríguez warned.

"He's been there since the year one," Joe snapped. "Why change His position now? Anyway, I want preach with me."

"You know he's the soul-saver kind?" María asked with mounting indignation.

Joe grinned in a way that was half pain, half vengeance. "Man, do I know it! If anybody knows it, I do."

"Then you know his kind don't belong in this sort of operation." She went on pounding home the logic with intensity. "He belongs in an evangelistic tent. What is he doing here? We think he's N.I.A. . . ."

Joe laughed. "Not this preacher we got here, sister. I know this man good. He's as N.I.A. as the Good Humor man is Mickey Mantle."

"He's still a misfit."

"There isn't one here who ain't," Joe retaliated, and he stared back at María, challenging her to come up with anything to that. "Now, Señor, you tell your niece here that if that preacher don't go, I don't. I'm going to look forward to one thing on this voyage." His eyes came back to fix on Sebastian in that boring, mesmerizing focus. "When my preacher friend here pops his colon down there at fifteen fathoms or so, I want to scoop up a specimen and hang it up in my wife's bedroom so she can see what kind of man she's got for a hero. Right, preacher?"

Nobody said anything, and then Bingo suddenly cut in with, "Nobody asked the padre if he wants to go."

Sebastian looked quickly at Bingo, for it was a kind of challenge on the one hand and a kind of invitation to refuse on the other. Bingo's smile was there yet, but his eyes were darker, hard pebbles that bounced off the rays from the lamp overhead, the kind of eyes that reflected the bitter soul that once looked on the blood of his own father in the fountain, with the Virgin looking on, powerless to affect the situation.

"I started this thing, I'll finish it," Sebastian said. He wanted to say more to declare himself, but El Dorado suddenly hit the guitar and came off with a loud strumming chord that rang incongruously in the charged room. Then he launched forth with "Onward, Christian Soldiers" in a clear, sweet, almost childlike voice, his twisted smile aimed at Sebastian in a mocking salute. It caught the rest of them by surprise, and Rodríguez was so stunned that he forgot all about his cigar and let it hang like a stick in the corner of his mouth. And then Joe laughed, having caught the parody El Dorado was framing at Sebastian's expense. Even María had to smile indulgently. Bingo waited for the discreet moment and then began to snap his fingers to the rhythm of the song and do a little shuffle with his feet. It all had the touch of the bizarre to it, a room full of contradictions, sounds scraping against one another, threatening to cancel one another out but each trying to rise above the other.

El Dorado finished with an expert fanfare on the strings, his smile a streak of amusement and even apology, while his eyes bounced off the lights of his inner joy. But Sebastian couldn't tell if it was out of the delight of the deliberate parody of religion or an actual satisfaction in what he was singing.

The song seemed to finish the argument. María was leaning against the mantelpiece in a pose of resignation, apparently aware that it was foolish to press this any further; Rodríguez simply stared at the dead ashes on the end of his cigar, puzzled that the glowing end and his argument seemed to go out at the same time.

El Dorado's flourish died slowly in the hot room, unable to find any kindred spirit who would perpetuate it. Then Rodríguez said, "So you have the padre. But keep God out of it, old man of the sea!"

"Oh, I fully expect God to be out of it," Joe quipped and grinned his crooked smile at Sebastian.

"Good," Rodríguez replied. "Now, let us go see this Alphonse."

Joe, El Dorado, María, and Rodríguez headed for his big black Cadillac.

"Chico, you take the padre!" Rodríguez called back. "And watch him, watch him good!" Then they climbed in and the chauffeur shot the car away from the curb and out into Flagler Street traffic.

Sebastian climbed into the jeep beside Bingo, who didn't waste any time getting the pounding engine into life, almost as if he wanted the noise to offer excuse for the conversation he didn't want right now. They drove north for fifteen minutes. Once Sebastian asked, "Where are we going?"

"To Rodríguez's place on Highway One."

"They got Alphonse there?"

"Sí," Bingo said, and that was that.

They sped along for another five minutes or so. When they were well out of Miami and running along the half-deserted highway, Bingo suddenly cut into a gas station. "Fill it up, man," Bingo told the attendant and, without looking at Sebastian, added, "Padre, it is time to wash our hands, no?"

A bit bewildered and apprehensive, Sebastian followed the young Cuban into the station washroom. Bingo slammed the door, locked it, and turned on the water taps full force as if he wanted cover for what he was about to say. He put his hands under the cold water and said, "You should go home now, padre, back to your church, wherever it is."

"Why?" Sebastian said loudly over the running water.

"The operation, it gets too big now, too big for a man of the church."

Sebastian wanted to ask point-blank if this had anything to do with the beating last night, but he thought he'd let it ride, let Bingo tell him if it did.

"María tell you to tell me that?"

Bingo turned a perplexed look toward him. "Why María?"

"She told me that you had a bad experience with the death of your father—that business in Havana at the fountain.

She said that you didn't like clergymen or the church much since and you didn't particularly want me in this thing. . . ."

Bingo turned back to the water, scooped some up into his face, and blew it back into the basin. He grabbed a fistful of paper towels and began dabbing at his face. "It is not for that only. I know things, I see things, I feel things. I say it for the last time, padre—you get off now. This thing is bigger than seven of Rodríguez's family on Cuba. It is a job now for us Cubans, sí?"

"So what's it all about?" Sebastian pressed, but Bingo moved by him quickly, threw the lock, and was gone without another word. Sebastian followed a minute later, climbed into the jeep again, and realized that the conversation was ended. Bingo had removed himself behind a strange curtain of detachment. He kicked the jeep out again with that raucous thundering sound to seal it off for good.

Sebastian could only watch the road and wonder. How did a fly feel when a big hand was slowly closing and squeezing it? You could relax and play dead and wait for daylight. Or you could jump for freedom while you had the chance. Instinct told him now to jump. That deep dull ache in his back was a good witness, and now Bingo's strange behavior. This was getting to be a very sticky bog indeed for a preacher who had started out simply to counsel a friend in soul trouble—but then, if he was ever to find out, he'd have to stay in. There were too many other areas of commitment he had to own up to anyway.

He shifted in the seat, trying to find a comfortable spot, but there wasn't any. He doubted there would be any on this ride. Then Bingo cut quickly to a dirt road that was just vaguely outlined in the moonlight, halted the jeep, and waited.

"There's a bus in ten minutes for Miami—it comes right by here," Bingo said, his eyes fixed on the road ahead and the dense curtain of jungle.

"I got some marks on me, Bingo, that haven't healed

yet," Sebastian said finally. "Maybe in a few weeks I might feel different."

Bingo didn't look at him. He simply nodded as if he expected that answer and threw the jeep in gear. And the jungle fell behind them like a curtain dropping to seal off their escape.

Chapter VIII

****

The building was an old airplane hangar. It still had its original paint of faded orange, but the front of it was painted in a kind of jungle green to make it blend into the brush that surrounded it. It was set back about a hundred yards off the highway, behind a good front of swamp grass and tangled palms. It was apparent from the looks of the dirt road that led into the building that Rodríguez used this place quite often.

When they were all accounted for, Joe swung the sliding door back and told them all to get inside before he closed it again. They stood in the dark, conscious of each other's breathing and the wet warmness of each other floating in limbo. There were strong odors of diesel oil, mold, kerosene, and new rope—they went with rooms associated with ship repair—but above that they felt a kind of finality that goes with scuttled hulls that litter the lonely beaches of the world.

Then Joe threw on the ceiling floods. They hit the side of the "thing" sitting there on the flat trailer bed with impolite jabs of light. For a long time nobody said anything. Even Rodríguez could only stand and look, apparently paralyzed for the moment by what he saw.

Finally El Dorado said, in genuine awe, "This is a submarine? A ship?"

"What did you expect"—Joe's voice, from somewhere back in the shadows, sounded defensive—"the *Queen Mary?*"

Again that long silence held control. "Sometimes," El Dorado went on again, and he began to move toward it cautiously, as if it were some kind of prehistoric specimen, "sometimes it looks like a boat—but then, I dunno, it looks like a buffalo or something. . . ."

For Sebastian, who had seen the vessel before, the name Alphonse fit perfectly, perhaps more here now in this light than before. For the name surely went with awkwardness, bulkiness, double-jointedness, and inevitable disaster; he felt the same kind of embarrassment as he would in looking at a deformed child whose misshapen body could not function in any coordinated way. If he had never understood why Joe named this monstrosity Alphonse, he knew now. Her bow was blunt and scowlike, like the front end of an old steam locomotive; the hull was neither round nor angular; it was almost boxlike, and yet some areas bulged like a balloon blown up unevenly. The simple conning tower was a five-foot appendage, tacked on as an afterthought, as if it was a necessary evil. Alphonse had all the proportions of a child's drawing of a kite that had turned out to be a bathtub, straight lines clashing with angular ones. Everything about her seemed to reveal the bizarre or alcoholic ravings of a depraved scientist on an all-week binge, designing without intent or reason—she was a Frankenstein of the sea, constructed from the dead parts of decayed hulks, in every sense the deformed product of a twisted nautical mind, a cross between a whale, a tank, and the Goodyear blimp. And yet, as Sebastian knew, the mind that conceived this belonged to one of the most brilliant naval architects of his time.

"Sixty feet long," Joe was calling out from somewhere back in the anonymity of the darkness. "She's twenty feet wide and displaces one hundred eighty tons of water. From the top of the conning tower to the keel she's eighteen feet."

"You sure you can spare it?" El Dorado quipped, shaking his head slowly as he surveyed it closely.

"¡Dios mío!" Bingo said in a half whisper from where he stood hanging back a few feet from Sebastian, and there was a kind of terror on Bingo's face as if he had actually seen the incarnation of the spirit world.

"I take it that it *does* float," María said caustically.

"Who knows?" Joe called back. "That's what you'll find out in due time, sister!"

"It is good," Rodríguez said suddenly, recovering his composure and putting his cigar back into his mouth, now that he was sure his jaws could hold on to it. "Joe!"

Joe came out from the back, a little reluctantly, like a child who finally has to confront justice for his errors. "Yeah?"

"We start now."

"How do you mean?"

"I mean we start to work on this—this Alphonse now." Rodríguez began to rub his hands together as if he relished the thought. "I want you to work on this around the clock. Anything you need I will get. Electrician, plumber, anything, I will get them. But I want to say something." They all turned and waited, sensing the note of warning in his voice. "Nobody—understand, nobody—says anything to anybody about this. We work in shifts. Four work, one watch outside. Castro's compañeros must not know about this or find this place. If anybody talks"—and now he looked at each of them one at a time, his black eyes boring through them—"they deal with me." He let that hang a second for them to remember, and the he shifted his attention back to Joe. "Now, old man of the sea, what can they do to get started—now? I will bring beds, food, drink—but I want to see this Alphonse come to life." He was suddenly waving his hands toward the hulk, as if he had a wand and was trying to make it breathe right then. "It is a good thing, this Alphonse—it will do the job!"

"Yeah," Joe said with a disdaining sniff, looking up at Alphonse with genuine dubiousness on his face. "Well, sure, we can start putting the sealing paint on the hull now. . . . Then in the morning we'll need to work on the electrical system. . . . I got acetylene equipment, so we can start cutting the hole in the afterdeck to get ready for the diesel. But it's going to be close, señor, even if we can possibly get her ready for the twelfth."

"We will make it, amigo," Rodríguez said with finality. "I am going now. María, you stay here and help."

"In these clothes?" she protested.

"I got some old coveralls that won't take a thing away from you, baby," Joe said, delighted to see her discomfort at having to dirty herself with this mundane task.

"Tomorrow I find an electrician we can trust and send him," Rodríguez assured them. "¡Adiós, muchachos!"

They were left to face the blob of a vessel that seemed to grow larger in impossibility as they studied her. El Dorado wanted to know more about her, so Joe took them all up the ladder to the deck. "The conning tower ain't tied down yet," he warned, "so don't knock around it too hard." Then he went down through the conning tower hatch, taking a long extension light with him. They went down one at a time, the others waiting on deck. El Dorado was first. When he came back up, there was a look of incredulity on his face.

"I think I'll go back to jail," he said simply, and he

wasn't trying to be funny. It was the first serious remark he had made since coming into the group.

María went down next and returned five minutes later without a word. Light spots of perspiration showed up on her forehead and around her mouth. She said nothing and reached for a cigarette in her bag, her expression one of deep meditation.

It was Bingo's turn. When he came up, he was soaked in sweat, his shirt black with it, and he looked as if he wanted to throw up. He sagged down on the deck, stretching out on his back, his chest heaving with the exertion to get fresh air into his lungs. "It is like you crawl into your own grave still alive," he said, and his hands shook as he reached up to wipe the sweat from his face.

Sebastian went down last. He descended the ladder to the first level. Joe was waiting, his face glowing with the grease of his own perspiration, looking even more ghoulish in the light of the single hundred-watt bulb he held in his hand.

"Welcome to your purgatory, padre," he said, and he laughed at his own joke. "This is where you and I will command our lovely ship of the line—sorry you grew to be the Jolly Green Giant; it may be you'll be riding on your knees before we're through."

The space was no more than six or seven feet in diameter; Sebastian had to stay half bent over to keep his head from hitting the overhead. He wondered how long he could stand like that with his back in its present condition. He noted a few gauges here and there, and in front of him, not more than a few inches away, was a column that must be the periscope. He didn't know much about submarines, but this much he could guess at.

Joe kept the light close to Sebastian's face, checking his eyes and face closely to see the first signs of concern and uncertainty. Sebastian felt the tightening knot in his stomach. Sweat came easy here; the air smelled with the ozone of rotting metal and that aura of suffocation that goes with a sealed vault. He felt the fingers of his pulse begin to tap rapidly on a throat muscle, and he had the sudden urge to get out of there, to bolt back up the ladder to fresh air. If he was claustrophobic, now was the test, for he knew that to be able to stay in this pressing, squeezing box with thousands of tons of water holding him in was going to take all the nerve he had and then some. And on top of that, Joe was standing there waiting for him to show one jagged muscle that would indicate fear or, even more significant, doubt that God Himself was really strong enough of a reality to make any difference.

"Maybe it's too much for you to see the rest, preach?" Joe jabbed him then, almost hopeful that Sebastian would welcome the reprieve of investigating this coffin any further. "After all, this was your idea, you know."

Sebastian swallowed, cleared his throat in a poor attempt to show ease, said, "Lead on," and forced a steady look straight back at Joe, who yielded, turned, and descended the hatch to the lower level forward.

"This is the forward control room," Joe said, flashing the light around a pantry-sized compartment. There were two rusty-looking wheels jutting out of a panel to the left, a couple of valves and two wheelbarrow handles hanging out to the right. "El Dorado and María will bump elbows here," Joe added. "This runs the steerage, the ballast tanks, and the sonar. I expect El Dorado and María will know each other pretty good before we're through, right, preach?"

Sebastian grunted, not liking the implication in Joe's voice. Joe took him through another crawl space by what he called a "compressor room," which was nothing more than a set-in compartment, then up through a larger space that connected the upper control room with the aft engine room. "We'll put the cargo here," he said. Sebastian found it hard to believe they would ever get seven people into a space built for no more than three at the most. Then they went down a three-step ladder to the engine room area. It was a little bigger, but not much.

"Figure a thirteen-foot-long, five-foot-high diesel in here, and an electric motor and generator on top of it, and you can guess what Bingo's gonna feel like," Joe commented, keeping the light a few inches from Sebastian's face. It was obvious that Joe didn't believe it could be done; he was swinging the full weight of the impossible to Sebastian, spelling out for him the terrible dimensions of this thing. And all the time he was watching for visible signs of acquiescence on the part of Sebastian, making every word and description a test run that would produce the response he wanted. Sebastian wiped at a trickle of sweat that rolled down his chin, fighting the nausea that rolled up from his bowels.

"Your father said it could be done," he said, but not with any conviction of his own. "So we're going to have to try. . . .

Joe coughed, a laugh that was intended to be ridicule, and started back up through the hatch to the conning tower. When they got back up into the heavenly refreshment of the dank, heavy, stale air of the hangar, Sebastian had all he could do to keep from yielding to the shakiness in his legs and the heavy pounding in his head. His back ached terribly from trying to negotiate those confined spaces. And he was conscious that the others were watching him guardedly, looking for the same signs as Joe did, as if he was the gauge finally to whether they could do it or not.

"Okay," Joe said, "now that you picked your way to die, let's dress up this coffin. I'm turning in. The rest of you get on the sealer paint on the hull. El Dorado, you can show them what to do."

They got up slowly, suddenly overwhelmed with the gravity of what they had involved themselves in, reluctant to proceed with what looked to be a digging of their own graves.

But they went to it, only because they had no choice and with the thin hope that paint and repair would change their percentages.

Sebastian would remember those next three weeks in terms of the mental snapshots that stood out in rather nightmarish dimension, impressions that cut deep into his emotions and left indelible images: the grueling hours of painting and sealing, the constricting hours inside the boat, trying to be useful, to perform tasks that were totally new to him, working with only one single fan blowing down into the suffocating heat. Though neither he nor the others really knew what or how to do the work, he jumped from one job to the next, mostly holding pipes in place while Joe swore at the sweat burning his eyes, the metal that crumpled in his hands, the nuts and bolts that wouldn't grab. Hours of heat, bitter coffee, stale sandwiches that tasted of oil . . . and nights when he would wake up on the lumpy straw mattress and see weird blue flashes in the hangar from the acetylene torch as it cut into the thin skin of Alphonse, while the acrid smoke burned his nose and throat and had him coughing most of his time on the cot. And all the time there was the unchanging Alphonse, looking no better for all the sweat, sitting flat and bulky and defiant of all attempts to make her live despite the bright coat of gray sealer and her relined insides. She began to take on the real proportions and immobility of a corpse, lying there without feeling, oblivious of wires and pipes and valves that poured new power into her, unresponsive to the bold efforts at this mouth-to-mouth resuscitation. At night he would mumble over and over the same prayer, "O God, let her live. . . . O God, let her live. . . ." And he could wake up the same way, the same words tumbling out of him in a crazy kind of chant, as if he were saying the Mass or something, and he would jerk to reality to find maybe Bingo or María or El Dorado shaking him awake to tell him it was his turn. And he'd see in their intent looks as they watched him, their own eyes heavy with exhaustion and growing defeat, the accusation that the God he was invoking was not actually doing much in reply.

Twice in those weeks Alphonse was almost lost for good to freak accidents. The first was after the Cuban electrician had spent two and a half grueling days rewiring the entire system. When Joe threw the switch to test the power, a short started a flash fire, and smoke poured out of the hole in the afterdeck and up through the conning tower. Joe tried using a carbon dioxide extinguisher, but the smoke got thicker. Finally he dragged a hose over and opened up full force, letting the water pour in until El Dorado finally yelled, "Joe! You'll have to spend a week pumping her out!" But it seemed as if Joe had gone mad; he shoved the hose deeper and yelled for more force, until both Sebastian and El Dorado bodily pushed Joe aside and pulled the hose out.

The second occasion came when they were lowering the monstrous diesel down into the after hole with the help of a winch. El Dorado was operating the winch while Joe and Sebastian and Bingo guided the big engine down to its berth. Suddenly, with the diesel still hanging ten feet from her moorings, the winch jerked the chains. The single loop wouldn't hold and the engine crashed down into the engine room with a terrible, clanging, tearing sound. Joe seemed to go crazy. He leaped off the deck and landed on the surprised El Dorado with a vehemence that was next to murder. It took Sebastian, Bingo, and María's well-aimed shoe to put Joe out of commission and save El Dorado from sure strangling. The engine took an awful knock on its housing, too, and they had to spend time repairing a jagged slash in the lower deck.

And there were the in-between hours during which they waited for delayed supplies; Joe took this time to teach each of them, especially Bingo and María, what they were supposed to do on board. Time and again he would show María the importance of ballast control on a sub and how to run the valves and read the depthometer. At other times he would show her the principle of sonar from the battered *Blue-jacket's Manual* he had kept from his Navy days. She listened and repeated all the information and even went through the test procedures without a flaw.

With Bingo it was different. The intricate job of running a diesel and then switching from diesel to battery-powered motor in an undersea craft was a complicated affair. Bingo would follow Joe so far into the engineering side and then lose him, and Joe would have to go over it again. Sometimes El Dorado would strum his guitar to match Joe's statements, as mercilessly pounding as a sledge, and Joe would stop, glare at El Dorado, and shout, "Cut that out, for pete's sake!" And he'd go over it with Bingo again, while Bingo tried not to look nervous, but it was obvious the young Cuban was getting anxious by the way his Spanish came out riding hard over his English, even to the point that Joe couldn't understand him.

If it wasn't that, it was El Dorado telling Joe that the single propeller that drove Alphonse wasn't enough to properly maneuver a ship that size. Or that the ballast tanks weren't big enough to get them diving or coming up fast enough. "And air, man," El Dorado insisted. "With the compressed air tanks we can carry, we only got enough air down there for four or five hours at the most. What if we get stuck on the bottom for longer than that—and with seven other people sucking up air all the time?"

Joe would wipe his sweating face with the back of his hand and turn instead toward Sebastian and say, "Speak to the man there; he's the one who got us into this mess!"

And El Dorado could only look hopelessly and helplessly at Sebastian, waiting for the answers that he knew Sebastian couldn't give.

There were times when the underground conflict between Sebastian and Joe came to the surface. Joe made no pretense about his feelings about God or Sebastian. When the two of them were thrown together on a job, Joe took pains to spell out new words of profanity that weren't even in the dictionaries. Sebastian found that the only way he could counter was to use the Book. When Joe finished with a stream of swear-words that cut slashingly into Sebastian, Sebastian would come back with: "'Behold what manner of love the Father hath bestowed upon us that we should be called the children of God.'" Joe would glare at him and invariably smash his thumb with a wrench in his anger—and his mouth would start to form four-letter words again—but after a while, knowing he would get a Biblical homily or text in return, he took to sticking his bruised knuckles into his mouth instead.

"A closed mouth gathers no foot," Sebastian would say to him lightly, and Joe would move off muttering to himself.

But something else was happening in those three weeks. Joe was the most pointed example. The ship was reshaping him, or at least goading him. She was doing the same to all of them. For Joe, it was always Alphonse—nothing else mattered. People, lives, equipment, none of it meant anything. For him it seemed that making that ship live had become an obsession; as if he himself had killed her and was now on a crusade to revive her. He swore, kicked, tore out equipment, screwed it back in, pounded angrily at stubborn fittings that didn't go right. He seldom slept, drank cup after cup of coffee mixed with whiskey, and smoked incessantly. He became more intense; his face took on a scraggly growth of beard that made his eyes reflect the fires that burned within him in fitful flashes. He became domineering, arrogant, irritable, lashing out sometimes with a fury akin to madness. Once he came up through the conning tower hatch waving a length of fuel line and lifted it for all of them to see. "You see that?" he yelled in a near scream. "Somebody didn't bolt it in right. You know what will happen to us if we go down to even fifty feet with a fuel line that isn't fitted right? She'll fill up with oil, you hear?

If we're gonna drown, curse it all, let's not do it in oil!" And he threw the fuel line down on the deck with such fury that pieces of it flew in all directions.

And that fury got to others. Even María, who was a classic example of composure, found herself crying over a simple screw that wouldn't go through a piece of sheet metal. At other times she would shout in jubilance over a completed job, no matter how simple, and once shocked El Dorado when she suddenly kissed him on his grease-smeared cheek after they had finally gotten an instrument fixed into a panel and running correctly.

For Bingo, it was a new world. There was no finger-clicking rhythm, less impulsive jigging; his energies were now channeled to the common obstacle that the ship presented. When he wasn't helping with the fitting, he was pouring over the submarine manual of Joe's, working and reworking over in his mind the matter of the diesel and electrical power systems that would be his responsibility.

What was happening was as old as man banding together to face a common adversary; they saw each other less as misfits now, less as amateurs pitted against ridiculously superior odds. They were coming gradually into a fusion with one another, to overcome that symbol of all they individually had fought within themselves since they were born, the eternal conflict of man at war with nature, with man, with the universe—even with God. They were united in their common battle to scale the mountain in that hangar, pump life into that lifeless heap, put power into that empty shell. Each had his own reasons, perhaps, but what mattered was that it was happening. They had had little going for them as they were, a tattered band of fumbling, confused, frightened people, a peculiar composite of wills and world views that ran constantly at crosscurrents to each other. Now at least they were becoming a kind of loosely joined flying wedge aimed at that ship—and this had to come if they were ever to master the more complicated business of actually operating this chunk of iron on their limited knowledge of submarines.

In those three weeks, Sebastian had no opportunity to inject any spiritual ideas to balance the individual obsessions they had on other levels. Now and then his countering Scripture verses to Joe's swearing brought some amusement to El Dorado, but apart from that there never was a moment of relaxation when an opportunity might present itself. To them he was a necessary appendage only because Joe demanded it; they did not see him as a contributor at all. Though he sweated with the rest of them and worked his share, he was not counted in the percentages they needed to get through the February twelfth operation. And because of this, they did not accept him, either as a member of the crew or as a clergyman. He was as irrelevant to this program as the hangar they worked in—useful only for a simple immediate purpose but eventually to be reduced to a nonentity.

On the three Sundays he had there, he managed to talk them into letting him go to church in the neighboring town. It took a lot of argument, and María was the most resistant to it, but in the end Joe let him go, probably because then he would have an opportunity to swear at Alphonse in the way he wanted to without the countering Biblical rejoiner. Each time Bingo was ordered to drive him to the church and make sure he got back.

The church they found in the small town bordering the highway and ocean was a big Spanish structure that had once been a Catholic mission but was now owned by an independent Protestant group. There were at least fifty steps to the big red doors, and Bingo said the first time, "You will have satisfied God by the time you reach the top—you won't have to go inside, padre."

Each time Sebastian asked Bingo if he'd like to join him. Each time the young Cuban shrugged and said, "Me and God we part good friends a long time ago. I think He is glad, and I think I am too."

There was no point in arguing that, so Sebastian climbed his fifty "penance steps," as Bingo called them, and worshiped with the small band of faithfuls.

But for all of that, when on the one hand he sensed a new kind of molding process among them while at the same time a disregard for him as any kind of essential ingredient to the cause, on the other, he would remember that last Sunday night, just before Rodríguez came to order them to the Keys. That night the fusion he thought was established showed itself as really a very weak paste; and on top of that, the apparent nonentity that he assumed he was among them was dramatically demonstrated as being quite the opposite—at least in one dimension.

He was sitting on a log outside the hangar, taking his turn at watching the dirt road that led out to the highway. The work had stopped for a while. Joe had retreated to his manuals to ponder, to rework the percentages. El Dorado sat just inside the hangar door, strumming his guitar quietly and singing the "Whiffenpoof Song" in slow, dreamy tones, his voice sliding up and down the scale and over the words like liquid mercury. Bingo was somewhere going over the engineering procedures for the fiftieth time.

While he was sitting there, his mind racing over the thin lines of survival they all had to face inevitably, he felt María behind him. The relationships among all of them had become instinctive because of their close work together. He had been thrown together with her on various jobs—on many occasions, when working on a piece of equipment that Joe had instructed them about, their concentration brought their heads and faces inches apart. Sometimes he would look around or up quickly and find her eyes only inches from his. To look into those black-green pools of changing light and endless depth had a peculiar mesmerizing effect on him. Always he would manage a light remark: "You've got a grease smudge on your cheek" or "You've got a shiny nose and black hate in your eyes. . . ." She accepted these remarks without comment, but he sensed that her close scrutiny was anything but admiration—she was studying him, probing him, examining him, looking for those flaws she was sure were in him that would support her suspicion of him.

So when she took that last step over the log to sit down beside him, he was glad for her company, for the magnetism she communicated, the vitality of her personality, the stark beauty she offered to the battle with Alphonse.

And as she sat down, he was conscious of the tight brown tweed skirt she was wearing, the one she had on the night they came here; only just beginning, too, to become aware of that smell that was peculiarly hers, the scent of orange blossoms and sweet lily. And he had just gotten ready to acknowledge her presence next to him when in one swift, agile movement, surprisingly full of strength, she had knocked him off the log so that he sprawled backward in the grass, and the next thing he knew she fell on him and kissed him, holding him down with her strong arms, her mouth on his acting as a kind of lock to keep him in that state of disbalance.

He was caught by the swiftness and suddenness of the act and the creeping tickle of delight way back in his senses, and in that instant when she seemed to know this she lifted her mouth from his and said, her breath warm on his cheek, "All right, either you are a man or you aren't. . . . If you are a man you'll do what any man would to to honor a woman who makes such a deliberate play for him, or else you'll make a fool of me."

She made another dive for his mouth, and he almost let it come again, for the man in him, the tired, beaten, pressured man he now was, begged to let it happen. But somewhere beyond this magical, spell-binding moment he saw the storm signals flying. This was her professional way of proving him; this practiced kiss, this rough way of straddling him, it had been done many times before, undoubtedly to get information she wanted. And now she was testing his true colors, using the method that would cut through the façade of any man who professed a role of clergyman but who would respond in an other fashion if he were not.

And he reached up quickly and held her by the shoulders, holding her off, her face still very close to his, her eyes very intent on his face and reaching out to engulf him, and that soft, precocious smile on the velvety curve of her mouth. Firmly he pushed her back and dropped her on the sweet-smelling grass, sat up, and looked down at her. Something was pounding feverishly inside him, demanding to get out, to be expressed, and he waited a moment to let it subside.

"That is a very dangerous way to prove whether I'm a clergyman," he said mildly, but he still had to take his time, waiting for the shakiness to get out of his voice. "Although I must admit that the Libertad is a very good teacher." He got up and stood over her, and she didn't move from her careless position where he had shoved her, her eyes still black liquid and not wavering at all. She had the look of a girl who had been caught in the act and was trying to look innocent.

He thought of other things to say, but he was still experiencing a peculiar kind of vertigo that the kiss had set off in him.

"Better call your uncle," he managed finally. "He'll want to know, I'm sure, if I behaved contrary to my professional image. . . ."

And he left her there, still lying in that obvious solicitous curve, as if she was trying to overcome him even to the very end. He went back inside the hangar and to his cot. But he didn't sleep. His heart still thumped now and then, either missing a beat or racing too fast. He was still a man, after all. She had cut through his well-insulated nerve endings on that score. He still had the smell of her lipstick on him, and the taste of her still lingered in his mouth. It had been a rough, coarse, practiced kiss all right, without feeling—but it was her, all her. And then he thought of Barbara Churchill, and that last moment when he had kissed her. How different! Hers was like a touch of spring, a warm breath of life and meaning. . . .

And then he had to smile, even in this whirling aftermath, for María had been dealt a blow too. Not many men had moved away from what she offered. She had embraced him in the fullest confidence that he would show himself to be other than what he claimed. Now she was left with further conflict of her own, and he wondered what kind of thoughts shook her mental castle right now.

He would have lingered on that until sleep came, but there was a commotion out near the front of the hangar, and he rose up on his elbows to see Rodríguez in the tangle of work benches and equipment. This time there was no cigar. That meant something big, something immediate.

And he kicked off the cot as he heard Joe and Rodríguez begin to go at it, and he knew now that the fire was heating up.

Chapter IX

****

They stood around in the neutral politeness of spectators who have not yet picked a side while Rodríguez and Joe carried on a furious kind of verbal Indian wrestling. Joe fought the move in a voice that had the sound of smashing mirrors, for he had come now to the breaking point. He appealed on the grounds that there was still too much to do on Alphonse: fathometer placement, sonar, compressed air tanks fitted, and what about getting someone in who could test out the equipment finally?

"You act like a sparrow who wishes for an ostrich egg," Rodríguez replied. Without his cigar he was like a blind man without a cane, having to use his hands to demonstrate the finality of his position. "There are no men among the Free Cubans who can help you—electrician, welder, diesel man, sí, but that is all. Anyway, it is too dangerous to operate here now, amigo. I have had Mathews coming to my house to ask about you. And if Castro's compañeros find what you are doing here, then what happens, ha? My men say there is a black car that goes up and down the highway outside this place every day; somebody already smells something. So you go to Bronco Key—tonight! And you do what you have to do to this—this Alphonse down there!"

Rodríguez reached for a cigar inside his coat pocket as if he was weary of talking without it. Joe argued some more, but he was like a dead snake with only its tail yet twitching. Rodríguez had a way of putting his foot on a man's neck when he talked; this was the Spanish aristocrat coming out in him, and few men could stand against it long. Joe tried, squirming under it, for he knew the percentages better than any of them, and he was not willing now to commit himself to what he figured was still a total disaster. The weeks of fighting Alphonse had given him a new side of biliousness; he was less accommodating, though this was a side he had never really shown, and a new fire of vehemence came out of him, the kind that Alphonse had built in him, the kind that turned white hot in a blacksmith's forge as new instruments of battle were dipped in and pounded into shape. Only for Joe not much was coming out of that fire; Alphonse still defied any touch of the new alchemy.

They went at it some more for about five minutes, and finally Joe simply threw a wrench he was holding into a toolbox ten feet away, a decisive act that said he had nothing left to argue with. Rodríguez lit his cigar and said, "Good," and that was that.

The problem then was how to transport Alphonse to Bronco Key off the Sugar Loaf, just north of Key West, the site Rodríguez had chosen to finish up the fitting. "You sure ain't gonna ride this thing through Miami like you did coming in," El Dorado said with a sniff to Joe.

"Here are all the papers," Rodríguez cut in, before Joe could rap back at El Dorado. He handed a sheaf of them to Joe. "You are cleared for underwater experiments at Key West, courtesy of your Uncle Sam. It took me a long time and mucho money to get those, amigo."

"These are forgeries?" Joe said, shaking his head in wonderment.

"They are good enough to get you by anybody who stops you," Rodríguez replied, a bit miffed that Joe would be so blunt in his description.

"You plannin' on goin' straight through Miami and down Highway One?" El Dorado asked again, his eyes showing his disbelief. "What about the underpass clearances of thirteen feet six? To say nothing of what a side show freak this—this thing here—presents to everybody . . ."

"We leave the conning tower bridge off and run it down separate," Joe said simply. "With it off and the low-bed trailer we got plenty of clearance . . . and we got tarps to cover her, so nobody will know what we got . . . anything else?"

Nobody had anything more to say.

They decided to split up for the trip down. Joe and El Dorado would start out immediately with Alphonse, using the night hours, hoping they would not pick up any watchful Castro agents or N.I.A.; however Sebastian knew each of them was thinking, as he was, that it was going to be tough traveling with that load without drawing attention. María would go by bus. Sebastian and Bingo would take the jeep.

"You stick with him, Chico," Rodríguez said to Bingo. "But first you let the padre check out of his hotel so it looks like all is well, sí? And you, Chico, you go to Mrs. MaConnel like you do always. But then go to the padre, comprene? So everything looks like you say normal, sí?"

"Normal as fruit bats in a vegetable patch," Joe said sullenly. His eyes stayed fixed on Alphonse, and it was as if he was addressing his remark to the ship there in front of them as lifeless as a beached whale.

Rodríguez said no more. He puffed once on his cigar and sent up a blue column of smoke as a kind of salute to them and then was gone.

Later that night, after the rest had gone, Sebastian drove back to Miami with Bingo. When they got to the Flamingo, Bingo asked if he should go in with him. "No need to," Sebastian replied. "I don't think we need worry about problems at this point." Actually it wasn't true; if problems were to come at all, it would be now. But Sebastian didn't want Bingo lingering when he should be checking on Jane. "I'll see you later." Bingo shrugged, but there was that clouded look of uncertainty in his eyes.

Sebastian got out, walked to the front door of the hotel, and went inside; only then did Bingo move away from the curb.

He got his key, explaining to the night clerk that he'd been out on unexpected business and that he would check out that night. Then he took the elevator up, approached the door with his key, and waited a second or two, not sure he wasn't going to walk into another welcoming party. But the key slid in as it was supposed to, and the door unlatched on the proper turn. He moved inside, threw the light switch, and stopped short as he saw the three of them there, one almost behind the door who immediately slammed it shut, another inside leaning against the wall, and the third sitting in the only chair by the night table.

"Come on in, Mr. Sebastian." He recognized the seated man as Mathews, the N.I.A. man he had met casually at Rodríguez's garden party. His eyes were blinking as usual, as if he were trying to see through a screen of smog.

Sebastian had no choice. He moved into the room, giving one wary glance at the two men who leaned against the wall, arms folded, barring any attempt he might make for a sudden bolt out the door. He hesitated a moment until Mathews waved him to a seat on the bed next to him.

"The N.I.A. sweatbox for information?" Sebastian said, trying to get to the heart of this immediately.

Mathews smiled, and he didn't seem like a difficult person to confront. He had a relaxed way about him, from the casual brown tropical suit to the long-stemmed pipe that hung loosely from one corner of his mouth. He looked no more intent than a man having an after-dinner smoke.

"We are not quite that sadistic, Mr. Sebastian," he replied. "Anyway, we have the information of most importance. Let me come to the point. We know about the submarine and Operation Freedom Seven."

Sebastian felt a sharp jab of disappointment. "May I ask how?"

Mathews smiled again, anticipating the query. "Well, you can't come into Miami with a submarine like the one you got without arousing some suspicion, now, can you? MaConnel is clumsy that way, or else he figures he couldn't care less. As for the operation, we've known for some time that it was coming off in February."

"Peter Rabbit?" Sebastian offered, and Mathews looked surprised that he knew the name.

"Could be, yes."

"So are you going to scuttle the operation?"

"Perhaps. We're not sure yet."

"Then what do you want from me you don't already know?"

"There are some facts of this operation *you* undoubtedly do not know," Mathews went on, talking around his pipe. "Facts, I dare say, that might change what you think you are doing from a rescue operation of seven Cubans to something of far more complicated dimension. All we want to do is show you these so you know what you are up against."

Mathews then flipped on a slide projector he had sitting on the small table beside him, and one of the men turned off the lights. The first slide that went up on the ivory wall was that of a man in a dark beard wearing the olive uniform of a Castro militiaman. The face above the beard was craggy, with high cheekbones, giving him an imperious look.

"This is Manuel Varga," Mathews explained in a dry professional tone. "He is the assistant to the top man in the Castro secret police. He is the man who is arranging to get Rodríguez's family to your rendezvous point—he is also coming out with them, a point which you probably did not know. Rodríguez thinks he's coming out as a defector, but we feel otherwise. . . ."

Mathews threw another slide on the wall. It was a picture of Rodríguez and another man, both in white tropical business suits. "Here is Varga on the left with Hector Rodríguez when they were in the sugar business together in Havana back in nineteen fifty-eight, just before Castro took over. When Rodríguez fled Cuba, he took all the cash and bonds of the business, leaving Varga high and dry. Varga had to fall in with Fidel just to survive. Varga has never forgotten that . . . and by piecing together what information we could get in the past few years, we feel that Varga is coming out deliberately to get to Rodríguez and assassinate him."

Sebastian sat almost stupefied by what was being said. He felt disbelief on the one hand and a sense of credulity on the other, just the way Mathews calmly and confidently made his revelations.

"Now, we can't let Varga get through into Florida here to bump off Rodríguez. Rodríguez happens to be a key man in the Free Cuban community here. If he got assassinated by Varga, it would go bad on the N.I.A. and put us in a very embarrassing light with the Cubans here, as well as with the rest of Latin America. For, as you may know, it's the N.I.A. who gets blamed for everything these days."

Another slide clicked into place, and this was of María, looking young and attractive in a white bathing suit. "This is María San Roman, whom you have already met. Here she is participating in the Pan-American Games just before Castro took over Cuba. She won three bronze medals for her swimming. She is an intelligent, highly educated person with, as you can see, other obvious attributes." Another slide went up, and this one was of María in the olive green of the Castro militia. "This is María in the hills with Castro, just after the Pan-American Games. María had taken the vows for the nunnery just before the Games, but when she realized that the Catholic Church wouldn't do anything to resist Batista's corrupt regime, she quit that and joined Fidel. María is that kind of woman: she can't stand inconsistency between what a person or group stands for and what action they take. A year later, disillusioned with Castro's communism, she fled Cuba. She swam fifteen miles out before being picked up by a shrimp boat."

Mathews hesitated, removed his pipe, and laid it down by the projector. "This may shake you up, reverend, but we are sure María San Roman is riding with you on that sub of yours to defect back to Cuba."

Sebastian looked at Mathews quickly to see if the man was serious. Apparently he was, for his eyes were not blinking, as if the seriousness of what he had said had cleared the smog.

"Why go back?" Sebastian asked, finding this almost too much to accept.

"Several reasons: I told you she hates inconsistencies. When she came here to Florida she felt democracy would be the answer. When we failed at the Bay of Pigs, she became disillusioned again. Probably the last straw came when President Kennedy was assassinated. She decided then that there was nothing more here than what she had in Cuba, and as much as she sympathizes with her uncle's political ambitions to start a new and more powerful Free Cuban movement, she also knows this is hopeless. And there's one other reason."

Mathews threw up another slide of María, this time in the brief red costume she wore in her role at the Libertad. "Here is the other side of María, the ugly side. María has been shaped by what she considers the corrupt American way of life. Even since the Tractors for Cuba campaign, when she had to help raise funds for that operation, María has been faced with the sordid fact that men—American men in particular—will give money or information in exchange for what a beautiful woman offers in return. This has soured María, embittered her. Now she wants out, she wants freedom from an American society she has come to hate because of the exploitation of her charms—she feels she can only get this by going back to Cuba."

"How do you know she intends to do this?"

Mathews put the pipe back in his mouth, holding the slide on the wall as if he was appreciating the beauty of María and the sadness of her experience. "She sent a radio message to her mother by the underground a week ago saying she'd see her in February. We know she could only plan to do that if she defected. Her father is dead, but her mother is married to one of Castro's big men."

"Does her uncle know?"

"Of course not. It'd kill him. María will probably go ashore with you at Cárdenas and conveniently get lost in the terrain—all you can report then is that she was captured. Rodríquez will accept that."

"Won't you be embarrassed by her defection?" Sebastian asked.

"Of course. But we can't stop it. Her going over will rock the Free Cuban movement, once they find out she defected; Castro will probably play it up. But it isn't worth our trying to stop her either."

There was a pause, during which it seemed that the air

conditioner was working harder to try to clear the heavy, stale air that had built up in the room. "Is that all?"

Mathews dug out his tobacco pouch and began to fill his pipe bowl slowly, as if he was reluctant to go further. "One more thing: if you get into Cárdenas and manage to get out, you'll have to reckon with our fleet pickets."

"Oh, so we have to fight the U.S. Navy too?" Sebastian wasn't trying to hide his sense of indignation now.

"We can't control that. The fleet exercise began February first and goes through March first. It's really our way of hitting the Castro subs who are running enemy agents into Florida and other areas of the Caribbean coast. They'll be depth charging any underwater sound that doesn't answer as friendly. And if you get caught in that, they won't wait to try to sort you out from the rest."

"That's encouraging. Why don't you scuttle this operation now before it gets launched? That way you save all these lives."

"Can't do it. We figure it's best for us to let it go. At least now we know how Varga is coming out—now we can be sure to get him before he gets in here. Otherwise he might find some other way of getting in that we don't know about—and then we've got chaos."

"So seven people get clobbered just to get one man you *think*—only think—is coming out to do damage." Sebastian argued. "He could be a defector, really wanting freedom; what then?"

"Chances of that are a hundred to one. We know what we're talking about, reverend."

"Okay, then why can't we surface when we get out of Castro's range and turn him over to your pickets?"

"No good. Varga won't allow himself to be taken by us. He'll keep you under all the way; he'd rather die that way, than in our hands. He's a man taking a long chance, and he'll run it long."

Sebastian stood up suddenly and began pacing up and down by the bed, wanting to work off the mounting load of confusion and cut through the entangling webs.

"You come up here to tell me all this—for what?" he asked bluntly, angry that this man could spell out their destruction so calmly.

"So that you can make up your mind whether you want to stay in this thing, naturally," Mathews said, and he held a paper match to his pipe bowl.

"You mean you've got a bad conscience over my getting killed with the rest of them at the hands of your own guns, maybe?"

"Something like that, perhaps. Of course, it would be an embarrassment to us if you fell into Castro's hands; and it wouldn't help us any to know that you got killed with the rest, thinking you were being destroyed simply for a rescue operation. Now you know it's more than that—you are in a complex political situation, reverend. Even Rodríguez is in this for his political image. If you get those seven people of his out, he gets a big political boost among the Free Cubans here. He's aiming to be top man, and you may be the one to hand it to him. I don't think you want to be linked with carrying a defector to Communist Cuba and a volatile assassin back, and on top of that, if you come out, helping Rodríguez in his political mountain climbing—or am I wrong?"

No, of course, he was right. Sebastian knew it before he asked. Here again was the dilemma: how far could he go as a minister when his legitimate motives served lesser ends? Where did his ministerial activity stop and the political begin? Could he rationalize the political overtones by those seven people wanting to come out?

"How many of the others know about this?" he asked.

"None of them knows about María, probably. Santos knows nothing, we would judge. MaConnel is probably not concerned either way, but it would surprise me if he didn't have some idea. The kid Bingo has a pretty good idea—he's been useful to Rodríguez in the gunrunning game and for information, much like María."

"And the fleet exercises?"

"Rodríguez has a good line to this kind of information. He'll probably give you these facts just before you're ready to launch," Mathews said dryly.

"Can't you help?" Sebastian pleaded, turning to Mathews in a direct appeal. "Can't you at least call off your fleet long enough for them to get out?"

Mathews shrugged. "That's not our responsibility. Anyway, if the Navy knew we had anything to do with a clandestine operation of this nature, we'd be in hot water all the way to the top. They don't intend to alter their plans to wait for one sub coming out, no matter how much we say it's top priority. While they wait for you, half a dozen others could get through, understand?"

Again there was silence as Sebastian tried to find a way out, continuing his short pacing by the bed.

"Are you telling me all this to get me out of the operation?"

"Like I said, there's no reason for you to get it with the rest of them."

"Why not, in the name of God?" he shot back at the unmoving, phlegmatic man, who acted as though this were nothing more than a parking lot problem. "Joe, Bingo, El Dorado, they're all going to do it."

"But for what?" Mathews countered. "Except for Bingo, the Cuban kid, who is probably the only one who is in it for the glory of Free Cubans, the rest have their own reasons and are prepared to take their own risks—MaConnel for money, El Dorado for a breath of air before a stretch in jail, María to get a free ride back to Cuba."

"And what about me? Do you think I'm in it just for the tourist special?"

Mathews puffed on his pipe, which gave off a crackling sound like burning leaves. His eye stayed on Sebastian. "We think we know why you're in it, too," he said slowly. "You've been sold the typical bill of goods on seven people who want out of communism, and your—shall we say—spiritual sensitivities are rubbed raw. The nobility of your calling, reverend, undoubtedly is what moves you—very fine, very idealistic, very church, but you're playing in the wrong league."

"And you, Mathews, what are your noble ambitions?" Sebastian flung back at him, trying to control his voice to that of a debater rather than a refuter.

"Ours concern the security of this hemisphere, Mr. Sebastian."

"And seven lives don't count in that, not even twelve lives?"

"Sometimes feelings must take second place to the job—we don't like it either, but that's the way it is."

"Well, then, that's the eternal difference between politics and religion. You see things in terms of a hemisphere—we go a step further and try to see God's view, that every man has value. I'll put my aims straight for the record, Mr. Mathews: I want God to be out there, I want to demonstrate a living Christ, to show that He still loves mankind, that in all that bleeding mass of Cuba, where people are clawing their way out, God is there to help them up. . . . That may sound idealistic to you, sir, and to your partners here, but that's the way it is. And when you drop your depth charges on us out there, you can think about that."

Nobody said anything. It was as if he had said a prayer and they were embarrassed to argue further.

"I take it you are going, then?"

"I don't know. I need time to think."

"How much time? An hour maybe?"

"That should do it."

Mathews got up and dropped a card on the table. "When

you make up your mind, call me. I need to know what you decide to do for the record."

"Would you like my personal effects for the record so you know where to send them?" Sebastian flipped back.

Mathews gave a thin smile. "If you decide to go, that might be a good idea. Good night, reverend; I'll hear from you in an hour."

He was left alone, then, in that room full of stale air, with Mathews's rightful arguments echoing in his ears. "God, why can't it be a simple rescue operation? Why can't it be a simple case of black and white?" He was startled at the sound of his own voice.

But he knew it never could be. What was he hoping for anyway when he committed himself to this crusade in the secular arena of life? This grim battle for survival was complicated with a variety of considerations. There was no straight line to action here. It was either in or out—and suffer the consequences. Mathews was right. He was involving himself in a complex political issue, the results of which could cast him into an entirely different role than a minister in a cause of good will. This was far stickier than his Negev experience with the Israeli-Arab issue—there it had simply been a matter of staying ahead of events, but here he was enmeshed in them, and his actions would have a direct bearing on both sides of the political issue. Was he willing to be cast in that kind of image? Did he have the right? And could he defy his own government's wish at the same time? Was his desire to be identified with human suffering dangerous and impractical after all?

He sat down on the bed to pray, to grope for an answer, but as he began to talk to God he sensed that he was trying to form a rationale for why he couldn't get involved.

Then the phone rang. It was Jane. "We never did keep

our dinner date," she said. He noticed the low key of her voice, dragging against her uphill battle.

"Jane—" he began, but her voice cut him off quickly.

"Never mind. I know where you've been. . . ." She paused, and he heard a shaky sigh over the line, a sound of fatigue and fear pressing on the already thin lines of life. "What I called for was to ask you again not to go. . . . Try to understand now . . . I need Joe. . . . He's all I've ever needed or wanted. . . . You can live with yourself so long." He caught a smothered gasp. "I tried . . . I tried to make God a substitute for a lost human relationship. . . . It works to a point, sure, but then you realize you've got to have the man you love too . . . but he's gone farther and farther away now. . . . Well, I wish I could cry, Mr. Sebastian, I wish I were like other women . . . maybe it would help . . . but all I do is ache all over. . . ."

Sebastian swallowed against the sounds of a human life breaking up, as if each watertight door were crumbling and death were rushing in. "Jane. . . ." His mind whirled to find some solution. "Jane. . . . I'll bring Joe back to you . . . you hang on a little longer."

"No!" It came out of her with explosive finality. "No, if you insist on going on this suicidal—if you get him back, then you can take *me* to him, understand? That's been the whole problem. . . . I've been forcing him to come my way, to my God. . . . It's time I yielded. . . . I'll cross the bridge to him, to his way of life. . . ."

He couldn't answer right away. She was telling him she was going back on God, throwing her faith aside. "You don't have to cross—all the way, Jane. Meet Joe halfway on that bridge. . . . Give me this one chance with him. . . ."

There was a long pause, during which he heard her breath coming in short uneven pants as though her heart were running away with her. Then it quieted, and her voice was strangely calm. "You try too hard, Mr. Sebastian. . . . Joe told me about the game between you two—about God in the middle. . . . He knows you can't win. He's so sure you'll lose, he's even happy to die just to see it. . . . You try too hard. . . ."

"I have to do it this way, Jane," he said, wishing he could sound more certain himself. "All I'm asking you to do is trust me . . . give me this chance . . . give God this chance. . . . Just don't do anything until—"

"Until when? Until I'm sure enough days have gone by to be sure you won't be coming back? Then what do I do? Drop a wreath in the Atlantic in memory and go on in this hell?" He didn't know what to say to that either, but she finally said, her voice toneless now, "Say good-by to him for me. . . . Tell him—tell him to keep his socks dry . . . he's so sensitive to dampness . . . he makes a lousy sailor that way. . . ." He was left with the silence of the line and the room and the racing crosscurrents of his own dilemma. Then he numbly dialed Mathews's number, knowing now he had no choice.

"This is Sebastian. . . . I've decided to go on with the operation."

There was a pause and then Mathews said, "All right. If you can tell us when the operation is being launched, we might be able to help you."

Sebastian frowned; that didn't sound right. "You mean you got everything on us but the date of the launch?"

"That's right."

"Then why didn't you try to get that from me before?" Sebastian challenged, puzzled by this development.

"If you weren't going on the operation, we figured there'd be no point for you to give us that information," Mathews replied in that same dry voice, a kind of exaggerated indulgence. "We had other sources of information, anyway, who possibly could give it to us. . . . But now that you're going we're willing to give you some idea of fleet maneuvers at the specific time you are coming out. It could be you might find a hole through. . . ."

"You mean you actually want to help us?" Sebastian quipped. He didn't want to sound sarcastic but it came out that way anyway.

"Mr. Sebastian, if we could just get Varga alive we'd be happy. . . . We don't like blowing up twelve people to get him either, I told you that before."

Sebastian didn't know whether to believe him or not, but there wasn't time to think it over. If he was tipping the operation to total disaster, it was a chance he'd have to take. Right now Mathews seemed to hold the only real percentage that counted.

"Okay, it's for the twelfth," he said with a sigh and wiped at the sweat running down his face.

"That means you're coming out on the morning of the thirteenth?" Mathews asked.

Sebastian didn't know. "No, I think it's the morning of the twelfth. We launch on the eleventh—or is it the other way?"

"You better be sure, reverend," Mathews prodded him. "If you plan to come out on the thirteenth, the whole fleet is jamming up in a sweep in the Straits. If it's the morning of the twelfth, you got a break; the fleet will be mostly to the east toward the Bahama Bank. . . . Now, how about it?"

"The twelfth," Sebastian said, but he wasn't sure. "Hold on a minute." He put down the phone and looked out the door to see if Bingo was coming back for him. The hall was empty.

"Okay," Mathews said when he came back on, "it looks like your guardian angel is with you, reverend. Between the hours of oh-five-hundred and oh-seven-hundred on the morning of the twelfth you'll have a corridor through. If you miss that time the fleet will close the gate. . . . Have you got that?"

"Sure. . . . But I thought you didn't want Varga to get through?"

"At your hotel desk I left a package. Inside is a small object shaped like a shoehorn. One side of it has a suction cup. All you do when you get out there in the Straits that morning on the return trip is stick that gizmo on the ceiling of your control room—it will send off a sonic beam that we'll pick up by sonar helicopter. Do you understand?"

Sebastian licked his lips. "How about telling Joe MaConnel about that? He's running the ship."

"No good, reverend. MaConnel doesn't trust us. Neither does Rodríguez. If they find out you talked to us, it could go very bad for you. It's your show from here on in. And may I add good luck?"

The line went dead. Good luck? It will take more than that, Mathews, Sebastian said to himself as he left the room and took the elevator down to the hotel lobby. The setup was like Moses and the Red Sea operation, only there was no Moses here.

"Just me, God," he said aloud as he got his things together, went to the desk, checked out, and asked if a package had been left for him. It was there in his box. "And poor Alphonse," he added. "What a combination. . . ."

He went back to the empty lounge and opened the package. There it was, just like Mathews said: shaped like a shoe horn, weighing about a pound, small enough to slip into his back pocket, which he did. He saw Bingo pull up to the curb in the jeep and went out, thinking about Jane, wondering how long she could hold on to those thin lines of life. Or even to her sanity. He climbed into the jeep, wishing he could stay and help her, but he knew he couldn't do anything for her now, except somehow get Joe back to her.

So he sat back and grabbed a hold as Bingo shot the jeep out for Bronco Key. He didn't like what was coming, and the scraping fingers of tension began digging around his stomach. "The fear of man bringeth a snare. . . ." Yes, well, then, O man of God, better start dogging the hatches, for the storm is about to break.

Bingo started whistling "Hello Dolly." Sebastian forced himself to smile and try counting the palm trees as they flashed by—and then he dozed.

Chapter X

****

Some time later in the night, he took over the driving from Bingo. He tried now and then to get a conversation going, but the howl of the motor was too much. Soon Bingo dozed off too, so he was left to himself and the long, tedious drive on Highway One.

As he drove, he considered the mounting sense of doubt in his mind. He wasn't sure of Mathews. And what really brought him to a sense of panic was the fact that he hadn't once asked Mathews for his credentials. He had accepted him and his partners as N.I.A. on their word—and María's. The thought that they could represent other interests—maybe even Castro's—depressed his already leaden spirits.

After a while, he forced his mind to other things. He began to feel tired. His back ached and throbbed from lack of sleep and the hours of working over Alphonse. When did he last have a good night's sleep? Weeks ago, maybe. . . .

His mind shifted to María. He found it hard to believe she would go back to Cuba willingly. A woman with so many gifts should be free to use them for the greatest good. But was he sure what was best? Maybe there was something in Cuba he didn't know about that was made for her. He thought of her life in the Libertad and how she had become what she was here in the free-wheeling society of affluence. He would have liked to think his own country and society had more things to offer. But that was the naïve minister coming out in him. There was nothing here to guarantee freedom from corruption. Man was man, anywhere you put him. Then he thought of her kiss again, and the sweet smell of her, and even the taste of her was fresh to him again—how much of that kiss was a test of him on that scale she had built from the reaction of other American males he didn't know. But he felt a new sense of understanding of her; at least he knew why she remained so icily cold and distant, so calculating, why she seemed to look at life and everybody in it with a sharp disdain.

Then, as though his mind were tethered like a dog on a short chain that jerked him back when he tried to wander afield, he thought of Jane. How close was she to self-extinction? Would she do it, despite her faith? What if she did? What if he got Joe back to a Jane dead by her own hand? How would he reconcile that? But she wouldn't; faith was stronger than that. But was it? Hadn't he been pushed to the very edge in the Negev—when God slipped out of focus and all he had was a mucky blur? Maybe he should have followed her advice, tried to scrap the operation, stay with her, find some other way to get Joe back on track with her. But it was a little late for that now. He shifted painfully in his seat as he realized the dilemma he was in. This operation had to go off with some measure of success. Something had to come out of this. If any of them lived—and he had to believe God would allow this or there was no point going on with it—something had to emerge to communicate some spiritual truth to Joe to help him get out on that bridge to Jane. How he would bring this about, he had no idea—there was not one crack of spiritual daylight in the whole operation so far.

"We are there soon," Bingo shouted suddenly above the pounding motor. Sebastian nodded and thought, what about Bingo? What torture for him? A boy caught between a natural affection for Sebastian on the one hand and an inbred hostility toward him on the other because of the image of the church on him. A boy who was afraid to have him in this operation for fear that the presence of a clergyman might bring disaster such as he'd known once in his life already and yet was willing to warn him of the gravity of what was coming out of concern for him. To resent his profession but to be concerned for him as a man—how then could he ever begin to reach out to touch that young life?

They crossed a long bridge across an endless sweep of ocean, and Bingo instructed him to turn off and stop as they came to a jungle-lined strip of highway. The dirt road was rough, so Bingo took the wheel. They ground and bounced their way for a good mile over what at times was no more than a path through the jungle. Then, finally, they broke into a clearing and the ocean was in front of them, spray from the surf bounding up over a crude breakwater of coral reef. The sun was just coming up, and the scene was peaceful, mixing the ingredients of a soft sleepy red sun with the azure blue of the ocean and the lazy glides of the white powder puffs of the sea gulls. The scene was such a contrast to what he'd known thus far that Sebastian sat in the jeep even after Bingo had gotten out and walked to the small lean-to at the right.

"'In the morning will I praise thee,'" Sebastian said softly, and then he was jarred by the slashing sound of Joe's voice.

"You figurin' on putting that scene on canvas, preacher boy?"

He looked up to see Joe's head and shoulders coming out

of a clump of jungle near the coral breakwater and realized with a start that the jungle was a cover of camouflage that hid Alphonse. Though he could see the battle-gray paint now and then through the cover, and the flat back of the trailer, he had to admit that it was a pretty good job.

He got out and walked forward, passing the lean-to, where María, clad now in tight black stretch pants and a short-sleeved green blouse, was cooking a pot of coffee over a charcoal fire. She gave him a quick glance as though he were no more than a shadow passing by, for in her own mind he probably wasn't much more.

"You talk to Jane?" Joe asked when Sebastian got to the jungle-draped Alphonse. He was addressing Bingo too, who had come up behind Sebastian.

"I talked to her over the phone," Sebastian said. "She's . . . okay, Joe."

"You see her, Bingo?"

Bingo nodded. "Only to say good night. . . . She going to bed when I get there." Sebastian calculated she must have phoned him some time after Bingo had seen her. "She looked okay to me, Joe."

Joe looked at them for a minute, either weighing the possibility of pursuing the conversation or trying to read something in their faces to contradict what they said. Then, with a shake of his head to dismiss Jane from his mind, he said, "Okay, let's get to work. Get some of that stuff María calls coffee and shag your tails up here, understand?"

So began another day of feverish, sweating, desperate, fumbling work on the corpse of Alphonse. They put in the fathometer, a small boxlike thing with a long pipe that went through the lower hull. The small clock face would record the feet under their keel from electric impulses bounced off the ocean floor. With the sonar and fathometer crammed into the forward control room, El Dorado quipped that the compartment was no bigger than a "broom closet in an igloo," which began an argument between him and Joe about the advantage of having the fathometer in there, the beginning of arguments that were to build up to frightful heat in the days to come.

Joe, of course, won, only because he was kind of senior in command, though nobody said he was. El Dorado finally grinned his surrender as Joe began to bristle more and more over the question about his judgment, but El Dorado got the last word in anyhow by singing one of his original rhymes:

> *"A is for sonar, it bleats the sound of ships,*
> *B is for the fathometer, it blips the sound of fish,*
> *C is for—"*

"Oh, shut up, for pete's sake!" Joe snarled at him. El Dorado's grin remained, but there were hard shafts of light in his dark eyes that spoke of the fire of resistance building in him.

With only a few days left, time had now become a lowering guillotine soon to brush their necks. Joe and El Dorado had had no trouble in carting Alphonse and all the equipment on the trailer from Miami. The official papers that Rodríguez had supplied seemed to pass the scrutiny of the highway patrols that stopped them, but one officer had taken their license number for a routine check. It might not be long before they'd realize they'd been had. It would take them a while to search all the keys here, but they'd find them sooner or later.

On top of that, there were coastal patrols that moved not more than two miles off the Bronco Key site they were on. Twice within two days, a blue patrol boat came within a mile of shore to take a look. They all hid behind the reef, and the camouflage on Alphonse apparently convinced them. But it was bringing a new case of jitters to all of them, and tempers were getting short.

As jobs of more technical complexity were pressed on them, Sebastian found himself consulting Joe's manuals on the submarine. Though he didn't understand all the blueprints that Joe's father had left in one of the books, he managed to follow the operational procedures fairly closely and to make some sense out of what was supposed to go where. The long technical description about the elongated bow chambers, he could not follow at all. But he read all he could, even though he knew that the details might not be of any value to him. He wanted to know—just in case.

Two days later, they installed the compressed-air tanks, which was a sweating, back-breaking job. They had to lower the oxygen cylinders down into the narrow conning tower hatch, down through the forward compartment hatch, and finally into place in the compressor room just behind the control room. When they finished that full day of work, none of them could move—they all lay around the lean-to, trying to regain both the strength and the nerve to go on—except Joe, of course, who kept pounding and hammering like a twitching nerve.

On the next to last day, Joe welded the conning tower bridge into place, swearing at the job all morning, shouting at nobody in particular that bubble gum would have done a better job. Then, just after lunch, he insisted they all get inside Alphonse for a mock drill. The temperature by then was almost 100 degrees, and the humidity was in the nineties. They argued about it, for their tired bodies and minds could hardly face up to one more constricting time inside the hull in heat close to 150 degrees Farenheit. But Joe pummeled them with his raking voice until they obeyed; none of them felt like facing up to him, for he had become a kind of terror. His manner was that of a broken high-tension wire twisting and jumping on the ground as the volts shoot through it, unable to make the right connection for that power. To argue with him was to grab that voltage, and none of them wanted that experience at this stage.

So they climbed into the suffocating hull. The first to

complain was María in the forward compartment, who said she didn't intend to "be poked, prodded, squeezed by any man in this poor excuse of a place for operating a submarine." To which El Dorado shouted back up through the forward hatch, "Well, I'll tell you one thing, I'm not winning much either, 'cause I don't usually fraternize with women exactly like this!"

Sebastian had to smile despite himself, but Joe only frowned at the irritation. Looking back through the after hatch, past the cargo compartment, and into the engine room, with its dim light coming from an inadequate power system, Sebastian could just see the top of Bingo's head above the gleam of the monstrous diesel. Though he was dressed only in swim trunks, the sweat poured off him, and without the benefit of an after hatch for air, he was forced to sit there, his mouth hanging open in a desperate attempt to keep breathing.

"Okay, crank her up," Joe said, and Sebastian gave the order through the telephone mouthpiece hanging around his neck. Then came the racking cough of the diesel turning over on empty fuel chambers, which sounded like a wheezing asthmatic fighting a bronchial infection.

They stayed at it for a half hour. They blew tanks, flooded tanks, practiced switching from diesel to battery power, made runs on nonexistent underwater sounds to give María practice on the sonar, ran a mock trial on the fathometer, did some "maneuvering" exercises to give El Dorado some polish on the bow plane wheels, which must have seemed juvenile to him after so much submarine experience of his own. Joe was never satisfied, though he couldn't tell if what they were doing was right or wrong. He found problems in the way María threw the ballast levers or worked the other equipment; he jumped El Dorado for being too casual and Bingo for being so slow in making power switches. He nagged sourly at Sebastian for not relaying orders over the phone quicker or not being quick enough to push the periscope button when he wanted it. He would have kept them at it longer, except that Bingo finally fainted in the heat of the engine room and they had to carry him out, with María sniping at Joe for his "crazy boat fever that was going to kill them all before they ever got into water." She was so mad that she began rattling at him in Spanish, and all the rest of them looked at her in wonder, for they had never heard her use Spanish before; but Joe only took it with a shrug and dug for a cigarette while they finally got Bingo to come around.

That night they sat around eating the half-warm chili María had fixed in a hurry, their tired senses waiting for just one false move, one ill-timed remark. They acted as though they were eager for something to happen, anything to allow them to let off the pressure.

It was El Dorado who finally started it. Putting down his half-empty plate of beans, he said, "Those ballast tanks, man, will never do."

Joe looked up quickly at him. "What's eatin' you about those tanks?" His voice was heavy with backed up hostility.

"They're too small, anybody can see that," El Dorado replied, and his normal gentility of spirit was diffusing for a new flood of tension. "You don't have enough room in them to take on water in a hurry to get you under when you need it. The same when you blow to surface. If you have to dive or surface in a hurry out there, you won't have it in those tanks. Your old man must have been a little bit crackers to design a boat like that."

Joe came off the ground in a gliding dive at El Dorado, who jumped out of the way, getting his switch blade out in a blurring motion. They jockeyed for a moment, each of them intent on having it out, until finally Sebastian and Bingo jumped in on Joe and María stood in front of El Dorado. But holding on to Joe was like holding a bag of live fish, and it wasn't until María's voice cut the atmosphere that the flaming tension was lessened.

"Stop it!" She said it twice, and both Joe and El Dorado looked confused, as if they had just awakened from sleep-walking. María's black eyes flashed and her body was taut and vibrant, a pulsing line of beauty and indignation. "All we need right now is to tear each other apart!" She looked at El Dorado and said, "Put that knife away," and El Dorado looked at the gleaming blade in his hand as if he was surprised it was even there. "Let him go," she said to Sebastian and Bingo, and they dropped their arms from around Joe. And quietly, almost as if they were all embarrassed by what happened, they sat down again. Joe and El Dorado exchanged mean glances for a few minutes, but then El Dorado picked up his guitar and began to strum quietly, as if he knew the only way to clear the atmosphere of ugliness. To the tune of "Clementine" he began to sing:

"There's a fish called mighty Alphonse,
How she hated salty brine,
Got all dressed but couldn't saunter,
For her nerves she couldn't find."

Joe only glared at him, while the rest kept back smiles, for they knew that El Dorado was having the last word anyway.

"Came the day that she would venture,
And her feet did touch the brine,
But she shivered at the future,
And withdrew to safer clime."

And then car lights flashed from the jungle road, and they stood up, wondering. It was Rodríguez's black Cadillac. It parked near where they were sitting, and they waited while he got out and walked over to them, looking at each of them, then back at Alphonse, hid behind the jungle growth.

"You're a day early, señor," Joe said. "I didn't expect you until tomorrow, when we launch."

"Urgent business brings me," Rodríguez said, and his face in the flow of the charcoal fire was as set as if it had been coated with wax and left to harden. He lit his cigar and said, "I have paid much money today to find out that someone has talked to the N.I.A."

Nobody said anything. They stayed frozen in their various poses as if they'd been caught by a camera. But their eyes moved slowly one to the other, looking for hints of weakness, of guilt.

"Who?" Joe prodded, his voice carrying tones of disbelief and menace.

"Perhaps the padre can explain," Rodíguez said, and they all turned to look at Sebastian. The disappointment in their eyes was being replaced by indignation. The fire of their anger would reach them soon, melting off whatever good will they might have had for him. They had accepted him at least for the sweat he gave on their behalf, but whatever respect that he had gained was about to be dissipated. Sebastian looked quickly at Bingo, who was staring at him now more in confusion than condemnation—and that was like a cold hand of death; for this to be added to the young Cuban's already questioning mind about clergymen was too much.

"I told you!" María's cry was shrill.

"Shut up!" Joe slammed back at her, but he had turned to confront Sebastian, his own face characteristically puffy with anger. Then he swore, letting it come out in long thrusts like stabs from a bayonet.

"Well, did you or didn't you?" he said, then, and moved in closer to Sebastian so that the heat from his anger was overpowering, mixing with the acrid smells of diesel oil, sweat, and salt water, all that went with the body of Alphonse.

"They came to me, I didn't go to them," Sebastian said, holding on to the narrow edge of calmness, though he knew he could die at Joe's or Rodríguez's hand easily enough.

"Don't double talk me, preacher boy," Joe raked. "What did you tell them, and when are they moving in on us?"

"They knew everything already—about the sub, the operation, even about Cárdenas Bay." He went on to tell about Varga coming out and the fleet exercises. He paused a moment, debating whether to add the bit about María's plans, but when he looked at her standing there, already as willing to kill him as look at him, he thought he'd let that go for the moment.

Joe had turned to Rodríguez, wanting some answers. Rodríguez didn't look too comfortable about having his plan aired before he was ready. "It is the only way for my family to come out," he said bluntly, no apology in his voice. "Varga—he come out to get away from Castro. . . ."

Joe laughed at that. "Manuel Varga? Castro's number-one hatchetman, who has put more of your people against the firing wall than any other man in Castro's secret police? Who sold you that garbage? If the preacher boy, here, is right, the N.I.A. is going to let us go—they want to clobber Varga before he can get in here to do whatever dirty work he has in mind. That wasn't in the deal, señor. . . ."

"You get paid to go in and out, that's it," Rodríguez snapped. His eyes had gone to narrow slits as his own anger stoked up.

"And what about the fleet exercises?" Joe continued, his voice rising with the mounting sense of incredulity all this was producing in him.

Rodríguez said it was true; he had only just found out about that bit of information and intended to tell Joe about it.

"So we get pounded going in and coming out by both sides," Joe finished for all of them. "We got as much chance as a gopher digging a hole through the Rock of Gilbraltar. . . ."

"We might get cover going over, Joe," El Dorado cut in then. "The Bahama Cup race comes off on the eleventh—they'll have to let that go, it's the race dedicated to the President of the United States—that could slow up the pickets. . . ."

Joe sniffed—the chance was still a long one. He turned back to Sebastian. "One thing they couldn't know, preacher boy, and that is *when* we are launching—did you tell them *when?*" His voice was almost appealing, begging, hoping he hadn't and at the same time carrying the promise of violence that would follow if he had.

"Yes," Sebastian said, and all Joe could do was stand there and stare at him, not really believing. "But I gave that in an exchange—"

"You don't bargain with *anybody* in an operation like this!"

Sebastian let that ringing denunciation die in the sound of the surf behind him, and then he said, "I gave them the date of the launch in exchange for the only possible way out—if there is one at all."

"What you gave them was the time when they could close the gate on us, that's what," Joe fired back.

"What is that way?" Rodríguez asked.

Sebastian looked from Joe to Rodríguez and saw nothing but a deadly design on his life. "I'll keep that to myself, señor. To give it up means I lose what value I have to this operation and maybe my life. I'm going to take the chance on what they offer. . . ."

"You don't understand the problem like we do," Rodríguez said harshly.

"Maybe not. But it's the only real percentage going for us now. I'm willing to try for your family on it, señor."

"Well, I ain't," Joe retaliated. "If the N.I.A. knows we're going, then Castro has a pretty good idea too. If Peter Rabbit gave N.I.A. that information, he's sold it to the Castro underground too. That means Castro's boats will be waiting. Nobody in his right mind would try it now."

There was a silence confirming what Joe had said. Even Rodríguez was unable to come back with anything. He stood by the fire, looking suddenly very old and tired. Up to a point he could buy a man or even threaten him—but there came a time when neither would work. Joe was the key; without him there was no operation.

Sebastian knew then that he would have to get Joe back into it himself. So he said, "We made a deal once, Joe, remember? I was willing to put God in the balance in this operation. I'm still holding my end of it—I intend to go."

None of the others would know completely what he meant, but Joe did. He stood staring back at Sebastian and made a move as if to swing at him. "You wouldn't go without me. . . ."

"Don't be too sure," Sebastian countered. "El Dorado is a pretty good submariner. The rest of the crew know their jobs. We might do it—and that leaves you high and dry. You want it that way?"

They all waited, watching Joe, for the weight of decision had suddenly swung his way.

"You want to go with this creep?" he shouted at them. "This Operation Freedom Seven has become Operation Eight Ball with Varga in it—Rodríguez can tell you what it's like to be behind the eight! The N.I.A. knows, can't you understand? Castro knows! Doesn't that register with you who have fought these people all these years? What chance have you got?"

They didn't answer, for they too were caught between the rightness of the operation and the thin lines of survival they had left. But because they didn't answer, it was like a contradiction of Joe's appeal, and for a moment Joe's shoulders sagged as if he'd lost something vital. Then he walked stiffly out of the circle and toward Alphonse, picked up a bottle of whiskey from the supplies, and climbed to the conning tower and disappeared inside.

Sebastian looked at the rest of them. They simply stared back, allowing him no reprieve for what he had done either. María's eyes burned steadily on him and there was a satisfied smirk to her mouth, as if she had finally proven him to be of the lesser breed, the kind she'd known here in the Great American society. Bingo didn't even look at him, as if it were all too much for him. El Dorado went back to his guitar; he had no choice either way, to go or stay, for he belonged to Rodríguez. And Rodríguez simply lit up another cigar, seemingly relieved that the worst was over at this point and that somebody at least would be going for his family.

Sebastian turned and walked to the coral reef and jumped down on the sand. The tide wasn't in yet. He sat there long into the night, sometimes praying, sometimes quoting Scripture to himself, feeling the torment of having lost them and putting a whole new dimension of uncertainty into the operation.

At intervals during the night Joe's drunken voice came from deep inside the hollow cave of Alphonse—sometimes it was laughter, then a discordant song, and then the sound of weeping. It was the cry of a man confronted with the hopelessness of it all. Sebastian felt Joe's wounds, the loneliness that the alcohol was bringing out of him, the deep pains that were peculiarly his, all the agonies of his inner life reaching out from inside the boat that was a symbol of Joe's own life of futility, frustration, broken dreams, and blind alleys. It was a cry against God, too, against what He had done to his wife—Sebastian knew it to be the cry of a man who had lost touch with the human love and companionship of the one closest to him. And then the cries ended and there was only the night, almost visibly scarred, like the aimless streaks of a child's scribbling on a clean blackboard.

And Sebastian wept too, for the overwhelming sense of sorrow he felt for Joe, for all of them, and for the painful pressures he had added to their cause.

"'O, spare me, that I may recover my strength, before I go hence and be no more,'" he repeated the Psalmist. And then he added, "'But lift them up, O Lord, that your name might be sweet on their lips and not cursing, that their agonies turn to joy and they no longer be strangers to you.'"

The tide moved in and hit his feet, and he roused with a start—and he heard that familiar bawling voice, raking, rubbing the world raw. It was Joe, and he was calling them back to Alphonse, to the job, to the cause. And the first streaks of dawn were in the sky.

Chapter XI

****

It was as if nothing had happened. Except for the swollen tissue around his mouth and eyes that the liquor had left on him, Joe was the same. He acted as though nothing had happened the night before. As Rodríguez watched, Joe drove them into the task again, turning them on the last of the fittings and adjustments. They responded to him, a bit bewildered that he showed no alteration of purpose, no indication of reluctance. If anything, he seemed to throw himself into it with even more fierceness, bellowing over their fumbling efforts and chiding them for their slowness to respond to his instructions. Some new spirit had gripped Joe, perhaps no more than defiance—defiance of Sebastian, of the N.I.A., of Castro, or of God. But whatever it was, it got to all of them, so that they thought less of any of these other factors and more again of Alphonse.

Later that same afternoon Joe announced that they could launch Alphonse that night on schedule, on the tide. There was nothing more to be done. All the fittings were in. He had wanted to get Alphonse in the water for a trial run, but there was no time. The real test of whether they could all perform as expected and if Alphonse would hold up was yet to come.

They sat around the rest of the day trying to get their strength back, drinking coffee or sleeping. Sebastian sat outside the group most of the time. Though he ate his meals and drank his coffee with them, he felt no easy communication. He had cast himself into a new role by consorting with the N.I.A.—and he was alive only because of a thin scrap of information that even yet they weren't sure was important to them.

But later in the night, as the time approached to launch Alphonse, they sat around the charcoal fire while El Dorado strummed his guitar lazily. Joe, however, didn't sit—he fidgeted around Alphonse, checking, rechecking, refusing to accept the fact that all that could be done was done. Rodríguez sat outside the pale of the fire, fanning himself with his hat, for the night was warm.

The first glimmer of spiritual daylight came then, breaking into the circle so quickly that Sebastian almost lost it. El Dorado, while still stroking the strings of his guitar, said, "You think God is on our side, padre?"

For a moment Sebastian couldn't believe he had heard right or that the question was actually addressed to him. He glanced quickly across the fire to where María sat, her greenish-black eyes staring into the coals as though she hadn't heard. Bingo was lying flat on his stomach on a blanket, looking into the fire too, and his eyes flicked just once toward María as the question got through to him, the look of one who sensed that an old wound was about to be slashed open again.

"God doesn't take sides," Sebastian said, eager to communicate what he believed, but taking it slowly lest he appear to try to force his way in. "But then I'm sure He's for any attempt that is motivated by concern for the good of the individual. . . ."

"And that's us?" El Dorado said, still picking at the guitar strings aimlessly.

"Don't you know?" Sebastian replied with a smile.

"Yeah, well, I get kinda confused, padre. We're going for the Rodríguez family but we're taking this man Varga back. . . . You figure God's got a problem about that?"

"It depends if Varga is a defector or not."

"Supposing he isn't—then what? How does God weigh it then?"

"Seven people who want freedom will outweigh one man whose motives are questionable, don't you think?"

El Dorado frowned. "I'm asking you, padre. . . . I don't know."

"I think so, El Dorado. . . ."

"Why don't you leave God out of it?" María cut in for the first time and swung around to lay her head down on a rolled blanket, a gesture that indicated her disdain for the subject. "Then you won't have to worry about whose side He's on."

"Can you leave God out of anything?" Sebastian replied mildly.

"I can very easily," she replied, aiming her words toward the stars as if she didn't even want to acknowledge that they were intended for him. "I leave Him in His world, and I operate in mine. It's much simpler all the way around."

"So there's no God in your world?" El Dorado said.

"Of course not." She turned her head slightly to look at El Dorado. "How can you reconcile a world of suffering as we Cubans have known it with a living God in the universe? Has God done anything for you, El Dorado? A black Cuban in America is no better off than in Cuba, maybe worse. You have any evidence He's alive in your world?"

El Dorado acknowledged her words with a stiff grin, because she had hit on his sensitive area, his skin color and his station in life. "Oh, I don't know, María, I live free in my own way. . . ."

"Sure," she snorted. "Take what you need with a knife—and now all you've got is a prison term ahead of you."

"Well, there's Señor Rodríguez—maybe God sent him to bail me out," El Dorado said with a laugh.

"I'm sure my uncle will agree that God had something to do with it," María snapped back with a mocking jerk to her head. She lit a cigarette. It was amazing to Sebastian that all of them here had to have a prop to lean on just to talk—Rodríguez had his cigar, María and Joe their cigarettes, El Dorado used his guitar, while Bingo had to snap his fingers and do a dance.

"That money comes from years of work in Cuba," Rodríguez offered, without much feeling for this conversation. He was more interested in what Joe was doing around Alphonse, and he kept looking beyond the fire to where Joe tinkered around the equipment, not too far out of earshot.

"You can leave God out if you want to," Sebastian said. "That doesn't prove that life is simpler or that you are better off."

"The burden of proof is on you," María said flatly, dragging on her cigarette, her eyes fixed overhead again. "Anyway, it's easy for an American to talk about the reality of God; have you ever been tested on that score? Watch your family shot by a firing squad for no other reason than a simple complaint about lack of vegetables in the market—then try going to church. Have you had that kind of test?"

Sebastian hadn't, of course. "Not quite that dramatic or severe, maybe, but I had one experience that tested the reality of God to the core of my being—"

"A bad case of constipation, no doubt," María flipped back caustically and blew smoke back over her head.

El Dorado laughed and hit a chord as if she'd made a real score with that one. Sebastian smiled. "You think you're the only one who has suffered in the world?" he asked her. "You think you're the only one in the world who had tragedy, disaster, violence? There are thousands who have and still hold on to God. . . ."

"So—why? What's the reason?" she challenged.

"Yeah, padre," El Dorado joined in. "If the people who believe in God don't have any edge on the folks who don't, it stands to reason there's no point in believing, right?" It was a genuine problem with him, a groping kind of query, for El Dorado wasn't shutting out God yet like María had.

"The edge comes not so much in avoiding the calamities," Sebastian returned, wishing he were more schooled in this, for he wasn't coming off too sharp for their minds, "but in the realization that God is going to bring some good out of it. God's love operates to heal. Anyway, you can't charge God with all the disasters; most of them are manmade. When man gets through wrecking your castle, at least you can know God is still there ready to help patch up the holes. . . ."

"But does God step in to stop the wrecking?" El Dorado paused in his strumming, intent on the question.

"I believe He does."

"Will He keep the Castro boys off our backs and the U.S. Navy from jumping down our throats?" El Dorado smiled in disbelief.

"I have that faith," Sebastian said simply.

"Because you're along?" El Dorado asked.

Sebastian looked at Bingo, but the young Cuban hadn't moved from his position of staring into the fire.

"A lot of people carried their images of Christ when they fled Cuba," María said sourly. As much as she must have wanted out of this conversation, she seemed bound on finishing it her way. "It didn't help them much."

"He got you out, María," Sebastian said lightly.

"I swam out," she retaliated, and her eyes swung around

on him, cold and black with hostility. "I left my images with a dead church that couldn't do anything about Batista or Castro. I could have swum to Key West if I had had to—God had nothing to do with it."

"What about the shrimp boat?" Sebastian interjected. The question caught her off guard, and for a moment she looked startled.

"Yeah, what about the boat?" El Dorado picked it up, curious now. "I heard it was fifteen miles out. . . ."

"So a shrimp boat came along by chance and picked me up," she defended.

"If it was a Cuban shrimp boat, chance maybe," El Dorado contradicted. "But if it was Bahaman or American, then that is God. No shrimp boat from outside Cuba could go that close by chance, María, hey?"

"It was a Bahama boat blown off course," she rifled back, dismissing that possible miracle immediately.

"You aren't giving God much of a chance to prove Himself," Sebastian continued, glad to keep pushing her to talk, for she was building up to exasperation now, a good sign that she had debated this many times before.

"I gave Him His chance in Cuba; now I've given Him time in America. . . . He's just as dead in both places. Maybe even more here, in your great society, with its corruption and its belly lined with dollars instead of morals. . . ."

"You just haven't touched the life of God in Christ yet, that's all." Sebastian added, wanting to get to the heart of the matter, "Reach out in your own soul's need and you'll find Christ—that's why He came, so you could touch God through Him."

María had gotten up on that, brushing off her pants, as if this was a signal to wind up the discussion. "And how do you touch this Christ?" she asked pointedly, skeptically, with a note of challenge in her voice again, and she looked directly at Sebastian.

El Dorado paused in his playing and grinned. "Through

the padre here, who else? I'm surprised at you, María, that all you learned in the church hasn't taught you that yet—it's what they call the apostolic succession or something; the padre is the holy man. You touch him, you touch Christ, see?"

A knowing smile brushed María's mouth, a sharp creasing line tugged by a nerve ending. Sebastian knew what she was going to say.

"Yes, I've had my—my touch?—with the holy man here. There was nothing divine in what I felt, I'm afraid—he's as mortal as the rest of us!"

And she marched out of the circle toward the surf, flipping her half-smoked cigarette in an arching trail of fire into the night, her way of thumbing her nose at the world in general, but now it was for Sebastian and all he represented.

El Dorado watched her go and then smiled at Sebastian with one corner of his mouth as if in apology for what she did. "You got a lot to prove to that Señorita, padre, before she will light a candle to the Virgin again, comprene?"

"And how about you, El Dorado?"

"Me?" El Dorado frowned at his fingers, stroking the strings of his guitar. He didn't seem to want that direct a question. Across his face came a look of strange longing, as if he were looking at something expensive behind a display glass. "Padre, I come a long road in my young life . . . lived too much. I wanted to touch something good, too, but around every corner was the teeth of hell, and I got bit every time. I was born wrong on every count, I guess. I came out of my momma's belly runnin' for my life and I been doing it ever since. . . . When my momma brought me here and got me citizenship that was supposed to be the millennium, but all it meant was I run a little faster to keep up and got bit a little harder. . . . So now, padre, I bite first like a dog who knows he's got to get in the first fang. I don't touch no more, padre, I take. . . . Some people are born under a star called God; me, I was born under a sheet-iron roof that leaked. I spent my childhood duckin' the rain pourin' in and I always wondered, if God was God, why did He always let it rain so hard on that roof. . . ." His fingers came back on the guitar again as he added, "And it's been raining ever since, padre. I ain't seen no sun yet, and I been lookin' a long time. . . ." And then he began to sing in that childlike, plaintive way:

"Oh, sun, where you been hidin'
Wrapped in the robes of God?
Here I am, you can see I'm pinin'
For a touch of your golden rod."

The stark realism of El Dorado's words was too much for Sebastian. He could find no handy response—anything he might have said would have sounded too simple. He had come again to that point where words were useless, a point that had always puzzled him, for he had been taught that words were the best and the only needles with which to inject spiritual truth. He had learned his lesson once in the Negev; he was learning it again here. For El Dorado's words seemed more powerful than his, they were a symphony of sound and meaning, an ode to a man's life of wandering and searching and to a philosophy that couldn't be readily refuted in just a few glib formula sentences, no matter how spiritual.

He looked at Bingo. The young Cuban was watching him intently with a look that said, This is where I stand, where El Dorado stands, cast in shadow, looking for light, but not expecting any.

There was no challenge in that look, simply resignation, as if to say, Now that you know, let it rest. And then his eyes went back to the fire—and the song diffused into the night, joining the sound of crashing surf that beat with futility against the impenetrable rock of the reef.

"Anyway, why does God need the N.I.A.?" Rodríguez suddenly broke in, as if he'd finally found something to say to the subject.

The statement sounded so out of context that it made El

Dorado laugh; even Sebastian had to smile. Rodríguez looked stonily back as if to say that no man should laugh at his own death warrant. Then El Dorado hit the guitar and began singing "Dominica" and the night lit up with the new notes. And then Joe was yelling, "Okay, let's get with it!" and the sound of it was harsh, like a knife ripping through canvas.

They had planned to launch Alphonse in the only way possible, on this reef. The clearing had three main outcroppings of coral rock jutting out into the ocean. The two side spurs of rock were close in and the tide only barely touched them. The third one in the middle shot one long arm of scraggly red coral out a good fifty yards beyond the other two, and the tide at its peak would put a good thirty feet of water off its razor-sharp edge. At high tide, about now, there was an eight-foot drop, and after examining it at least twenty times Joe figured there were no rock shelves jutting out that might hook into Alphonse as she dropped in.

The plan was simply to back Alphonse up to this ledge on the trailer. With the back wheels up to the edge of the rock, there was still twenty feet of trailer bed jutting out over the reef and over the high tide. If it worked right, the trailer's back wheels would push solidly up against a ledge of coral, thus tipping the trailer bed and allowing Alphonse to slide slowly off; the momentum of her slide would carry her out far enough to clear the end of the reef and the trailer. It was not a very elegant way to launch any boat, and El Dorado insisted that even a drop of eight feet could damage her.

"If she can't take that, she won't take what Castro has in store for her," Joe muttered in reply.

They cleared the jungle brush off Alphonse, and then El Dorado backed the truck cab back and hooked it to the trailer. Backing up the reef head was a slow, painful maneuver, with Joe running around Alphonse as if he were lowering a gold-plated casket into a grave and didn't want a touch of dirt on it.

When they got to the edge of the reef, to the point when the trailer would slide down off the shelf to give Alphonse the gravity needed to slide off, Joe held her there for a good five minutes. He measured the clearance of the trailer bed, the long drop, the turn of the tide swirling in over the rocks on either side.

"Okay, let her come!" he yelled, and the trailer came back, eased down slowly over the ledge, and Alphonse began to move from her planking platform on the trailer bed, inch by inch at first and then faster as the trailer dropped farther on to the thin shelf. Suddenly the wheels of the trailer slipped from the rock and the trailer crashed down to the axle on the reef and hung up there. Alphonse shot off the trailer bed, the last thirty feet of her, and hit the water with most of her stern first. The geyser of water was like an uncontrolled fountain, spraying all of them as they stood on the reef. Alphonse rolled over to one side, then back. Loud sucking noises came from her, and her decks went under, so that all that hung out was the conning tower. For one horrible moment it looked like she was going down—and then she seemed to make a peculiar heavy roll to starboard and her decks came back up, gleaming black in the moonlight. Then she settled there, bobbing up and down as though she were nodding approval to them all for what they had done to her this time.

"Venceremos! We shall win!" Bingo's voice pierced the moment of awe they all felt, not quite believing Alphonse was actually afloat.

"Viva Cuba libre!" Rodríguez shouted back, and they all cheered. Sebastian found himself yelling until his throat ached. Even María, who stood looking so stoic and composed, wiped at her cheeks. El Dorado pounded Joe on the back, but Joe simply stood there quietly looking down at the boat, rubbing the back of his neck in bewilderment and disbelief. He had done what his father had never lived to do—launched "MaConnel's Folly." And there she sat, riding the surf, defying the critics, rising to her moment of glory. In this moment, Sebastian felt nothing separated them as they stood there—their feelings of pride in this accomplishment welded them together.

Then Bingo started to do a jig on the rocks, his feet flying nimbly on the wet coral, and El Dorado ran back and got his guitar and pounded out "Dominica," the one song he knew best, and then the Cuban national anthem. After they had secured Alphonse to the rock haven with heavy lines, they went back to the fire, still heady with their victory, and Rodríguez broke out the rum. They danced and sang and drank—and Sebastian sat quietly aside, letting them have their moment, sharing as best he could with the coffee. He watched Bingo and Rodríguez dance first, then Joe and María went through a fast Spanish number. María was beautiful in the way she did it, as only Spanish women can, and she did the twisting, contorting, and writhing in front of Sebastian, as if she delighted in tantalizing him, trying to batter down his defenses and almost mockingly communicating to him that he was not really a man at all if he could sit there and take it.

But he took it. Biting down on his back teeth, he took it. And no one pushed him further. They were content to let him sit while they unleashed their emotions. They had won the battle here, a real one. But he was still only an incidental part of it, still shut out from its core because of what he ultimately represented in life; he could tap his toe and swing his coffee cup with the rhythm and try to join them in this small way, for he had suffered too and the lonely man in him cried for some identification with what they had now. But they would not cross over to him, and he in turn could not move toward them. It was that peculiar gulf that makes ministers a breed apart, maybe, and no amount of common sweat or blood or effort could change it. But he wished just for that moment that one of them would have asked him—anything, maybe to sing a song of his own, even do some kind of jig, if there was any way that a man of God had to express joy to God, anything that would have allowed him to share this tremendous moment of exultation. Instead he sat there with feelings of joy and sadness running through him, now and then lifting his cup to María as she did another dance for him in that same mocking solicitation and noting her steady, intent gaze on him, the changing lights of those eyes coming back always to the deep black of her feelings for him.

And as he watched them, Sebastian saw too for the first time what the strain of these weeks had cost them. Scraggly growths of beard covered Joe's and El Dorado's faces, singed in places where the hot sparks of acetylene torches had hit. Bingo's face was caked with patches of black fuzz mixed with dirt. Sebastian felt his own bony cheeks; they were scratchy too, and he smelled of grease and salt water and the decay that was Alphonse. Even Rodríguez, who had had to chip in his feeble effort here, stood in a dirty white shirt looking completely out of character except for his cigar, wiping at the sweat and grime on his sunburned face with a soggy grease rag he thought was a handkerchief but which didn't matter much to him at this stage. And María too had gone through a change—she had chopped off her long hair at some time, which Sebastian hadn't noticed till now—and it must have been in anger, for the ends looked frayed and uneven around her neck. There were smudges of dirt on her cheeks and lines of fatigue under her eyes and around her mouth, but that couldn't hide the beauty she lent to the whole lumpy scene of tangled wires, hoses, broken tools, and men stripped shamefully by the carving knife of adversity.

Sebastian felt a strange sense of affinity with them, a warm sense of comradeship, even stronger than he sensed with his fellow ministers back in Nashville. It startled him, for he knew this should not be—they were still, after all, hostile to him; they were still in a real sense spiritually out of tune with him. They were in essence pagan elements, even now dancing their defiance of Deity, just by the way they took pains to mock him with their gyrations and contortions. The feeling stunned him for the moment, for he knew the Biblical record that spelled it out: "what concord hath Christ with Belial? or what part hath he that believeth with an infidel?" But he did have a part with them, and it was impossible for him to see them apart from himself, for Alphonse had forged them, even beyond their capacity to realize, into a unit of indistinguishable flesh and spirit. And though he viewed them and they him as a man apart, something transcended this difference and afforded this moment when they could carry on this way almost for his benefit.

But before he could analyze this further as to whether it was good or bad and what action he should take, if any, the festivity died almost abruptly as it had begun. It was as though Alphonse had called them to the immediate task at hand; one minute they were singing and clapping their hands, and then they were sober and meditative, as if some arresting sound had come in the night to break through the high notes of exuberant abandon.

And Joe said, articulating it for them, "It's the morning of the eleventh. We better load up. We probably got some leaks inside the boat, too, so let's get to it."

So they turned to the bigger test at hand, most reluctant to leave what they had here for this brief moment. Cuba was still a long way off. Alphonse had not yet been put through her paces—they had not yet proven her under water. But they had at least drawn a new straw of hope. They had come further than any man would have predicted. They had put their unskilled hands to a monstrous task; it would have caused many a Naval engineer some shaking of the head to consider what they had done. So that now something of the fear of what lay ahead was diluted—some of their uncertainty, too—and their brief celebration had taken up the clogging debris of that fear and washed it out into the night.

It was El Dorado who ran the colors of their optimism to the top of the pole as he sang to that "Clementine" tune:

"Periscope above the water,
See the mighty Alphonse now,
Like a knight in shining armor,
Where she once was just a scow!"

Chapter XII

****

They filled the sub's tanks with fuel from the portable trailer and put aboard minimal amounts of food and water. Sebastian watched Joe carry on three rifles and later place the dummy thirty-six-inch torpedoes into the forward and after tubes. He didn't say anything; he knew it would be useless, since this was a command of war anyway as far as they were concerned.

They changed into the black turtlenecked sweaters Joe had provided against the cold they could expect in the lower depths. They went over the plans with Rodríguez again, checked the rendezvous point on Cárdenas Bay, and computed time factors on the tide charts. They figured to go straight into Cárdenas the only way they could, on a 220 course directly south from Key West. They would have to wait for high tide to go into Cárdenas area, since there was only twenty feet of free water under keel at low tide a good mile out. That would be at two in the morning. That had been figured for the Rodríguez family too, for they were to be in the fishing shack on the point of Cárdenas Key at three. "You give them three lights, you get five back—understood?" Rodríguez said.

Joe nodded. They computed their chances of getting through the Bahama Cup race going over. Joe wasn't too sure of it, but they figured it would offer some cover.

Then there was nothing more to say. They stood around as if wanting to discuss it further, as if what they had said was far too simple in terms of what lay ahead. But then Joe rolled up the charts and without a word to Rodríguez walked down to where Alphonse waited. The rest of them followed—except for María, who lingered to say farewell to her uncle. As Sebastian turned to follow Bingo to the sub, he caught Rodríguez's eyes on him for just an instant—the look held a promise that if anything happened to this operation it would be laid at Sebastian's door. And the hard, steady, gray-black smoke of his eyes was enough of a down payment on that promise. Sebastian didn't bother to say anything, for it was not a time for words. He paused once just above Alphonse to watch María face her uncle for the last time—she took a long time. She was tearing out the roots of her love for him, one at a time, not making a sound. For her, this was the finish, and Sebastian sensed she was finding it harder than she thought.

But Rodríguez simply patted her on the shoulder, kissed her lightly on the hair as if she were no more than a child going off to school. In a few hours he would know the betrayal—and it might be the end for him too.

Then they were all on the cramped bridge of Alphonse. Rodríguez stood above them waiting for word to cast off the lines, looking as lonely and misshapen as laundry on a clothesline. El Dorado, María, even Joe—they all looked like people on a carnival ride waiting to begin, not sure of what to expect, wondering if they should change their minds. But there wasn't time for that. Sebastian would have liked time to rethink the whole thing, go over the percentages, be safer, surer. Up to now he had half expected some kind of intervention to stop the whole thing, something that would save them all the trip and the dishonor of backing out. But it hadn't come. Now it was time, and there was nothing to do but go.

"Crank her up," Joe said, and Sebastian relayed the message into the phone to Bingo. There should have been something more dramatic in this launching, culminating four weeks of emotional, mental, and physical strain. But all they got was rumbling, coughing sounds from the belly of Alphonse, sounding like some sick animal bellowing in the pain of impending death. And then the engine caught, and the conning tower bridge rattled, threatening to shake loose from its mount. Smoke boiled up from her stern exhaust a full minute and then Joe, as if afraid she'd explode before she got five feet from the rocks, yelled to Rodríguez, "Let go the lines!" María ran down on the deck and gathered them in, and they began moving out to meet the first big test of the Bronco surf.

She jerked, yawed, and at times seemed to want to dive nose down for the bottom, but she snorted, sprayed foam off her flat snout, and plowed through the test passably but hardly in elegant or marinelike fashion. She was like an old woman taking her first steps after a lifetime in a wheelchair. El Dorado shouted, "She handles like a cow draggin' a plow, but she floats!"

Joe only stared dismally at her decks, still awash and refusing to rise, and said, "Yeah, well, what will she do in a dive?"

Nobody wanted to answer that one, but surely it was in all of their minds, as it was in Sebastian's, that erratic behavior like this carried underwater was a sure design for disaster. But they plowed down the inner water lanes anyway, and when they were within twenty miles of Key West Joe shifted her out to the main shipping channel. Bingo was allowed then to come up for air. His eyes showed the jubilance and pride of his accomplishment—the engine was the heart of Alphonse. He had started her and run her, quite a feat for a novice. It was good to see him with his shoulders back, his chin raised to the spray, telling the world that this "gusano" was more than a gusano, and Castro better watch out.

They spotted the sails of the Bahama Cup race at about ten-thirty, and Joe acknowledged that the Navy had no ships in the area yet. They stayed on the surface content to run as long as they could, but when the first Navy reconnaissance planes came over, checking on the race, Joe gave the word to dive. They went down through the hatch without hesitancy. Whatever fear or doubt they had, they knew this moment had to come.

Joe was the last one down, and he sealed the conning tower hatch with one twist of the wheel. Now they were shut in. That constricting feeling came hard into Sebastian's throat, and the sweat started to run easily. The smell of diesel fumes was heavy here, the roar of the engine loud enough to smash the fragile boat from the inside. But Bingo made his power switches as he'd done a hundred times in his dreams, and the relays cut out the diesel and brought on the electric motor without a hitch except for the dimming of the lights.

But from then on it was one long slide to the edge of disaster. They were not even twenty feet under and the little green Christmas tree light over the depth gauge hadn't gone on yet—that meant there was some outer vent not closed. In the same instant that Joe made a move to reverse to surface, Bingo yelled that water was pouring into the diesel fuel chambers. That meant the air intake valve hadn't closed. They had to reverse their descent, go back up, close the vent, and go under again. Then, when it looked like they'd made it on the second try, the boat pitched over on a sickening 45-degree list to starboard.

"Geez!" Joe yelled. "We're runnin' this thing like a Chinese laundry!" And he stormed at María to open her ballast evenly on the dive; she had flooded her starboard tanks too early. They managed to get Alphonse retrimmed, but their rate of descent was only about ten feet every two minutes.

"That ain't no record, man!" El Dorado warned.

When they got to forty-five feet, Alphonse seemed to tremble and shake, and peculiar sucking sounds ran through her hull as if some sea mammal outside were trying to get a good bite of her. These sucking, creaking, moaning sounds were too much for Joe, and he called for full planes to surface. They staggered up the ascent in jerky jumps, and when they finally managed to get to the surface and break the hatch they stood around on the bridge quietly dragging in the fresh air and numbed into poses of serious contemplation as they realized now that they were riding a whale running with a harpoon in its back. But if they had any idea of returning, it was too late. Joe pointed out the first of the U.S. Navy destroyer picket fleet astern, moving on a parallel course a mile or two.

"No place to go but Cuba," he said, as if he sensed what they were thinking.

So they spent the next two hours drying out the diesel fuel chambers, and then, with Castro waters under them, they did another test dive. It went off fairly well, but they hadn't gotten more than thirty feet down when María suddenly said, "Joe, I got sound!"

Joe immediately dropped prone on the deck, sticking his head down into the forward hatch to look at the sonar gauge. Sebastian stooped down to look over his shoulder, relaying what was going on to Bingo by the phone.

"How far is it?" Joe asked, his voice sounding tight in the quiet humming of the electric motors.

"She's under us," María said in awe, and her eyes came around to focus questioningly on Joe.

"Has to be a sub," Joe said flatly. Sweat was leaking out from under his battered yachting cap.

"Russian?" El Dorado offered, looking over his shoulder at the sonar reading. "Or Castro's?"

"She's going west—probably to Havana," Joe returned. "That would be Russian. They're trying to go under the cover of the Bahama Cup too; Castro must need supplies bad these days. . . ."

They waited until the sub's screws disappeared, and just as Joe made a move to get up, María indicated another sound, the same kind, going under them.

"A Russian pack," Joe said. They waited, counting three of them going by, Joe timing each pass to eight minutes each. Then he said, "Okay, that's our break." María and El Dorado looked up at him quickly, wondering. "If Castro is ganging up on us around Cárdenas, we haven't got a chance with the way this boat is acting. But if we follow that Russian pack on the Havana course, we could get into their waters without arousing suspicion. Castro's gunboats won't be looking for us in the middle of friendly sub traffic. . . ."

"They'll be sure to pick us up, those subs!" María protested.

"You just get that sonar on the stern of the next sub that goes by, babe," Joe said with a smile, "and hang on to her about twenty-five yards back. She'll never know she's towin' anybody on a sonar string. All you got to do is stick to that scope."

María twisted around to stare at El Dorado, hoping for some further argument to this. El Dorado shrugged and said, "Could be he's got a point," and that was that.

For four hours they played the dangerous game of dogging the Russian sub ahead of them. The strain was visible on María. Her unpracticed hand at sonar was already obvious, and to have to master this kind of computing game with bouncing sounds, some of them not really clear, was forcing too much weight on so fragile a frame. Joe hung over her most of the time, but after a while she became more nervous and told Joe to get off her back.

All this time Sebastian could only stand in his hunched-over posture and wait. There was very little for him to do. Except for relaying messages to the engine room by phone, he was just so much extra baggage. He was here only to be observed, anyway: to have his pulse taken, blood pressure measured, muscle reflexes computed, palpitation and sweat noted, to indicate how much of his God was so much paste in stress. They might as well have hooked him up to an electrocardiogram or encephelogram and plotted charts on his body secretions. It was this that was beginning to irritate him most, to have Joe peer at him intently now and then like he was a chunk of meat turning on a barbecue spit, checking him for those telltale signs of disintegration.

But he knew he would have to take it and bide his time, to wait for that moment when the thin ledge they were holding on to broke in their hands. He wasn't sure what he would be able to do himself when that time came—he sensed no greater stability or certainty than they did now. He was the least familiar with the operations they carried on and least equipped to exploit a weakness anywhere here. But he would wait, and sweat it, and pray he'd know what to do when it came.

At eight o'clock in the evening, the Russian sub made a course change south. María reported it and Joe said, "Okay, they're now turning on the Havana leg!"

"You gonna follow them right in?" El Dorado asked, perplexed.

"No, sir, Ellie!" Joe sang back. "In one hour I'm going to break loose out of this pack, when I see the eighteen-mile light off Havana. Then we follow the coastline to Cárdenas, using the shore markers. How's that for comin' in the back door?"

Nobody said anything, but Sebastian had to agree it was good. And just to prove that his calculations were not awry, Joe made the course change to 130 south out of the Russian sub chain at exactly eight-thirty. Nothing happened. They were clear. It was obvious that he knew he had scored the victory. And so confident was he that at nine he ordered them to surface to recharge and get fresh air. With the lights of Havana astern, splashing the sky with throbbing pulse, he called Bingo topside and pointed it out. "There's your doll, kid," he said. Bingo stood there a long time watching, and no one could know the longing in his heart at that moment.

An hour later they dived again, and Joe cut Alphonse in close to shore to get the six-mile light through the scope. They changed course to 90 and were on the last leg to Cárdenas Bay, and the fifteen-mile light just two hours away. It was then that Sebastian felt a dribble of water coming down from overhead and pointed it out to Joe.

"We got a leaky hatch," Joe commented sourly. Then, mostly to himself, for he didn't want to compliment Sebastian with a straight remark, he added, "If you want the easy way out, preach, all you got to do is step under that spray when we're down around a hundred feet. It'll put a hole in your head messy as a forty-five slug." And he gave that slow grin of menace, the sign of a borderline psychopathic which he called humor.

As they moved farther down the coast and closer in to their rendezvous, Joe became quieter. Now and then his tongue darted out to wet his dry lips. He couldn't smoke in the already heavy air, so he rolled a cold cigarette in his mouth, trying to draw something from that.

They stayed under, running at about forty feet. Alphonse was holding her own so far, except for those eerie sucking sounds and her inability to hold really steady at her depth, bouncing five feet up or under her running course. Bubbles of sweat began to show up on her bulkheads too.

At eleven o'clock they picked up the sounds Joe had been expecting. "Castro's antisub boys!" he yelled the warning as María flashed the signal. "Ellie, take her down to sixty feet!"

They went down to the new depth painfully slowly, the sound of the high-pitched whine of the screws passing overhead. They counted five going north, another eight going south.

"Either they don't know we're here," Joe commented, aiming his remarks at the ceiling, "or they're heading to Cárdenas to lay the trap."

The sounds passed overhead and disappeared. They went on running at sixty feet, Alphonse taking on new pressure sounds in her hull, a kind of thumping and knocking. The water coming down through the hatch over Sebastian's head was a fine, needlelike spray, and it stung him hard when he got his head in the way.

"There's one more sitting up there," María warned as Joe got ready to take Alphonse up to a safer level.

Joe hesitated, dropping down to look over her shoulder at the sonar gauge to be sure. "Yeah," he said quietly, his voice carrying the subdued tone of one confronted with a tough math problem. "Washing Machine Charlie. He doesn't know what to make of us yet. He's probably checking back to his patrol HQ about sub traffic in the area."

They kept running, waiting for the boat topside to make a move. Nothing happened. The boat stayed with them. "No," Joe said, his lips pouting in the new thought pattern, "he's not going to drop any eggs. . . . He'll tail us, notify others in the patrol fleet, and they'll set up a fix on us before too long. All we can do is keep going, hope he drops off. . . ."

They went on for another hour. At midnight the sound of

the small boat was gone. "Don't get your hopes up," Joe said to María. "He's out there somewhere, not too far, close enough to know where we are, far enough to give us the idea he's gone. . . ."

"Shall we lay on the bottom awhile and see what happens?" El Dorado offered, poking his sweating face around to look up at Joe.

"No time," Joe said. "We got to get into the Cárdenas reefs and find our way through. We'll just have to take our chances. . . ."

They got to the Cárdenas area at twelve-thirty. By using the fathometer and sonar they were able to creep into the scraggly, reef-pocked shoals. As they came into thirty-five feet of water under the keel, Joe took a look through the periscope. "We're clear," he said, "and Cárdenas Key, I think, is right off the starboard quarter. We'll drop her down here and wait. . . ."

It was near one o'clock then. They had to wait until two for high tide. Joe ordered the engines shut down and asked Bingo to come up and join them. They sat there around the forward hatch in a tangle of their own legs—El Dorado, who had come up to give María some room to relax in, Joe, Bingo, and Sebastian.

"What if we get caught here in shallow water with a patrol boat on top of us?" El Dorado asked, leaning his head on his arms, his knees drawn up under his chin.

"Pray, what else?" Joe said with a laugh that didn't come off well at all in the heavy, tight air that had built up to a peculiar pressure in the tension of the past few hours. Nobody said anything to that, and then El Dorado began to hum softly, an aimless kind of melody, rising and falling in a sad wail, running hauntingly through the boat, riding over the hum of the fans, almost caressing in its plaintiveness.

"Maybe the padre ought to read something from the Book," El Dorado suggested.

"Oh, shut up, for pete's sake!" Joe snapped at him. "You'll have the whole Cuban fleet picking you up on their phones—and that goes for that caterwaulin' you call singing, too!"

El Dorado didn't look up or respond, and Joe had to hunt for another cigarette, to find something to do.

"I'll tell you what I think," he said morosely then, staring at the bent cigarette in his fingers. "You might as well know. . . . It's too easy, Castro letting us come all this way without a challenge. . . . I think he's letting us in, and then, when we try to get out, he drops the rock on us. . . ."

"So?" María asked, lifting her eyes from the sonar and peering impatiently through the hatch at him.

Joe took his time, and then, aiming along the line of his cigarette toward Sebastian, said, "Well, maybe our preacher friend here knows now that when he shot his bolt to Mathews he was giving it all to Fidel—"

"We can't be sure of that," El Dorado cut in, not so much in defense of Sebastian as trying to support his own thinking. "Only one boat hung around to even check."

"All it takes is one, Ellie," Joe countered, "one to alert the whole fleet—and that puts us at a thousand to one. It'll be fun for them, like dropping a stick of dynamite in a mouse-hole."

Nobody said anything to that. The weight of it was overpowering, especially sitting there at thirty-five feet under the ocean. "Well, the padre likes odds like that anyway," El Dorado offered then, almost factually, but yet wanting to be sure. He looked up to stare at Sebastian. "Like, what's a thousand to one when the Book says one shall chase a thousand, right, padre?"

"I don't hear the man of God blowing any trumpets," María chimed in in her usually caustic way, her eyes still on the sonar screen.

"No, but he's sweatin', right, preach?" Joe jabbed, his

face creased into the lines of a deeply meditative clairvoyant as he kept aiming across the stem of his cigarette at Sebastian's nose. "He's been sweatin' the percentages that have been dropping on him the last couple of hours. He's got God riding on every move, and that's enough to make any man of the cloth sweat. . . ."

"Does it really matter if he sweats?" María interjected, sounding weary with the conversation.

"Jesus sweat blood," El Dorado said, unwilling to let it die yet.

"Give the preacher time, that'll come too," Joe added snidely. "How about it, preach, you got a miracle coming our way yet?"

"Play your own games, Joe, leave us out," María insisted, apparently disturbed at the way things were going.

"It concerns all of us," Joe said in a gesture of wounded vanity. "He's the man with the magic wand . . . remember?"

They waited. Sebastian wanted to let it go. They were like a pack of dogs wanting to sink their teeth into something that would give blood. But for Joe it was more important; the whole point of his taking Sebastian was to humble him, disarm him, even defrock him by the pressure of circumstances. For Joe, the operation was really secondary to this main objective—and now that he had the time and the opportunity, he wanted to start driving the nails. But for El Dorado and Bingo, it was something else; they looked at him now too, waiting for some rejoinder, anything that would support his reason for being here and maybe even give them some hope.

But he had hardly got his mouth open when the high-pitched whine of screws came to them loud and strong.

"Two of them, Joe!" María yelled.

"Sure, sure," Joe said and he laughed, as if he had made a point which was now being vindicated. "Washing Machine Charlie has picked up a buddy to do search and destroy!"

"Padre, you got that wand in your pocket, you better use

it now!" El Dorado called, his eyes rolling to the ceiling, where he expected to see the ocean fall in on them any minute.

Joe laughed again. "Don't complicate things for the padre!" and his voice scraped over the jagged edges of his personal vendetta against Sebastian. "God has to have the right conditions to work in, right, preach? Now here we are—it's kinda complicated: thirty-five feet under the ocean, two Castro patrol boats poking their finger down here tryin' to find us—you gotta have a church, organ music, choirs, all of that. . . . You can't expect God to get all messed up in this kind of thing. . . ." The screws passed and came back again, even closer this time, and Joe's voice went on, pounding against that sound, as if he wanted to keep shouting all this while he died. "No, sir, Ellie, God don't hang around places where the odds stack up too high against Him . . . so don't go squeezin' the preacher for miracles."

The sound of the motors faded out again. And it was quiet, almost embarrassingly so, with the ring of Joe's voice still there in the sub. Sebastian stared at the puffy, bulging lines of exhaustion on Joe's face, seeming to swell and distort even more as his bitter spirit rose to a head like pus in a boil, and debated whether to say anything right then, for he felt that allowing Joe to vent his hate like this would relieve some of that backed-up vehemence that could make it dangerous for all of them here. But Bingo and El Dorado were watching him too, waiting for something, anything to balance the heavily one-sided tirade, something to counter Joe's final judgment.

"It'll come, Joe," Sebastian said in the eerie silence. "When you run out of your string and ask for a little more rope from God, it'll be there. . . ."

Joe laughed, an exploding jab of ridicule, and then María snapped, "Do you have to go on with this crazy debate?"

And then the screws came back on them suddenly again,

materializing out of nowhere with no warning, and this time something clicked loudly and the explosion smashed into them, lifting Alphonse off the rocky floor of the reef and smashing her back down again. The air was filled with a shower of cork and fiberglass.

"He's taking an awful chance dropping a charge in this depth!" El Dorado shouted to Joe.

"Naw, he ain't!" Joe yelled back. "He's lobbing those things in from a stern catapult . . . wants to drive us in further toward Cárdenas, where we got no room at all! He ain't sure yet where we are exactly, but he figures we got to be in here somewhere. . . . We better move in closer or he's bound to get us on the next jump. Bingo, get on the engine!"

They crept into even more shallow water, with the depth charges fading behind them. "Mucho water back here!" Bingo called out on the phone. Sebastian repeated the warning to Joe, and they went back to check. It was the beginning of the collapse, Sebastian knew, for they could hear the sound of the water coming in aft now.

" 'Though a thousand fall at thy side and ten thousand at thy right hand, it shall not come nigh thee.' " He repeated the Psalm to himself.

But it had come nigh. And as he followed Joe into the engine room, the stink of death was on them, and the rattle of it was in Alphonse as she trembled like a steer heading for the slaughter barn. And the water pouring into the engine room was like the sound of blood running through the broken main artery of some beast.

"Not yet, God, not yet," he said over and over in his mind, and he saw Bingo's terrified eyes behind that long, slashing tongue of water pouring in from overhead. It was all he could do to keep the terror out of his own throat, for this was indeed an ugly way to die.

Chapter XIII

****

The water flooding the engine room was from a broken water pipe feeding the stern ballast tanks. Joe and Sebastian worked together to seal it—it still leaked some when they finished, but it would have to do.

They crawled forward, and María reported it was all quiet. "Okay, let's take her up," Joe said. It was about five minutes to three.

They broke the hatch. When Sebastian got up to the conning tower bridge, he saw that they wouldn't be easy to pick out here on the surface. There were a lot of jutting reefs and hooked coral that stuck bony fingers up a good ten feet out of the water. With only their conning tower showing, they hardly showed against that backdrop.

Joe called the rest of them topside, and when their eyes were fixed on the mass of land showing up to their right, he flashed the three signals from his six-inch battle lamp. The light seemed to illuminate them, and Sebastian wondered if those Castro boats would see it. They waited a long time for the return signal, and then Bingo said, "There!" and he pointed to the dim, winking, feeble light that appeared high on that black blob of land.

"I count five," María said, and El Dorado confirmed it.

"Get the rafts over the side," Joe ordered. "El Dorado, you stay on the boat and be ready when we come back. . . . If we don't show within the half hour, set the time fuses on the bombs and swim to shore. . . . You got a chance with the underground. . . ."

Joe and María went in one of the rafts, taking two rifles with them. Sebastian and Bingo went in the other. The night was still and black. The water felt oily and chilly to the touch. They rode the high surf into a beach area that was mostly rock. When they had pulled the rafts up on shore, Joe looked over the area with his binoculars. Ahead of them was a high mound of rock and a gradually ascending slope of tangled swamp grass.

"Come on, come on," Joe kept saying. "We can't stay here all night. . . ."

"Something shows," Bingo said softly then, from next to Sebastian on his left.

"Yeah," Joe said after a while. "That must be them. . . . They're comin' down awful fast; that can only mean that the security militia is on their tail. . . ."

Sebastian looked to his left—Joe was farthest over, Bingo next to him, and María should have fallen in on Sebastian's right. Not seeing María, he turned quickly—and caught only her shadow moving off in the night, going down the length of beach toward the clump of scraggly reef. It was María's planned move—to make an escape at the precise moment when their attention would be fixed elsewhere.

Sebastian got up quickly and started after her. "Hey!"

Joe shot out after him in a low, growling, half whisper, but Sebastian kept going, running faster after that illusive shadow. He caught up to her by the rock, and all he could do was throw himself forward and drag her down by her shoulders. They rolled over in the heavy wet sand, and Sebastian grabbed her by the ankle so that she sprawled over on her back. He jumped on her quickly and pinned her shoulders down to the sand with his hands, leaning over with his weight to keep her from struggling. Her breath was hot on his face, and her eyes were wide in fright and desperation, mingled with the hate she now had for him.

"God damn you forever!" she hurled at him, and she spit, then, and it hit him on the cheek, moist and hot. But he held on to her, forcing her squirming to stop under his body.

"You don't believe in God, remember?" he replied, grunting with effort. "And even if you did, you can't get Him to damn His own. . . . Even you ought to know that." Her body arched to shake him loose, but he wrapped his legs around hers and held on, so that he kept her pinned there, his hands holding her arms down against the sand over her head. He took time to get his wind as her body heaved with her heavy breathing, until she choked on something in her throat, and he realized that through her anger there were tears.

"All right, now you listen to me even if it's for the last time," he said, holding her steady, his face only a few inches from hers so that he could see the trace of the tears on her face curving over her jaw line as she kept her face away from him, toward the sand. "That spit makes up for all the times you wanted to do the same thing to some other American male. . . . You've evened up something of the hate you've got inside you, anyway. But let me tell you, dear lady, you can run to Castro if you want to now and break the heart of that old man you love back in Florida—and for what? Just so all the beauty and loveliness of yourself—the inner beauty of you that you don't even know you've got—can be turned ugly under what you know is in this country. At least in the States they complimented you for being a woman. I doubt you'll get that much here." She squirmed again, but he held on. "So all American men are the same? Well, here's one who's got you where he can do as he pleases with you—but I won't, because like a lot of other American men you haven't met yet I'm seeing the loveliness of a Spanish lady deep inside where you haven't even looked, that place nobody has yet touched. . . . That's what I want to protect, to defend, to see blossom as it should. . . . At least you can remember that much when you get swallowed up in the baggy olive drab of Castro's militia. . . ." She squirmed again to get out from under him but he held on and added, "Go ahead, if you want to, sell what's left of your soul—but you'll have to live with that one thought: there's a beautiful part of you yet that hasn't been touched, and you may never see it or experience it where you're going now. . . ."

He jumped up, for there was the sound of voices coming to him now, and his duty was with them; he could do nothing more for her. He ran off, letting her lie there in the sand, wiping at the moist spot on his cheek with his sleeve. He didn't look back to see what she did; he was more intent on what was going on with the others.

When he came up to them, he knew the tall, bearded man in the stiff-brim olive cap and militia uniform had to be Varga, talking mostly with his hands to Joe. The others, pulled together in a loose knot off to one side, had to be Rodríguez's family. The woman standing close to Varga, the tall, regal, but much older-looking wife of Rodríguez, he faintly recognized from the photograph. He tried to count the others in the dark, but they were all blended in the crepe paper of the night—but something about that group puzzled him, something seemed wrong.

"Ask him if Castro knows we're here," Joe told Bingo to translate.

"He knows English," Bingo said.

Varga, having understood the question, made a great

gesture of appeal. "Castro does not know—I work seven years for this moment," he insisted. "I cover every track, sí? But he is questioning—he has arrested five security officers in the last week, because he is not sure who is going out!"

"Are the coastal patrols alerted for a sub?" Joe asked then.

"Santa María!" Varga blurted out. "Tonight before I come, word comes through the underground—someone has said there is invasion. There are many ships, American ships, in the Straits. Castro is nervous this night. His boats run like cattle—north to Havana, south to Guantánamo. . . . They are much too busy to look, señor. It is perfect—what you say—cover, no?"

"How long will it be before they miss you?" Joe asked, rejecting Varga's optimism.

Varga couldn't say it fast enough in English, so he went to Spanish, his voice much agitated. "He was supposed to check in at Pena de Hicacos at midnight," Bingo said. "He is worried. That was three hours ago; already they are searching, and if they check the road here and the check points, they will know. . . ."

Joe let that sink in and then he added, mostly to himself, "There's two bogies out there who know we're here; by now they got everybody on the alert." Then he added, "Okay, get into the rafts. . . . Preacher, where have you been?"

Suddenly another sound came to them in the night, and they all stood still, shocked into poses of alertness, but crouching, too, as though they were afraid of what the sound meant. It was a low, moaning cry lifted into the night, almost animal in sound.

"What's that?" Joe asked, turning to point his rifle in the direction of the shack on the slope.

"It is the other one," Varga offered, his voice hesitant, uncertain.

"What other one?" Joe prodded.

"María's mother, Joe," Bingo said, his voice carrying a strange muffled cloak of awe. "She calls for María. . . ."

Joe looked confused for a moment. "Go on, get these people into the boats," he snapped at Bingo, but none of them moved, except Varga, who was anxious to get going. The Rodríguez family stayed where they were, seemingly kept together in mutual understanding of what that voice meant, reluctant to move without something being done.

Again the sound came from the hill, and then Señora Rodríguez stepped forward and in careful, precise English said slowly, in a voice almost drained by weariness, "Señor, she found out we were going. . . . She said that María had gotten word through to her that she was coming to her this night, and when she found out we were going out, she was sure that María wanted her to come out with us. . . ."

"She is with child," Varga added, adding a new problem to the load. "She is due soon to deliver that child. . . . I told her she could not come, but she said she would come or she would tell her husband. . . . I told her there was not room."

"That's right," Joe said with finality and turned to push them to the rafts. But then suddenly María was there, materializing out of the shadows of the night. She did not look at Sebastian as she moved past him to Joe, and he caught only a faint glimpse of the tears that had dried on her cheeks.

"Joe! Listen to me!" she pleaded, grabbing Joe by the arm. "It's my mother up there! You know what it cost her to come all this way!"

"I made no deal for any more people than Varga and the Rodríguez family," Joe snapped back. "Anyway, what hanky-panky did you have in mind when you sent word you'd be meeting her? You thinkin' about going to Havana tonight, María?"

"There isn't time to argue, Joe," María tried again, and then there were lights above them ripping out the black cover of sky above the shack.

"Castro's police come now!" Varga warned.

"Let's go!" Joe ordered.

"Joe!"

"Listen, María." Joe's eyes were hard. "I can't take one more person aboard this boat—we don't have enough air to go around as it is. Besides, she's pregnant, ready to give birth. You want to take a woman like that aboard under those conditions—your own mother? She could die down there!"

"They'll shoot her when they find her in that shack!" María's voice rose to a shrill cry of protest.

"I'm sorry, María—"

"Wait a minute, Joe," Sebastian suddenly cut in, but before he could say more Joe spun around and jabbed a long, accusing finger at him.

"And I don't want any sermons from you either, preacher boy!" he bellowed. "I got a contract for eight people, and if you want to stand here telling me about the value of one life in the sight of God—"

"Well, I didn't sign that contract," Sebastian shot back. All the weeks of pressure he had faced and felt were coming up in him, and his voice had risen to a clip that had even María turning quickly to look at him, even if briefly. "I took all the sweat and hell of this thing from the start—and I didn't do that to come all this way to leave one person behind just because of a little shortage of oxygen."

"You want to run up to that shack with the militia ready to come through the back door?" Joe roared back. "You're holding us back as it is. Another five minutes and all hell will break loose! You're asking us to put eight lives—yes even thirteen—on the block for one. What kind of justice is that, man of God?"

"I don't go if she doesn't," María said flatly, defiantly.

"Suits me," Joe retorted. "You planned to stay here anyway, María, the way I see it."

But María had turned quickly and started in a hurried

trot up the slope toward the shack. Sebastian went after her. From behind him he heard Joe telling Bingo in an exasperated bellow, "Go on, take them out to the boat. Give us ten minutes, and if we don't show you take them back to Florida, okay?"

Then Joe was with them, pounding behind them, swearing all the way, the lights of the oncoming militia close enough to put them in a glare close to daylight. When they got to the shack, they found María's mother just inside, sitting on the floor, her face white in the lights and her eyes big with fear. There wasn't time for a reunion between mother and daughter; Sebastian simply picked her up and started down the path toward the beach. The lights were everywhere then and the sound of equipment banging around above and behind, punctured by shouts in Spanish.

The first shots thumped against the deteriorating night and broke it open like an egg, letting loose the struggling embryos of new fear. They had gotten down to the beach level when Joe went down hard on the sand, his rifle flying off against the rocks. But he was up in a second, yelling, "Go on, go on, for the luva pete!"

They piled into the raft waiting there and began moving awkwardly out across the ugly surf, searchlights feeling for them, shots rattling behind them, the sound of bullets hitting water in buzzing ricochets all around them. María's mother lay leaning against María, prayer beads in her hands, her eyes staring in disbelief of what was happening. Joe's black sweater was sticky with blood high on his right shoulder. It didn't look good.

They made it to the boat with the bullets falling short behind them but with the realization that they were discovered and the worst was yet to come. They got down inside, leaving the raft to drift. It took an agonizingly long time to get María's mother down the small hatch, as big as she was. Sebastian went down last, pulling the hatch closed as he did so. Once inside, things were hectic—Joe had to lie down, his legs gone out from under him, Rodríguez's family were jabbering excitedly in Spanish back in the cramped cargo space, and it was difficult to find a place for María's mother to lie down in that condition.

"Okay, preacher boy," Joe said, his voice thick with pain, but his eyes boiling with the night of increasing violence, "you wanted command; you got it! You better get this boat out and under before you get—get boxed in here. . . ."

Sebastian knew then that his hour had come—he had to rise to it now or the whole operation would break apart before they made another move. Cohesion had vanished, and confusion and panic were sinking claws into all of them.

"What'll it be, padre?" El Dorado sang out then, and Sebastian looked down at the black, shiny face peering up at him, wearing a smile that either was calling his bluff or trying to pump him with a shot of adrenalin.

"Joe?" Sebastian asked, not knowing what kind of order to give that would be right.

Joe's eyes opened again, and his face was pale against the sweater. María had come up from the cargo space to look at his wound.

"What else?" Joe rasped. "Flood tanks . . . get her off this reef and out to deep water . . . put your engine at slow. . . . María, get your hands off me and get on that sonar!"

She did as she was told. Sebastian put on the phones and checked in with Bingo. He relayed orders as best he knew how, for Joe wasn't always focusing on what was being done or what was going on. El Dorado called the shots on steering and gradually they moved off the reef until he sang out, "We got ocean under us, padre!"

Joe came out of his stupor at that and shouted, "Steer course three-twenty—that's Key West on a beeline! And take her down to ninety feet!"

Sebastian stood at the periscope well, keeping his head out of the way of the water coming down through the leaky hatch that seemed to become a steady stream as they went deeper. He went back once to the cargo space to see if he could quiet them down there, but he found that some sense of order had emerged. Bodies were squeezed together, almost impossible to identify. Some were sitting, some standing. Señora Rodríguez stood in the middle, and her quiet brown eyes told him she had command. María's mother lay back on a bed of sweaters and life jackets they had managed to collect. There was a gleaming coat of greasy sweat on her face; it was a tired face, like that of the others, even the children, the kind of faces he'd seen at the Cuban Refugee Center, as if they'd been giving too much blood and getting none back. Their eyes stayed on him, for they knew what was going on—that Joe's voice dribbling out in the control room was a sign of deteriorating command—and they looked at him, studying him, looking for strong lines in his face and body that would tell them he knew how to get them out before the ocean came in on them. And maybe they could tell, for under a dictatorship people come to determine bravery easily by watching faces; it wasn't easy to keep his own face calm there in the half light without revealing some of his own uncertainties and hesitancies.

Varga was standing by the open hatch, peering up at him, his black eyes watching too, testing, the shadow from his brimmed cap hiding some of the thoughts that must have been chasing around in his own brain. Sebastian felt that maybe now was the time to get the drop on him—maybe now he should get one of those guns on board and confront Varga, for the danger could be greater from him here within than from without. He wondered why he hadn't thought of this before and maybe told Joe or María about what Mathews suspected about Varga.

But while his gaze locked on Varga's, and the two of them seemed almost to be thinking the same thing, María's voice called out, "We've got sound, coming fast!"

And Sebastian knew there wasn't time to deal with

Varga. He would have to let the string run out on the course that was set. So he simply said to them, "You must all get close together and hang on to what you can—we will soon be knocked about. If you know anything to sing, then sing, loud and happy, sí?"

They just stared at him, not comprehending. He turned back to the control room. Joe was coming out of it again and had half propped himself up against the wall, so he could watch.

"Get me an aspirin, somebody," he said in a growl that carried the tremors of pain. Sebastian dug out the first-aid kit and gave him two morphine pills. Joe swallowed them and sat back.

"How many targets?" Sebastian asked of María then.

"There are three, I think. . . . They've crossed over once and are coming back."

Sebastian looked at the depth gauge. They were down to ninety feet: water was coming in the hatch like out of a half-open faucet. It ran off the deck plates and down into the bilge trap—but it was going to pose a problem if they had to go any deeper.

The first depth charge was far away, but as the screws snarled overhead they began to march in closer, and Alphonse went through corkscrewing motions as the charges played havoc with the thin lines of buoyancy that held her here. The cork and fiberglass showered down as before, and someone began to cry in the cargo space. María left her forward position to go back and check. The patterns came at even intervals, every ten to fifteen seconds, and Alphonse began to tremble as if she was ready to come apart.

"You got—you got to get a breather," Joe said. He seemed to be getting some life back as the pain lifted under the morphine. "Try a decoy. . . . Ellie, send out one of those torpedoes. I don't know if it'll run, even . . . but if it does, it might confuse 'em a little. . . ."

El Dorado's face appeared at the hatch; he was wearing

the sonar phones now that María wasn't there to help him. There were the usual streams of sweat down his face, but his eyes were alive, caught up in the combat of the moment.

"Yeah, well your torpedoes really got some big decoy in them, Joe!" he sang out. "You look at them at all?"

"What're ya talkin' about?"

"Just this: your daddy put in two sealing compartments of electronic foils that look to me to pop out when the torpedo is running! If they do it, that'll put up enough disturbance in the water for miles and confuse their sonar up there!"

"Yeah, sure," Joe said, unconvinced. "Those torpedoes ain't ever run, either, so don't count on it!"

But El Dorado went to work, checked the tubes, then pressed the button. There was the sound of compressed air as the torpedoes shot out. They waited. After a long ten seconds, El Dorado shouted, "She's running! One of them is a dud, but the other is going straight and true! Now watch those Castro campañeros run!"

It was a while before anything happened. Then it seemed as if the boats above were scattering. The sound of their screws moved off to the left as the torpedo did its work. "Joe, I get all kinds of crazy sounds—that torpedo is throwing up more noise than a herd of porpoises!"

The depth charging had stopped now too. Sebastian had to salute El Dorado by saying, "That's the work of a genius!"

"Won't last long," Joe responded dismally. "That torpedo will run out pretty quick. They'll be back on you in five minutes!"

"Well, we got our breather, man!" El Dorado sang out.

Sebastian knew what Joe was trying to prepare them for, so he said, "Joe, what's the chances of surfacing if we leave those Castro boats behind? There's a chance when we get on top—"

"Nothing doing," Joe said flatly, still breathing rather rapidly against the shock of the wound. "Those boats will pound you down as deep as they can and as far. They want to drive you under and set you up for the Navy ships in the Straits—they know what's out there and why. . . ."

Sebastian licked lips that were caked with the chalk of his own tension and indecision as the mounting sense of destruction built up around them. Finally he turned to Joe and said, "Joe, Mathews told me that if we made the Straits between five and seven this morning, most of the fleet would be on the Bahama Bank. . . . We could surface once those boats leave us and have a better chance."

"Mathews?" Joe said, and his eyes went puffy again. "So that's the gate he gave you, hey? Well, preacher boy, don't bet on it—if he knows Varga is aboard and he gave you a rendezvous for clearance, he's probably leading you into the fleet, not out of it!"

"He's batting a thousand so far on his hunches!" Sebastian argued. "You got to trust somebody!"

"Anyway, those Castro boats won't let you surface!" Joe slammed back.

"And, amigos, neither will I." Sebastian turned to see Varga crowding up behind him with a black, snub-nosed gun in his hand. "We will not surface . . . is that clear?"

"Geez," Joe said with a half groan, and then he laughed, that usual scraping laugh that mixed derision with hopelessness. "Well, preacher boy," he said, as if he knew this moment would come, "the bag of miracles is in your hands—this is what you came out here for. All you got to do is convince your God to turn one loose!"

The loud whine of the screws came back over them in reverberating caves of the ocean, and the depth charges came again. Once more the world was full of snapping, clicking, banging sounds—and there was cork and fiberglass showering in on them again, and the sound of crying coming from the jammed cargo space. But Varga stood there hanging on to the periscope well, his eyes not wavering, his gun steady.

Chapter XIV

****

"I suppose Mathews told you about this crumb too?" Joe shouted in between the rocking explosions, as if that was so important now.

"He told me I could expect it, yes," Sebastian said defensively. He had to move around to Joe's side of the scope, since Varga had the other. Varga stood there without moving, his head cocked to one side to keep from the water coming down the hatch.

"Why didn't you say something, for pete's sake!" Joe demanded. "We could have got the drop on him on the beach!"

"You knew yourself that he wasn't necessarily a defector," Sebastian retaliated, hating to be hung up on this hook of responsibility. "Anyway, you wouldn't have believed anything the N.I.A. told me. Did anybody think about Varga in all this?"

"Well, *you* should have, for cryin' out loud!"

"Stop vexing your spirits, amigos," Varga said crisply, slowly, working the English words carefully. "If you had tried to take me, you would have given some trying moments to the Rodríguez family. For you see, only six are here—the seventh, the most important, Carlos, is—what you say in America?—my ace in the hole in Havana." Now Sebastian knew why he felt disturbed when he had looked at the Rodríguez family on the beach. "He is there, kept there until I say he can be released to the Free Cuban underground. . . . When I get to Florida and finish my work, I will contact my people in Havana and Carlos is free, but—unfortunately—not until I finish. . . . So, you are now under my command, sí? And we do not surface—we go under to Florida, for I do not intend to fall into the hands of the N.I.A. or the Navy."

"You want to risk destroying all of us to save your own skin?" Joe roared out his outrage.

Varga smiled thinly. "You have already taken on a pregnant woman who means nothing to you and cuts down your chances of life; you will do as much if not more for Carlos. . . . He is the whole Rodríguez family, he alone can make your trip worthwhile. . . ."

"Mr. Varga, we can't stay down here forever," Sebastian tried, wiping the sweat from his chin. "You can hear what's going on. We are already on a dying ship—we can only live as we surface."

María's face appeared at the cargo hatch. She could not see the gun in Varga's hand, so she knew nothing of what was going on, for the explosions killed the sound of conversation in the boat.

"You've got to slow down or get out of range of those charges," she pleaded. "My mother already feels the pains. If she has that child here she'll die. . . ."

"Preacher boy can't do it!" Joe shouted back, and his voice was mocking, riding the crest of his weakness and pain. "He's got an appointment with the N.I.A. in the Straits! It's already going on six o'clock, preacher—how about it?"

Sebastian looked back at Varga, whose eyes never left him, standing there with his brimmed cap an inch from the water spilling down from the hatch. In that moment, when Varga brushed at the water that hit off the scope and splashed into his face, Sebastian saw the only possible way out. There wasn't time to think about it or consider the awful consequences if his judgment failed.

"El Dorado," he called, "take her down twenty feet!"

"Are you out of your mind?" Joe bellowed as if he'd been jabbed by a knife. "This boat is already popping her rivets! That'll put you below a hundred feet!"

Varga's eyes didn't flicker. El Dorado's head was at the hatch, peering up in some concern, questioning the order. "We got a lady with a baby," Sebastian said. He grabbed the hatch ladder as another charge smashed into them, but his eyes did not leave Varga's, watching him carefully now. "El Dorado, give us forty-five degrees on the bow planes."

Joe swore. "You gonna dive her in?" and he coughed on his protest.

"Bingo," Sebastian said into the mouthpiece around his neck.

"Sí," Bingo answered, his voice high pitched by the closing vice of pressure on him.

"Engines at one half. . . ."

"You going to power her down?" Joe yelled. "You'll blow!"

"Planes at forty-five degrees," El Dorado sang out.

And then they were tilting down, and the depth gauge swung quickly to 105 feet, and at that moment, when there seemed to be the sound of metal scraping under intense weight, a depth charge smashed overhead. Alphonse staggered and plunged downward sickeningly—and the water from the leaky hatch suddenly shot down into the boat in a knifing, cutting spray, backed up by the new pressure that jammed the boat. It was as Joe had said—at that depth the leak turned into a mean weapon. It caught Varga behind the ear, and the man hit the deck like a hundred-pound sack of mud. He didn't move. The gun flew across the deck and landed somewhere down in the forward hatch with El Dorado.

"Take her back up, El Dorado!" Sebastian yelled, for he could sense now that Alphonse had suffered a mortal wound somewhere by this jump to a depth she was never intended for, and she rolled lazily, like a dead fish.

"What's going on?" María shouted from the cargo space, her face white, her eyes large in the horror of the moment. She looked at Varga lying in front of her. And then, as if further questions only demanded more time that she didn't have, she ducked back as her mother cried out in pain.

"We got water back here, padre," Bingo said into the phones.

Joe waited, so Sebastian told him.

"Slow her to silent running," Joe said. "You got to fix it. . . ."

And then María's face was there again. She looked at Varga, then at Sebastian. "If you turn Varga over to the N.I.A. Carlos dies—Señora Rodríguez just told me!"

"I just put out of commission the man who was going to kill your uncle," Sebastian returned.

"That's more N.I.A. information!" Joe contradicted.

"That's right! You can believe it or disbelieve it—but it's done now!"

"What if you killed Varga?" Joe yelled back, his eyes jumping with fire as he reached out to cut the pins from under Sebastian, bound on his own act of destruction. "You got to live with that, preach—and that includes any way of sweatin' the information out of Varga on how to get Carlos out."

"We're back to a hundred feet, padre!" El Dorado cut in, and it was like a reprieve, for both María and Joe were getting ready to lower on him. María disappeared back into the cargo space again, and Sebastian asked Bingo about the damage in the engine room. It was the same ballast pipe they had fixed before. He went back to do what he could. After they had patched it, Bingo pointed out the bulging plates overhead where the new plate had been welded in, the place where they had loaded the diesel. He didn't have to say anything—it was hanging there by a margin too thin to last. Another close pattern of charges could do it, and Bingo knew it too. Sebastian looked at the greasy pallor of the young Cuban's face and saw the frailty but the determination to try to hold on. "Venceremos!" Sebastian said, trying to help him, and a little smile, tired and drawn, appeared to say he would try.

Sebastian passed through the cargo space on his way back to the conning tower. María was on her knees beside her mother, who had bitten her lips to bloody patches in the pains. "She looks close to me," Sebastian said. "We better rig some kind of a screen so the kids don't see it all. . . ."

"She can't have it here!" María protested, and he looked down into a face that had lost its pointed, hard, worldly look and was almost childlike in its fear, appeal, desperation.

"She'll have it when it's time," Sebastian said simply, but he hated to think of the complications involved. "If you remember any prayers and can find it in yourself to believe a little, you might try that. . . ."

He went on, leaving María, stopping once to check Varga, who was still out. Only a faint ripple of pulse was there, but there was nothing he could do for him, though his heart cried out for something to keep the man alive.

It was now ten minutes past six, time yet to make it through on Mathews's promise. The depth charges had stopped, too, so he checked with El Dorado.

"We're probably moving deeper into our own waters," El

Dorado explained. "The Castro boats are dropping off astern. . . ."

"They don't want to chase us into our own territory?" Sebastian asked hopefully.

"Maybe, but it could be they spotted one of our picket ships coming up and are pretty sure they'll finish us off. . . ."

Sebastian pulled out the "shoehorn" sonic beam box that Mathews had given him and showed it to El Dorado. "Mathews said to stick this on the ceiling when we were in our own waters; he said he'd have copters up there to pick us up and follow us in. Should we chance using it now?"

El Dorado frowned. "Padre, you could chance it, but if one of our destroyers is anywhere around up there, that beam will bring them on us in a rush. . . . Besides, they could use their underwater ASROC missiles to fix on that beam, and we'd be dead ducks. No offense to Mathews, padre, but it's risky. . . ."

"Okay, we'll wait to see if the Straits are clear first," he said, feeling a new weight of disappointment and frustration building in him. "Let me know if you get sound."

He went back to the cargo space and rigged a screen out of old canvas tarp to shield María's mother from the others. He had hardly finished when El Dorado called, "I got sound, padre!"

He went back to check. "She's at thirty-five hundred yards. . . . It's not Castro's kind of sound, it has to be ours."

Joe, who had fallen back into a kind of stupor, came to life and said, "Of course, who else? The N.I.A. didn't hold up, hey, preach?"

"It's after six," Sebastian defended, wanting to hang on to something now, for it seemed as though this was all breaking up in his hands. "We should have made it earlier, that's all. . . ."

"So now what?"

"I don't know."

"You better make up your mind," Joe went on, his voice like a jackhammer pounding into Sebastian's hide. "You lost a lot of air through that hatch. You got about twenty pounds of oxygen left, that means about twelve minutes to live. . . ."

Sebastian lifted his head to study the enemy from this new quarter. Joe was right. "We haven't much choice then, have we?" he said, and it was as if he had arrived at the point he knew he had to reach from the first day he climbed on that PT boat.

"The ship is closing faster now," El Dorado said, and his voice was quiet, almost gentle, as if he hated to say it, to add anything more for Sebastian to think about. "She's about twenty-five hundred yards. . . ."

All he could do was wait. If Mathews's copters were up there, they might intervene. If not, well, what then?

"Her sonar is on you," Joe cut in again, his voice factual, as if he were reading it out of a book. "And she'll know what size you are—that you run about sixty feet, just the size of a good midget sub that Castro would use to run his agents into Florida. They're probably hungry to get one up there anyway, to let Castro know they mean business. . . ."

"You got any suggestions?" Sebastian said to him pointedly.

Joe shifted clumsily against the damp steel bulkhead, propping himself up as if he wanted a better look. "No, but I can give you the alternative ways of dying."

"That's a real help. . . ."

"I didn't expect it any other way," Joe retorted. "I told you this would happen. I told you you couldn't win in this business. I told you when you put God up for ante that you'd lose. . . . Now I'm gonna tell you how, so maybe then you can at least have the last minutes to see the shape of it. . . ." He paused and coughed once, as though he was getting ready to make a speech. "You can stay down here and take what they dish out, which will be plenty and final . . . or you can take your time and suffocate as your air runs out . . . or you can try going up, and with this boat going up at five feet every thirty seconds it'd take you ten minutes to make surface, all the time running through a shower of charges. . . ."

"That all?" Sebastian said, too tired to raise up any more defenses.

He grabbed the periscope well as El Dorado said, "Coming over on a pattern!"

"Grab hold down there in cargo!" Sebastian yelled.

The chug-a-chug-a-chug of the screws went over, on by, and then back again. They made the sweep four times, thumping out the signal for what was coming down, as if they wanted to be real sure before unloading. On the fifth pass, it came—the sound was crushing, worse than what the Castro boats had given them, and Sebastian yelled, to relieve the awful pressure of those explosions in his ears and to yell that they were killing their own people. And in between the blasts he heard Bingo's voice over the phone: "Jesucristo, Espíritu Santo . . ." and it startled him that Bingo was praying, trying to rebuild the bridge back to God that he had torn down years before.

"O God," Sebastian said, his lips up tight against the wet brass of the periscope well, "help us all . . . help us all. . . ."

And then, as he heard the ship coming back again, he suddenly saw it coming through the distorted focus of his memory, hazy in its outline, but there nevertheless. And he knew he would have to try it, wild as it might be. So he got down next to Joe, who was still half out, and he yelled for El Dorado to come help him. Then María was there too, coming to report on her mother but waiting instead to see what they would do.

"Listen to me, Joe," Sebastian said, holding Joe off the steel bulkhead, hitting him lightly on the cheeks. "Your father said it in one of those manuals: this sub was built with angular reinforcing bow chambers—Joe, you got to listen now; we can't do it alone unless we know—your father said this ship could blow forward ballast, keep her stern tanks full, and shoot to the surface on full power. . . ."

Joe opened his eyes and stared at Sebastian as if he'd said something unforgivable. "You run out of miracles, preach?"

"Look, the only miracle God gives sometimes is what He puts in your hands," Sebastian countered, and then the charge hit them again and there was the sound of breaking glass as the guages smashed under it. It seemed to snap Joe out of his gradual slide into unconsciousness.

"No good, preacher," he said. "That's why . . . they called my old man nuts. . . . No sub can blow up through the water at the speed you're thinkin' and not crack open under that pressure change. . . ."

"But those chambers, Joe," Sebastian fought back. "You've got to tell me if that's what he had in mind."

Joe laughed, as if he thought all this was too comical to keep serious. "Sure, he had it in mind!" he snapped, and he looked at El Dorado and laughed. "But you can't do it and live!"

"We've got to do it," Sebastian said, for all of them, "or die here."

"And what do you do when you get to the surface?" Joe shot back, and he leaned forward to emphasize what he wanted to say. "You got no identification . . . no flag. . . . They'll be running you down, if they don't see colors in a hurry after you break surface, even ten seconds after. They'll run you over; they won't stop to ask questions. . . ."

Sebastian couldn't say anything to that. He looked at El Dorado and María, then at Bingo, who had come up from the engine room some time during the exchange. Their eyes admitted the futility of the situation. None of them had thought of a flag or any such identification. It seemed ridiculous to think of it, for whose would they run with anyway?"

So Sebastian put it to them, because he didn't want everything hanging on him alone. They stood there holding on to what they could while another pattern of charges hit close like a string of Chinese firecrackers going off, only a thousand times louder and more deadly. Alphonse was dying now, they knew it. He saw it in their faces—sadness, resignation.

He explained what he wanted to do, and they said nothing when he finished. They looked once back at the Rodríguez family huddled in the cargo space, as if somehow wishing they could have gotten them out first. El Dorado could only grin when Sebastian asked him—it didn't matter to him which way they went now. María looked at him with a long, hard look, trying to tell him she was in a dilemma—she was torn between what that wild ride to the surface would do to her mother and what was left if they stayed here. Bingo, his young face worked over with new lines of maturity that had cut into him in these few hours, simply stared upward toward the charges coming down, as if he didn't want to have any part in such a decision. . . .

It was up to Sebastian then, and it was right that it should be. He had brought them here; now it was up to him to decide the final move. They listened a moment to the faint bleatings of Alphonse getting louder in these depths, the sound of her life dribbling out inexorably through her battered plates. They looked at him, then, wanting to know, so he said, "Let's go the only way any ship should go, at least fighting for life. We'll blow tanks!"

Once he had said it, they seemed to straighten up, glad to know what was coming, trying to brace up to it. Bingo hesitated just for a moment and then took out a square of blue cloth from his pocket and extended it. Sebastian took it and unfolded it—it was a four-foot cotton flag with a white cross on a blue background; there were smears of red on two corners.

Joe had come to life again and he chuckled hoarsely, as

if this were a dirty picture in Sebastian's hands. "His old man's flag," he said, his voice accusing. "When his daddy died praying to the Virgin, he died with that flag on him. It didn't do him any good then; now it's the kid's last chance to try. . . . You got nothin' to lose, preacher. The ship up there will recognize that as nothing more than a piece of laundry in the wind, but you might as well fly it. . . . If you're going down in the name of God, you might as well tell everybody. . . ."

There was nothing in Bingo's face to contradict what Joe said, no indication that he was offering this emblem because of his confidence in what it stood for.

"You know what he carries it for?" Joe piped up again, and his voice continued to carry its note of mad humor. "Yeah, a snot rag. . . . He washes his feet, he wipes with that. . . . The grease and oil of a thousand lubricated engine parts are on that chunk of rag, preacher, so don't think it's been some kind of prayer shawl or even a good-luck charm to that gusano!"

Bingo didn't refute it. But for right now that piece of "rag" had taken on another dimension; for him it was the fountain again, different characters, same issue. Now he was pushing Sebastian, like Joe, to see if he would put this seal of God on these few moments of labeled destruction. He was no different from any of them right then. Even El Dorado and María looked on with the same interest of people watching a poker game when someone calls and someone else has to lay it out on the table. The whole operation had built to this one moment—for all men were the same, maybe, when they came down to the wire as they did here now; whether in curiosity or desperation, they wanted to know if the claims of God could be supported. For Bingo, there could be no real bridge building back to God until he saw how far Sebastian was willing to go; the flag became the symbol of the challenge. Sebastian realized that Bingo must have carried it a long time, using it as he did but waiting for this opportunity. And he knew too that there would be no reaching them with words or arguments about spiritual reality until he was willing to break that hatch and run this standard to the mast.

Now that he realized the shape of the trap he had fallen into, the crippling extent of it, far beyond what he had anticipated, he felt the sharp pangs of reticence. He wanted to argue, to charge these events to forces outside of God's responsibility; he wanted God off the hook. It wasn't fair to push God to reverse the very nature of the laws He had ordained. . . .

And this was what Joe was laughing about—even though he should die here, he was going out with a laugh, because not only was he sure they couldn't get out of this but that Sebastian, the confident ambassador of Deity, would have to commit the act of final insult himself on that name.

But there was no choice. And there wasn't time. "Okay," he said, clearing his throat, "let's put it all on the line."

Bingo turned without a further word and went aft to the engine room. El Dorado and María took up their stations in the forward control room. Joe lay where he was, staring at him with those incriminating eyes, a grin on his face as if chiseled out of cold stone, lifeless, without warmth, twisted by his amazement that Sebastian could continue to go through the motions in this situation.

"Stand by," Sebastian said, and Joe chuckled, as if hearing a command from him was ludicrous. He waited to make sure they were holding on to something and that the ship was passing over them, then he said, "Blow forward ballast!" The depth charges hit hard again, and the boat seemed to snap taut in the pounding. The lights went down too, but Sebastian was not paying attention to any of this now. He computed that they had about three minutes to make it, clear the surface, and try to identify themselves or wave off that ship.

Alphonse's deck tilted astern as she sank with her stern ballast full. When she was pitched to a 30-degree angle, he said into the phones to Bingo, "Engine full ahead. . . ."

Terrible sounds began as they started their crazy ride up, some of them coming from the cargo space and María's mother, who had to take this change of pressure on her already tortured body, most of them from the ship herself: sometimes a low moaning whistle, sometimes a noise like pencils snapping in somebody's hands, as the plates expanded rapidly with the pressure change . . . and there was the sound of water too, rushing behind the thin hull, splashing in the bilges . . . the sound of things banging around, falling apart, tumbling out of place . . . and the sound of his own yelling against the pressure that hit his ears, and a roaring last appeal to God not to desert them now, not to let the thin stream of humanity here be snapped into oblivion without one single demonstration of Himself . . . even if it was foolish to push a submarine like this in a crazy, rocketing ride to the surface a hundred feet up, expecting God to intervene, to reverse the laws of gravity and sea pressure whose natural right it was to smash the thin and fragile lines of a boat hung together by the weak patchwork quilts of welded plates and the ineptitude of the human factor who manned her . . . to answer the wild hopes of a boy who had lost his confidence in the goodness of God . . . to answer the bitter soul of a girl who had lost touch with anything good . . . to answer the black man, the drifter, who sang his heartache and laughed his anger and wanted so much to believe . . . to answer a man who still cried in the night, whose whole life was one of running, searching, railing, beating his fists against the brass door of his own defeats . . . and for six other people, who had hung on to one thorny rod of hope for this moment, so close to freedom, God, yet who in a few seconds could lose it all . . . and even for Varga, that insensitive bulk rolling around the conning tower like a piece of furniture . . . even he might look back if he were still alive to a moment when he came to life by a Divine intervention . . . and for me, God, because I committed them all to this, and maybe it was wrong, but I didn't want to have all of hell laughing in your face, either. . . .

And then there came a trembling sigh from Alphonse, and she rolled far to starboard, so that he fell hard against the hatch ladder. At the same time, El Dorado yelled from somewhere beyond the sounds of breaking things and sucking sounds and water, "She's got her bow out, padre!" and there was in that voice some cresting notes of jubilance, a salute to the impossible.

"Can we blow stern ballast now, El Dorado?" Sebastian shouted back, but María had already hit the stern ballast levers. So he waited, counting those precious seconds while the stern came up enough for him to crack the hatch. He heard Alphonse gurgling again, and there were those same snapping sounds in her plates, and he knew she didn't have far to go; she was dying, deep in her innards, in that place that kept her concept of soul alive . . .

He went up the ladder and hit the hatch. The water came down on him with a shock, but he fought through it; then he was up to the bridge, to sun and water and glimpses of fleecy clouds . . . and he turned to the left, and he saw her. A moan came from him, for there she was, coming back off her circle and so close he could see her anchor bays like two big eyes staring at him, her bow cutting the blue water in a murderous, purposeful ride to destruction. . . .

He knew there wasn't going to be time. He grabbed the periscope well and climbed up its slippery sides, and he fumbled with the blood-smeared flag with the small white cross against the blue—it seemed so inadequate, in this moment of rushing disaster—and he thought, how foolish! How insane! How even comical!

And he finally secured it, and the wind took it and snapped it out. He knew the captain must have tried; he saw the big, gray bow coming down on him, but it was turning, and the white beard under her bow slackened some so he knew the captain had cut speed. . . . Maybe he saw the flag—it would be good if he had tried because of the flag—but maybe he didn't see it and would have tried to turn anyway. . . . What did it matter now? But he saw that her turning wasn't going to be enough. . . . She came into Alphonse off the starboard bow, and her big gray hull went over the sub with hardly a sound as if there were some understanding between them. The sub heeled over, but that was all . . . and then the big destroyer passed, her speed carrying her a good 300 yards before she could turn back . . . and he saw the boat being lowered to come to their assistance.

He dropped down through the conning tower hatch. Already the Rodríguez children were scrambling around him up the ladder under prodding from their mother. He heard the sound of water rushing in from some place and knew Alphonse hadn't come all that way without serious damage. He went into the cargo section, where María was on her knees, bending over her mother anxiously. Bingo was there too, completely soaked, water running off his face as if he'd just come out of a shower. María's mother was doing her best to get up from the deck under María's urging, but the wild ride to the surface had squeezed her too hard, so that she could only lie there, breathing heavily against the contractions that obviously bit deep.

"We haven't got much time," Sebastian said, trying to be understanding of their predicament but at the same time communicating the shortness of life in Alphonse.

"We can't force her through that conning tower hatch," María argued, turning her anxious eyes up to him. "She'll never make it, she's too close."

"Padre, the hole in the engine room, where we put in the diesel," Bingo offered. "She pop like a cork when we surface . . . lots of room there. . . ."

"Okay, we'll have to try it," Sebastian said. So he and Bingo picked her up, trying to brush María aside as she hung on to her mother's hand, as if this was going to help matters any.

When they got her back into the jammed engine room that was knee high in water, Sebastian called to the sailors on deck to lend a hand. Through clumsy shifting and rough straining shoves upward, during which she screamed in pain, they got her up through the jagged, blasted-out hole. Sebastian yelled to the sailors that the lady was ready to deliver a baby and to take care. Then he sent María on up to be with her mother. He went back to the conning tower hatch and called two more sailors down to get Varga up. He didn't know if the man was dead or alive, but he wasn't going to assume anything at this stage.

Then it was Joe's turn. He got up dazed, staggering, trying to focus on Sebastian and then Bingo, but he was practically out on his feet. "Don't forget Ellie!" he managed to yell from topside as Bingo went up with him to make sure he made the boat.

Sebastian crawled up the deck that was slanting dangerously forward now until he got to the forward hatch over the control room. Something was wrong. El Dorado stood quietly in the dark hole, the water up to his waist. Sebastian saw that part of the forward torpedo section and bow was up flush against his back, pinning him there against the opposite wall of the compartment. He knew then that El Dorado wasn't coming out.

"Let me help you," Sebastian offered. He would have torn that metal apart with his hands rather than see El Dorado have to go like this.

A slow smile had come on El Dorado's mouth, and there was a quietness in his eyes that stopped Sebastian. "Padre, half of me below the waist won't move—I think maybe some of it's missing," he said. He had his guitar around his neck and was holding it above the water rising slowly in the compartment. He strummed the strings once, fondling them carefully. "Padre, there's that minister I cut up, remember? I want you to do something for me. Find him in the Miami phone book—his name is Parks, Reverend John—you call him, tell him I'm sorry for the way I humiliated him. . . . He was right; I never did intend to marry that cute white girl. . . . I was only lookin' for trouble. . . . You call him, hear?"

"I'll do it, El Dorado. I—I'm sorry it had to be our ship that did it. . . ."

"Pshaw! I wouldn't want it to be Castro's, that's for sure. . . . Anyway, things are kinda balanced up now. . . ." He lifted his eyes off the strings, and there was a faraway look there, like he was seeing something that he'd been seeking for a long time. "Don't you worry none about me, padre . . . Remember I told you I been huntin' for the sun all my life? Look at this place." He grunted in amazement as he looked around the dark, wet, flooding compartment. "Bright as noon . . . you said I could reach out and touch Him . . . this Son of God . . . this Jesus. . . . Just ask in your need, you said. . . . Well, I got the chance to ask and the kind of push I needed, too . . . and I got me the sun. Yes, sir, padre, I got me the sun. . . ."

The boat trembled again, and the water came up on the strings of the guitar where his black fingers rested. Then he reached up and took Sebastian's hand, gently, and it was like a child's touch, reassuring, full of confidence, a "though I'm sick it's all right" kind of touch. "Don't feel bad about losin' some of this pot, padre. . . . This old cat, Alphonse, had nine lives, and me, El Dorado, I had nine too. . . . I was gonna jump ship in Cuba, you know that? What did I have to go back to? Nothin' but ten years in the pen. Why didn't I jump? Well, I kept lookin' at you, padre, and I figured there's a man that's got everything to go back to . . . ain't got no business here . . . but he comes anyway . . . so I figured if he thinks it's important to come all this way to bring out eight people who ain't more'n a drop in the bucket, considerin', then maybe it's the least I can do—well, I'm real glad I decided to stay aboard. . . . So now me and Alphonse run out on our averages, but like I said, we ain't goin' ashamed. . . . No, sir, padre, we're both goin' in glory, man. . . . Muchas gracias for ridin' along. . . . The roof, it don't leak no more. . . ."

And the boat jerked again, and the death rattle was louder now. Someone was yelling for Sebastian to hurry up. Then, as if a curtain were drawn between them, El Dorado went back to his guitar while the water seemed to turn red around him. Reluctantly, Sebastian withdrew and climbed to the upper deck and the boat waiting for him.

"Where's Ellie?" Joe demanded from the stern of the launch.

"He's got an appointment somewhere else," Sebastian said. Nobody said anything. The sailor up forward pushed the boat away from the awash decks of Alphonse, and they moved off about twenty yards. The coxswain stopped there and cut the motor. They should have gone on to the destroyer, what with María's mother so close to her time, but somehow nobody wanted to just run out of there, with Alphonse slowly going under and El Dorado still inside. Sebastian saw that he had left the flag on her periscope well, and he thought that didn't look so good, the symbol of the church going under; it seemed like failure. But then he thought of El Dorado, and he knew it was right.

So with the sea strangely calm and the bright morning sun giving the water that snapping blue color, they watched as Alphonse settled deeper by the bow. And across that carpet of optimistic blue they heard it, coming through that hole in her bow where El Dorado stood, then carried too through that jagged gash in her stern decks, running on the light breeze blowing toward them—the sound of the guitar, faint at first, muffled in the casement of steel. It seemed to grow stronger, and with it came El Dorado's high-pitched, clear, childlike voice, singing in Spanish, the language of his youth, rising to points of exultation, flying like a young girl skipping to church, and finally shooting like an arrow with decisiveness. There was a pause, and it seemed as though he was repeating it, but it was lost as the bow sank and the sound was gone. But Bingo translated it for all of them, his voice subdued:

"See the sun how bright and glorious!
Shines upon this Alphonse now—
'Tis the warmth of God victorious
Chasing death and hell below.

"Now I rise to meet the morning,
Gone the night of bitter shade,
Look how bright the vision changing,
All for me, this splendor made!"

And then only the echo was left. Alphonse hung there for a few seconds, her flag snapping out into the breeze, as if she was proud of it and wanted them to see it—and then she was gone, with hardly a sound or a bubble.

There was silence a long time, except for the soft whimpering of one of the twins. They simply sat and stared, each one of them collecting the feelings, the thoughts, the emotions to be looked at later. Nobody tried to say anything. It was a moment to let remain as it was, cast finally as it was intended in some eternity past. And then the motor coughed to life and they moved off briskly toward the destroyer.

When they came near the ship, Sebastian looked at them —but he could see nothing in their faces of victory. El Dorado was dead, Alphonse had sunk, Varga was close to dying, Carlos was locked up in Príncipe Castle, probably forever. And just to nail the lid down on that pall that hung over them, Joe said, "You lost your flag, preacher."

Chapter XV

****

They were taken to the submarine base at Key West. When they landed, Joe, Varga, and María's mother were taken to the hospital; María was allowed to accompany her mother. The Rodríguez family went to a special building for immigration clearance. Bingo, who had astonished the destroyer's engineering officer with his account of Alphonse's wild ride to the surface, was led off for more of the same at the submarine engineering section.

Sebastian was put up in one of the spare officer's rooms. He stayed there for most of the day, waiting for clearance. He slept some, but it was fitful—he had too many loose ends to tuck in. Finally, at eight that evening, Mathews showed up. When Sebastian responded to the knock and opened the door, they both stood looking at each other like two boxers who meet casually on the street after a fight.

"I'm here to take you to Miami," Mathews said with a twitch of a smile.

"Special escort?" Sebastian replied, backing into the room to let him in.

"Could be. . . . Are you ready?"

"I need to call Jane MaConnel. Nobody would let me telephone today."

"I already notified her. . . . She flew in at three this afternoon."

Sebastian savored that a minute, then asked, "How much time you giving me in Miami?"

"The day after tomorrow we booked you on a flight," Mathews said drily. "You're open season now—the sooner we get you out of the area the better."

"What about the rest of them?"

"Varga died a few hours ago." Sebastian winced inwardly at that revelation, but he also knew there was nothing more he could do about it. "María's mother delivered a boy—María got to name him. Alphonse San Roman Lopez. How's that for a handle?"

"Lopez?" Sebastian asked, not fitting the name.

"María's father died a few years back—her mother married again . . ."

"Oh," Sebastian said simply.

"Anyway, she and María are going back by ambulance tomorrow," Mathews went on. "These Cuban women are made of stout stuff; deliver a baby one day, out shopping the next. Actually they want to get in on Rodríguez's homecoming party for his family tomorrow night. Joe won't get out for a week anyway."

"Then can I see them before we go?"

Mathews shrugged. "The hospital is about a hundred yards down the road."

When Sebastian turned into the private room at the hospital, he saw Jane first, standing on the opposite side of the bed. Something had happened to her. The bony, flighty, spectral look of fear had been rubbed down some—something had laid a hand on her, softened the line of her face, cut down the jagged ends of the pointed and prickly personality that had been developed by her nightmare of the past years. The Jane he'd known in 1959 was coming back, and the prospect excited him.

But it was Joe who first saw him move into the room, and he began to push himself up against the pillows as if digging in for an attack. His right hand shot out for the crumpled pack of cigarettes on the side table, and he had lit one up before Sebastian got to his bedside.

"Come to crow, hey, preacher?" he growled. Jane looked up quickly in surprise and smiled, and there was a message in that too—something had happened here between them, something Sebastian knew he would never find out, something they were keeping to themselves. "Well, you got nothin' to crow about in my book," Joe went on. "You lost Alphonse, Varga, Carlos, and—El Dorado. . . ." When he mentioned El Dorado, something of the petulant growl died in his voice, and he puffed up a cloud of blue to give him protection. "So in my book the best you got out of this is a draw . . . and don't start in on me with the old hat that we're all safe and sound and how can you charge it to anything but God . . . so if you're lookin' for converts here, forget it, understand?"

It was obvious Joe wasn't going to shift out of character now. He had everything going against him, of course—he was clean shaven, he smelled of fresh soap, and he was hung up there helpless with that shoulder. The vehemence didn't come off very strong or very true—but he was going to fight it to the last.

"Come on, Joe," Jane said then, and there was no grating, snapping sound to her voice now. It was a tone of indulgence, as if she alone knew that behind all that growling was something contradictory he was guarding. "Why don't you tell him the rest?"

Joe looked confused, embarrassed, as if a closely guarded secret of his was out. Sebastian felt he ought to ease it, so he said, "I only came to say good-by—and to make sure you two are okay. . . ."

"Okay? Why shouldn't we be?" Joe snapped in a huff. He reached over to the drawer of the side table and took out a check, handed it to Sebastian. "There's your fourteen hundred bills, preacher. I make debts, but I don't take charity. And we didn't smash the piggy bank either. Rodríguez paid up, and the Navy's going to give us a chunk of money for the plans on Alphonse. We hit the jackpot, preacher boy, like I planned it, so everything is just dandy—got it?"

"You want to shake hands on it, anyway?" Sebastian offered. Joe stared at the outstretched hand, a look of incredulity on his face. A few days ago he would have spit into it; now it was like a bouquet of flowers stuck out there. He looked up quickly at Sebastian, almost in an appeal not to push him too fast.

"I ain't promising anything," he said, and his voice was defensive but not half as gruff. "I ain't gonna run to no churches or start a rash of prayin', you understand? That woman of mine says she does, so don't you start no more trouble, get it?"

Sebastian knew then that this was as far as he could take Joe. And seeing him smile, Joe put his hand into Sebastian's, almost afraid it would stab him with holy dynamite. "Keep your bilges dry, Joe," Sebastian said and moved for the door, Jane following. Through the smoke screen he thought he saw that old go-for-broke grin, but now it was more like a kind of salute to the impossible, to the incredulous that had happened to him, to what was yet unfolding before him.

Out in the hall, Jane said, her voice riding a crest of hope, "He growled about you losing, but this afternoon he had to finally admit it: he said nobody could have known that he carried the shame of Alphonse on his back all his life. He always said he'd have to sail her to prove his father right, to rid himself of the doubts, the feelings of stigma. Then, he said, you came here straight out of nowhere and committed him to it in just one sentence—you forced him to sail her, prove her one way or the other. And when you shot her to the surface like you did—you of all people—something he would never have tried—well, that and what he said about El Dorado's death. He said, when you add it all up, maybe there isn't too much to argue about."

"You think Joe is out on that bridge with you, Jane?" he asked.

"All I know is I prayed this afternoon out loud and he let me, and during it, he put his hand on my head, like he was trying to touch God through me."

"That's good enough, Jane," Sebastian said and took her hand. "He's just one foot out of the Kingdom. Can you lead him the rest of the way?" She smiled, biting her lip against the tears. "You're crying, Jane," he added with a smile. "Not bleeding, crying." He knew it was time to leave her then, so he said, "Remember, if you need me again, just drop me a line."

He didn't say anything to Mathews until they got out on Highway One, on the way to Miami. Then he took out the shoehorn-shaped sonic detector and laid it on the shelf of the dashboard in front of the steering wheel. "You know now why I didn't have any use for that," he said mildly enough but wanting to jab really hard on the issue. Then when Mathews didn't answer, he went on, "You set us up out there," and he made it a point of fact, not a question. "You used me to lay the trap. Between five and seven, you said. Stick the sonic beam on the ceiling of the sub . . . but all the time you must have known it would bring the Navy down on us."

He tried not to make it sound like a whining child, but his sense of indignation was rising within him now. Mathews lit his pipe with ceremonial flourishes, and then he said, "Our information was correct. When we saw that single Navy destroyer coming through off the schedule, then we had to make the choice: try to break in on a classified operation and alter it or let it go and hope you'd make it out on your own. All things considered, it was the only choice we could make." Sebastian wanted to insist that it was the choice Mathews wanted to make anyway, but before he could voice that, Mathews went on, "Reverend, all of us want to be humanitarian in our choices in life. But in international relationships there are no black and white choices like in religion. I told you we had to keep Varga out, save Rodríguez. We've done our part to rescue Cubans, keep Free Cuban hopes alive too—but in this case we had to play it closer to what we figured was the bigger cheese, and that was the life of Rodríguez. And if you want to stay in this league, you'll have to learn to live with these things."

It sounded so natural, normal, even logical coming from him in that dry, factual, categorical tone of voice. It left Sebastian without a retaliation for the moment. And the matter of choices. He realized what Mathews was trying to say—for he had made a choice out there himself, Maria's mother over thirteen others, Varga over Carlos. Thinking about that now pushed him off balance.

"Anyway," Mathews went on, "you kind of made us eat crow too."

"Oh?" Sebastian said, still feeling bilious about it all. "Because we beat that destroyer?"

"No. The fact is, you came out with the biggest fish since Castro took over Cuba, one we've tried to get for a long time."

"One of the Rodríguezes?"

"No—Señora Lopez. Nobody else knows yet, not even Rodríguez, but she came out with microfilm showing Castro's plans for guerrilla infiltration of the hemisphere for the next five years."

Sebastian didn't know what all that meant—he simply sat there stupefied by the twists and turns of this incident that kept growing heads as he talked. He waited, digesting that.

"You didn't know she was coming?" he asked, with curiosity.

"If we had, we wouldn't have let that destroyer clobber you out there. . . . We've been trying to get her out for the last five years, but since her husband is the key man in Castro's guerrilla activities, she was under close security guard all the time. Lopez didn't trust her, she was too close to the Rodríguezes and he knew that she wanted to join María in Florida. . . ."

"So how did she decide to hook on to Alphonse?"

"Well, the way she told me at the hospital today, Señora Rodríguez told her a year ago she was going to try to get out with her family. . . . Señora Lopez wanted to go too, but they had to find a way to get by that security guard. . . . Then she got pregnant—by accident or design, I don't know, but I don't think a forty-six year-old woman would let that happen by accident—and they figured then that they'd wait until she was a week to delivery. Lopez would relax the security guard, knowing his wife wouldn't try to bolt that close to countdown . . . so Señora R. got the word out for February twelfth through Varga, who shot it to Rodríguez by underground radio. . . ."

"But she wasn't on the beach that night," Sebastian insisted.

"That's where María complicated things by sending the radio message that she would see her mother in February. Her mother was in a tough spot: was María coming in to defect or coming in to take her out? After all, she only wanted to be with María, in or out of Cuba. So she decided to wait in the shack for María to make the choice—if she chose to go back into Cuba, that meant they'd have to get by the road blocks and get the film back into Lopez's wall safe before he found out, a very tough deal indeed."

Sebastian was intrigued; and his earlier anger subsided. "So it was María's choice that swung it for her mother?"

Mathews laid his pipe down on the dashboard shelf. "Not quite," he said. "Joe told me that María could not have convinced him to wait for her mother by herself—it was when you stood up for her that the balance was tipped. Joe said he wasn't going to let you be a hero at his expense, whatever that meant. . . ."

Sebastian knew all right what that meant. "I almost didn't do it," he said then. "If I had played it the way you do, the big picture, I would have sold out María's mother there—for a few pounds of oxygen, yet—because Joe had a good point. . . ."

Mathews smiled thinly. "That is the major difference between politics and religion, as you once said, reverend."

Sebastian nodded, finding it difficult to argue with this man who made it all sound so right.

"How about the fleet invasion scare that got Castro's boats diverted—that your game?"

"No, we wouldn't have dared that. Probably Rodríguez flashed the radio alarm hoping the Castro monitor would pick it up. Apparently they did."

"I suppose it was you who beat me up in the hotel?"

Mathews shifted in his seat, looking uncomfortable for the first time. "Sorry about that, but we had to be sure of you. If you ran after that beating, we knew we could dismiss you then as just another kook—but since you stayed, we had to confront you with the operation and, as you intimated, use you."

Everything was being nailed down professionally and methodically now. There wasn't much more to say. "As long as we are tucking it all in," Sebastian went on, "how about that destroyer? Did he recognize the flag?"

Mathews seemed reluctant to answer, as if he knew how important that little item was to Sebastian. "I'd like to tell you he did—but the captain decided to make his evasion when his sonar told him you had blown for the surface."

Sebastian let that go and then asked, "What about Carlos?"

"We'll try to get him out. It won't be easy without Varga, but we'll try."

They drove a long time then in silence. Mathews put his pipe back into his mouth as a sign he was through talking. Sebastian looked at him once, wanting to get more satisfaction. But he knew it was done now.

They said no more to each other until they drove up to the hotel in Miami. When Sebastian opened the door to get out, Mathews held him by saying, "There's one other thing." Sebastian paused and looked at him. Mathews appeared to be debating something; then, as if he were still peering at a puzzle, he said, "I think you knew it was going to be a hundred to one against your getting out of this alive. Yet you went anyway. I've been thinking about that for the last couple of days, and I don't get any easy answers. I suppose it'll be found in what makes a man of God tick—I don't have much time to chase that around, but I'm going to think about it anyway."

Sebastian sensed it had taken quite a bit for the man to make this admission. He got out of the car and leaning back to look at Mathews through the open window, said, "Thanks for the ride . . . and may your pursuit of God be a rewarding one."

The next afternoon he picked up the paper and saw that Mathews had released the story. It told of the sub, the rescue, and the big play about Maria's mother, but wisely there was no mention of the microfilm that was smuggled out. The paper also stated that Señor Hector Rodríguez would give a speech that evening at his Coral Gables residence about the future of

Free Cuba. Sebastian decided to go—because there was at least one he still had to see.

When he got to the mansion that night, the grounds were jammed with people. A band was playing, Rodríguez was making speeches, there were cheering and fireworks, and the Cuban flag was run up the flagpole. It was like Bingo had said—they had hope again and the revival of a cause. It appeared that Rodríguez had not lost anything of his political ambition or power by the absence of Carlos; it seemed he was now at the apex of his popularity.

Sebastian managed to get to the house and decided to try the library first. Somehow he sensed she'd be there watching the festivities. He was right. She was standing leaning against the door frame leading out to the terrace, her trim, shapely body silhouetted against the flash of fireworks beyond her.

He stood behind her a long time, waiting, content to watch her, noting the beauty of her figure but also the almost fragile tilt to her body which did not become her, for she was by nature as resolute as a marble column.

"Come to find something to balance the books?" she said then, not turning to face him but knowing he was there, as if she had been waiting too. "Some sweetening to vindicate all those miles in the name of God?"

Her voice wasn't bitter or even sarcastic—just factual, not allowing any room for real questions at all.

"I suppose so," he said. "But I don't keep the score card—God does."

Another cheer ripped the night, and he thought he saw her shiver. She turned then and with her back to the door frame, her arms folded across the pale pink of her dress, the upper part of her face in the shadows, hidden from the bright moon, she said, "In a minute my uncle is coming for me to join him down there and beat the drum for the Free Cubans, so there isn't much time." Her tone was rather patronizing now, as if somehow she had to say all this to balance things up, either for him or for herself. "I actually didn't think you'd come, I was hoping you wouldn't, so I wouldn't have to go over it again. But then maybe it's best." She sighed, and it was the culmination of a lot of thinking, some indecision, some blind alleys and dead ends. "Let's get to the point—I'm still trying to sort things out, so I can't give you any conversion language, if that's what you expect. The biggest blow has been for me to realize that I couldn't make a choice for Cuba when I was so close—I found I had grown a bourgeois heart full of sensitivity, and when it came to a choice I had to pick human values, the very thing I criticized you for in this room, remember?"

He nodded.

"All right," and she took another deep breath, satisfied that the first admission was past. "You might as well know, too, if you don't already, that all of us were fighting that boat for one reason: we were fighting you more than anything else, trying to prove we could make that thing go without a miracle from God . . . and it looked like we did, everything went pretty normal, except for that crazy ride to the surface . . . and then El Dorado. . . . Only we who knew the dark, bitter spirit that was El Dorado can realize what happened to him when he sang that song before he died. . . ."

A splash of fireworks lit up the terrace, and he saw her face then, and her eyes were not changing colors like before. It was as if a fever had died in her. The smile on her mouth was almost whimsical; she seemed to be seeing things of new dimension, intrigued by the mystery of it all.

"What does it all add up to?" she went on, her tone almost professorial, taking it a point at a time, exposing it, thesis, antithesis, synthesis. "I don't know—I guess I'm a good Capitalist but maybe only a weak Marxist. Maybe now I can take the Libertad without feeling it's a dead-end street—you got that home to me in that wrestling match on the beach in Cuba. . . . I can see now that there could be something more beautiful for me beyond that." She paused again as the cheers pounded the night. "I can't completely unwind the spring of my bitterness and disillusionment toward God—not yet, anyway—but I touched something," and he saw her lips press firmly together as if she was finding it hard to express. "I touched a vein of—of understanding, and on that perhaps I can find my way back. . . ."

She turned quickly to face out toward the cheers, her back to him, as if she didn't want him looking at her. Then, in a lighter tone, to direct attention from herself, she added, "You must have made quite an impression on my uncle; he had all those statues of war heroes carried off the lawn today. . . . He put saints in their place, bought out every monument and memorial garden in town, almost. . . . Everyone from Jesus Christ to Augustine to John F. Kennedy is out there now. . . . That's ridiculous to you, probably, but for my uncle that's a long jump back to faith of any kind in the church, quite a move indeed. . . ."

Someone was calling to her now from down on the lawn below the balcony. She turned and walked up to him. The smell of sweet lily and orange blossoms was there, and her eyes still had those signs of the highly spirited person that she was, but he saw the contrasting softness of humility there, too. She reached up then and kissed him lightly on the cheek. "I know your heart belongs to someone else, maybe to God only, a woman can tell," she said. "But I wanted that to remember. . . . When I kissed you at the hangar, you knocked the trim out of me. It was good, clean. That's when the battle started about Cuba. . . . I fought it and you all the way to that beach, but I can leave you with that, at least: you measured up for what you stand for. That means a lot in my book. . . . Good-by, and keep your eagle's wings, reverend!"

His flight was booked for the following afternoon. He debated whether to stay longer but decided he could do no more here. His presence would only rob them of what they had found, force them to further introspection that might do more harm than good.

But he was concerned that he couldn't get hold of Bingo. He phoned the Rodríguez residence, tried Key West—he wasn't to be found. He hated to leave without one word with the young Cuban.

He finally went down to the lobby to check out. An envelope was there, and he opened it to find a check for $10,000 made out to him by Rodríguez. The note simply said:

You must come back and play billiards with me, padre! It would do me much honor. Adiós!

Sebastian thought of the check, then decided to send it to the Reverend John Parks in the name of El Dorado Santos to be used for the rehabilitation of Cuban refugees. He also wrote Rodríguez to that effect.

Then he went out on the sidewalk to hail a cab. That's when he saw the jeep and Bingo, sitting there casually as if he knew all the time that this was the day and the time.

"I take you to the airport, padre?" he sang out, jumping down to the sidewalk. The smile was there, the magnetism, but a cover of maturity was on it now—he had crossed the line, maybe too early, into manhood.

"I can think of no better way to go out," Sebastian said with a smile and threw his bag into the back.

"Ah, I got one better way," Bingo responded, and he pulled out a rolled-up flag on a stick, the kind that can be bought at any Woolworth store. Sebastian took it, unfurled it. It was about a foot square, a blue field with a white cross on it. It was simple but so meaningful now—especially coming from Bingo.

"What's this?" he said.

"Well, you lose your flag out there in the Straits, so now you got another one."

Bingo then took it and went around to the front fender of the battered jeep and stuck it in the flange that must have been used at one time for flying a general's standard. It hung there, the breeze snapping it out briskly. And with his hands outspread in delight, Bingo said, "It is now that you go in style, sí, padre?"

Sebastian swallowed and said, "Sí." He realized now what Bingo was trying to say, something profound, something deep and very significant, something he could not express adequately in words.

Then Sebastian got into the jeep, and Bingo shot out from the curb, pushing the machine at a fast pace across the causeway and finally into the busy Biscayne Boulevard traffic. He kept up the smoking speed, excusing it for fear he'd be late for the plane, but Sebastian knew there was an hour yet to plane time and he knew Bingo knew. What Bingo wanted was to get that breeze, to keep that flag straight out, to see people look, point and wonder.

"Venceremos!" Sebastian yelled in the exuberance of the moment.

"Viva Cuba libre!" Bingo shouted back.

And their spirits touched in that salute to be forever one in transcendence of time and distance.

Epilogue

****

Mr. John Holland
Dir. Operations
State Department
Washington, D.C.

Subject: Operation Clean Sweep
Class: Priority A
Med: Teletype—Straight

Enclosed you will find a complete report on Operation Freedom Seven, listed also as Operation Eight Ball. After examining the report, you will see that our permitting the operation to run under the quarantine of Clean Sweep was within our power inasmuch as we were complying with SHOOT-KILL of your orders.

You will also find the complete analysis of what Señora Lopez has given us. This should in every sense make our job easier in the future.

May I add here that the key to the operation as we have been able to piece it together is in a man who goes under CODE NAME SEBASTIAN. His real name is the Reverend Raymond Sebastian. I'm enclosing a profile on his experience in the Negev desert provided by the Israeli Secret Police and an agent of theirs, Miss Barbara Churchill.

This man Sebastian is no quick runner in the espionage bit. He seems to be operating out of his element, and he knows it. For some reason, he figures he has a responsibility to identify with the poor, lame, halt, and blind in the world—not very good credentials for any of our business. But he's no kook either. That's why I take the time here to spell it out as best I can.

This man Sebastian is no charismatic type—he's no great leader of men, nor does he pull the rabbit out of the hat. What he has is a peculiar quality of being able to touch the nerve endings of people in their relationship to God; he either gets the unbelievers to work like the devil to prove there is no God, and they seem to do it by pouring their sweat into the operations he gets into, or else he fans the flame of the weak believers into experiencing what God can do with impossible odds. I don't think he intentionally does this, but rather goads people this way.

Like all clergymen, of course, he's got the big principle about the value of every human soul. That could work against him; it apparently has in Operation Freedom Seven. He learned some hard things in that one. But in this case, the values he holds got us the score in Mrs. Lopez—I don't think we would have pulled it off without him.

I'm not saying we can use him at all in our force in the future. But I'm just warning you now that I think you're going to see him pop up some place else before too long. He's wiser now to us and how we work—but that wisdom won't hurt him. He knows now that he can trust only God, finally, and nobody else.

The only way I can possibly describe what happened in this operation is to quote from a Book you may not be familiar with: "*So Gideon, and the hundred men that were with him, came unto the outside of the camp . . . and they blew the trumpets, and brake the pitchers that were in their hands . . . and held the lamps in their left hands . . . and they cried, the sword of the Lord and of Gideon. And they stood every man in his place round about the camp: and all the host ran, and cried, and fled.*"—*Judges 7:19–21.*

If you can understand and believe that about a farmer named Gideon, you'll know pretty much what kind of shadow this Sebastian cuts. I leave it to you to figure it out.

H. B. Mathews
National Intelligence Agency
Miami, Florida